I0829331

HARPER'S JUSTICE BOOK 2

THE MAVERICK MARSHAL

R.J. SLOANE

The Maverick Marshal: Harper's Justice Book 2
By R.J. Sloane

Cover Design by Desert Life Media

Publisher:
Desert Life Media, LLC
Gilbert, AZ 85295

www.rjsloanewesterns.com

Printed in the United States of America

ISBN-978-1-960217-74-5

When justice is executed,
it is a joy to the righteous
but a terror to evildoers.
—Proverbs 21:15 CSB

To K.W.

Your bravery has changed the trajectory of my writing career and has inspired me in countless ways to pursue the stories God lays on my heart.
Be strong and courageous.

1 - Desert Rat

Arizona Territory
July 26, 1899

Flynn

THE HOOFPRINTS TOLD a story of desperation. Deep gouges in the hardpan where Kellerman's stolen mount had stumbled. Scattered droppings still steaming in the chill of dawn. The trail wove erratically, evidence of a rider and horse pushed past their limits.

I crouched beside the clearest track, a worn horseshoe with a chip on the left rear like a busted tooth. I'd been trailing him across the Arizona Territory for three days, and now the signs read clear as scripture. He was close. Maybe two miles ahead. Maybe on foot, if the horse had more sense than its rider.

The desert stretched out in every direction, endless and merciless. Sagebrush, dust, and sun-bleached stone waited to swallow a man whole. But I wasn't just any man. I was born in this godforsaken land, raised by a father who gave the devil lessons in cruelty. I'd crossed this wasteland more times than I could count, hunting men who thought they could outrun justice.

This was my ground, my crucible. Every shadow, every shift in the wind, every bird call held meaning. And I'd learned to listen better than most men ever learn to speak.

I stood, thumbing the brim of my hat down against the blaze of the rising sun. Leather groaned at my hips as I shifted. My gun belt spoke the language of reckoning. Somewhere out there, Kellerman was about to find out what justice felt like when it came with a badge and a loaded Colt. He hadn't just robbed the Flagstaff Land Office. He'd lifted a satchel stuffed with more than cash, with documents that stank of rot in high places. Filth decent folks prayed didn't exist.

If the whispers held water, this case might be just the break I'd been waiting for. Word was Kellerman wasn't acting alone. He was a cog in something bigger, meaner. An outfit with roots tangled deep in territorial politics. Corruption that could bury a man's career… or make it.

Truth was, in these parts, decent folks were getting scarce as water. And the ones left were too scared—or too smart—to look too close.

Tracker, my sturdy black gelding, stood patient as stone while I swung into the saddle. We'd covered hard ground together. He knew the rhythm of a manhunt as well as I did. A gentle nudge sent him forward at a steady walk, conserving energy while my eyes swept the terrain.

The wind carried the usual scents of creosote and dust, but beneath them lingered something else. The acrid tang of fear. The faint metallic bite of blood. Kellerman had injured either himself or his horse during the night. Either way, it gave me an edge.

Two hundred yards ahead, movement caught my eye. A flash of white against red rock—a city man's shirt, all wrong for desert travel. I reined Tracker to a halt and pulled my field glasses from the saddlebag.

There he was. Thomas Kellerman, formerly of the Territorial Land Office, stumbled through the scrub like a lost pilgrim heading straight for perdition. His pale skin was already burning despite the hat, and his gait screamed dehydration and desperation. The leather satchel still clung to his shoulder, his fingers locked around the strap like it held his soul.

Smart man. That bag was his only bargaining chip.

Not that I had planned on bargaining with a snake.

I nudged Tracker forward, keeping to the low ground where shadows masked our approach. Tracking wasn't just about signs. It was about thinking like the hunted, staying two steps ahead. And right now, Kellerman was thinking like a cornered rat.

Same as every other man I'd chased. Same as the one who fathered me.

His trail angled toward the railroad tracks that cut across the wasteland toward Canyon Diablo. Maybe he figured he could flag down a train or follow the rails to civilization. What he didn't know was that those tracks led straight to one of the most dangerous bridges in the territory.

A spine of steel and timber stretched over a canyon that had swallowed plenty of fools.

The sound of Tracker's hooves on loose stone finally reached him. Kellerman spun, his sunburned face twisted in terror. Then he broke into a shambling run toward the gleam of steel rails.

"Thomas Kellerman!" I called, my voice cutting clean through the desert air. "Deputy U.S. Marshal! Stand and surrender!"

He didn't stop. Didn't even slow. 'Course not. They never made it easy. Just kept running with an awkward, city-bred gait that might've been comical if not for the weight of his crimes.

I touched my spurs to Tracker's flanks, and we closed the gap fast. But as we neared the railroad embankment, I pulled up short. His hooves weren't made for railroad ties, and beyond them stretched the iron and timber bridge spanning Canyon Diablo's yawning chasm like a skeletal finger.

I dismounted and ground-tied Tracker in the shade of the water tank. Checked my weapons. Colt rode easy in its holster. Winchester stayed in the saddle scabbard. My heavy Bowie with its distinctive clip point blade and brass guard hung ready at my side. For what lay ahead, the handgun and knife would serve better than the rifle.

Time to finish this dance.

Kellerman had reached the tracks, scrambling down the embankment. His city shoes slipped on the gravel, the satchel banging against his leg, throwing off his balance.

"Give it up, Kellerman!" I shouted, climbing after him. "Ain't nowhere left to run!"

He glanced back, pale face streaked with sweat and panic. "You don't understand!" His voice cracked like a boy's. "They'll kill me! There are bigger forces at play. Bigger than your badge!"

My boots found solid footing on the wooden ties. Heat radiated up from the sunbaked rails, hot enough to cook a man's feet through his soles. Ahead, Kellerman backed toward the bridge's edge, where solid ground gave way to a bone-breaking drop.

"Then talk," I said, drawing my Colt. The weight felt right in my hand. Thirty-seven ounces of frontier justice. "Tell me who's behind the land fraud. Tell me why you've got forged documents in that satchel."

He clutched the bag like a lifeline, sweat dripping from his chin. "You want to talk corruption, Deputy? Real corruption?" His laugh was brittle, humorless. "Start with your own bloodline. That name of yours—it ain't exactly clean, is it?"

The words hit like a sledgehammer. My jaw clenched. Rage surged, white-hot and familiar. The same fury that had nearly gotten me booted from the marshal service more than once.

"What in tarnation did you say?"

"I said your family name belongs on wanted posters, not badges!" His voice rose, feeding off my reaction. "Everyone knows about Galen Harper. Apple doesn't fall far, does it?"

That did it.

I holstered the Colt and lunged, red clouding my vision. My hands reached for his throat, ready to silence him for good. He yelped and swung the satchel like a club. I ducked, but his free hand caught my jaw with a lucky punch that lit up my skull.

My boot caught between two ties. I pitched forward, off-balance, just as the satchel came around again. The world tilted. Then I was falling.

My hands shot out, fingers clawing at iron and wood. I caught the edge of a tie. The jolt nearly tore my arms from their sockets. My legs swung free over the canyon, three hundred feet of empty air below me.

Reckon my luck was holding true to form.

"Well, well," Kellerman's voice drifted down, thick with smugness. "Looks like the famous Flynn Harper ain't so tough after all."

I heard his footsteps on the ties, slow and deliberate. My shoulders screamed. Sweat slicked my palms despite the desert air.

"You know what's funny?" His face appeared above me, grinning like the devil. "Your family's name is all over these documents. Crime really does run in the blood."

He dangled the satchel just out of reach, taunting me. Thought he had the upper hand on a Harper. That was his first mistake.

His second was leaning too far forward.

I'd been hanging there, letting him think he'd won. Truth was, I'd been planning this move since the moment I started falling. A man didn't grow up with Galen Harper as a father without learning how to turn apparent defeat into confident victory.

I swung my body like a pendulum, building momentum, then launched my left hand upward. My fingers closed around the satchel's handle just as Kellerman realized his mistake.

He tried to pull back, but my grip was forged from years of hard living and harder fighting. The shift in weight yanked him forward. His eyes went wide with the kind of terror you only see in a man's last seconds.

For a heartbeat, we were connected. Hunter and hunted. Lawman and criminal. Suspended over a drop that would turn us both into red smears on the rocks below.

Then his fingers slipped.

Kellerman fell without a scream. Just a blur of limbs and panic, shrinking until he hit the canyon floor with a thud that echoed off the walls.

Reckon desert rats never did survive long out here.

The satchel was still in my hand. And I was still breathing.

Always had been luckier than I had any right to be.

I hauled myself onto the tracks, every muscle shaking like I had the fever. For a moment, I lay flat on the sun-warmed ties, staring up at the endless blue sky, lungs heaving. Sweet mercy, that'd been closer than a shave with a rusty razor. One of my more pious sisters must've been praying again.

Then I heard it.

A low rumble, distant but growing. The kind that meant my day was about to get a whole lot worse.

A train whistle echoed off the canyon walls. The rails beneath me began to vibrate with the weight of tons of steel and steam. I rolled to my feet and ran, the satchel clutched tight to my chest.

But I wasn't going to make it.

Wouldn't be the first time I'd bitten off more than I could chew.

The whistle screamed again, closer now. Black smoke rose above the scrub, and the vibration in the rails became a steady drumbeat that rattled my teeth. Twenty-five cars, maybe thirty. A long freight train that would take forever to pass.

My boots pounded the ties. Fifty feet to safety. Forty. Thirty. The train's headlight blazed around the bend like the eye of some iron devil. The engineer laid on his whistle in a long, urgent blast.

Twenty feet. Might as well have been twenty miles.

I dove off the tracks, hands reaching for the trestle's iron framework. My fingers closed around a steel beam just as the locomotive thundered overhead. The whole bridge bucked and shuddered like a bronc trying to throw its rider, and there I was, swinging in empty space above the same abyss that had just claimed Kellerman.

Reckon I'd be joining him soon enough if my luck ran out.

The first freight car roared overhead with a sound like the world ending. Then the second. The third. Each one sent bone-jarring vibrations through the iron framework that made my teeth click together and tested every fiber of my grip. Rust flakes rained down from the aged metal like bloody snow, stinging my eyes and coating my throat with the taste of old iron and decades of desert dust.

My shoulders screamed in agony as I hung there like a side of beef in a slaughterhouse, the satchel's strap cutting into my neck where I'd slung it. The leather bag banged against my ribs with each violent shudder of the trestle, a constant reminder of what I'd nearly lost and what I still might lose.

The wind screamed through the canyon like a banshee, whipping grit into my face and dragging sweat from my skin. The sun beat down like a hammer, baking the iron until it seared my palms. Somewhere below, a buzzard cried out, the sound sharp and mocking. I didn't dare look down, but I could feel the emptiness yawning beneath me, hungry and patient.

Car after car thundered past above me. Ten cars. Fifteen. The whistle shrieked again as the engineer spotted something ahead, probably cattle on the tracks miles down the line. The sound was like having your eardrums split with a dull knife, echoing off the canyon walls until it seemed like the whole world was screaming as loudly as my muscles.

The flesh of my hands felt like I'd been using them to pound railroad spikes. No gloves to provide extra grip. The rough iron beam bit into my palms like wolf teeth, drawing blood that made my hold even more treacherous. I tried to shift my weight, get a better grip, but every movement sent fresh bolts of agony through my arms and shoulders.

Twenty cars. Twenty-five.

For a brief moment, I saw my pathetic twenty-three years flash before my eyes. Shane's steady face when he'd kept us alive after Galen Harper abandoned us. Hayley's fierce grin as she stood beside me against the world. Young Ike with his law books, determined to build something clean from our cursed name. The older girls' worried faces as they prayed over another dangerous case.

All of them working so hard to build something decent from the wreckage that outlaw left behind. And here I was, the wild one, the one with Galen Harper's temper burning in my veins, about to prove Kellerman right. Maybe the Harper name was cursed. Maybe I was just the latest fool trying to outrun blood that ran too much like his.

I'd chosen the badge to prove I could be different. To show that fire could serve justice instead of feeding it to the vultures. But hanging there, bloodied and beaten, I couldn't help wondering if I was just chasing ghosts with a gun and a grudge.

Sure could use another prayer from one of my sisters about now.

The bridge swayed with each passing freight car like a ship in a storm. Except ships didn't hang over bone-crushing drops onto jagged rocks that would split a man open like a ripe melon. I forced myself not to look down at where Kellerman had landed, but I could feel that distant grave pulling at me like it was hungry for more company.

My left hand slipped. For a heart-stopping moment, my full weight hung from my right arm alone, and I felt something pop in my shoulder joint. The pain was like having a branding iron shoved into the socket. Somehow, I managed to swing back up and get both hands on the beam again, but the effort left me gasping and weaker than a newborn calf.

Thirty cars now. How long was this blasted train? Must've been hauling half of creation.

The noise was incredible. Not just the clatter of wheels on rails, but the groaning of the bridge itself under all that crushing weight. Bolts creaked in their housings like they were about to give way. Metal supports sang with tension that made my bones ache. The entire structure felt like it might shake itself apart and take me down with it.

A particularly heavy car passed overhead, loaded with what sounded like mining equipment from the way it clanked and banged like a dozen church bells. The extra weight sent a violent shudder through the trestle that nearly tore my hands loose entirely. I gritted my teeth and held on, muscles cramping from the sustained torture.

My vision started to blur around the edges. My body threatened to give up the fight.

Finally, mercifully, I saw the caboose approaching. The little red car seemed to take forever to reach my position, but when it finally passed overhead, the sudden quiet was almost shocking. My ears rang like I'd been standing next to a cannon when it fired.

I hung there for another moment, my muscles quivering like a green-broke mustang hearing thunder for the first time. Then, hand over hand, I worked my way along the beam toward the solid rock of the canyon wall. Every movement was pure agony, but I'd survived worse. Barely.

The iron framework held, and eventually I swung up onto a rocky ledge and climbed back to track level.

The train was already disappearing around a distant curve, its smoke trail the only sign it had ever been there. I sat on the warm rails for several minutes, flexing my mangled hands and working feeling back into my fingers before walking back to my horse.

Tracker looked at me like I'd lost my mind. Couldn't say I disagreed with him.

The satchel had survived the ordeal better than I had. Its contents were still secure when I opened the flap and examined what Kellerman had died protecting.

With hands still shaking from the ordeal, I spread the papers across the desert floor. Dozens of documents, some official-looking, others clearly forged. Land deeds, shipping manifests, and bills of sale, all bearing signatures I didn't recognize. Except one.

I held up a fraudulent deed dated three weeks ago, my blood running colder than a mountain stream as I read the signature at the bottom: A.C. Beaumont.

The name meant nothing to me, but something about the handwriting nagged at me. Too perfect. Too practiced. Like someone had spent considerable time learning to copy it just right.

One deed referenced a parcel near Prescott I knew had been sold years ago. Another listed a shipping company that had gone under last spring. The forgeries weren't just sloppy; they were bold. Brazen. Like whoever made them didn't expect anyone to look too close. Or maybe they thought no one would dare.

I gathered the papers carefully, my mind already working through the implications. Kellerman's dying words echoed in my memory: *Your family's name is all over these documents*. What had that miserable snake meant by that? And more importantly, who was behind this operation?

Couldn't be my father. Galen Harper was rotting in

the territorial prison in Yuma, hundreds of miles away. Exactly where the worthless piece of trash deserved to be. And when he got out—if he lived that long—I'd be waiting to finish what the law had started.

As the sun slipped behind the canyon walls, I gathered the papers together and stuffed them back into the satchel. Tomorrow, I would need to report Kellerman's death and head to Holbrook. But tonight, I would study every page in that collection until I knew them by heart.

Something told me this case was far from over. And if my family was somehow tangled up in these crimes, I would find out why. No matter where the trail led or who tried to stop me.

Shane and the others had clawed their way out of the purgatory Galen Harper left us in. I wouldn't be the weak link that dragged them back.

Because justice wasn't just my job. It was the only thing standing between me and becoming the man I swore I'd never be.

2 - Wanted Dead or Alive

Lavinia

THE AFTERNOON SUN streamed through the front windows of Beaumont's Mercantile, casting golden rectangles across the polished wooden floors. I hummed softly while arranging a display of canned peaches, their bright labels catching the light. The familiar scents of coffee beans, leather goods, and the faint sweetness of penny candy created the comforting atmosphere I'd worked so hard to build.

"Mama, look!" Beau's voice piped up from behind the counter where he sat cross-legged on a wooden crate, carefully arranging buttons by color into neat little piles. His dark hair fell across his forehead as he concentrated, tongue peeking out slightly—a habit that never failed to make my heart squeeze with love.

"That's beautiful, sugar." I smiled at his handiwork, noting how he'd organized them from lightest to darkest. "Papa will be impressed with your sorting skills."

Papa emerged from the back office, ledger in hand, spectacles perched on his nose. His graying hair was neatly combed, and his vest pressed to perfection despite the afternoon heat. Even after all these years running the store, he maintained the dignified bearing of a Southern gentleman.

"Indeed, I am," he said, ruffling Beau's hair affectionately. "Perhaps tomorrow you can help me count inventory in the storeroom."

Beau beamed at the praise, and I felt that familiar warmth in my chest—gratitude for Papa's patient love with my son. He'd never once made Beau feel unwanted or shameful, treating him as devotedly as he'd always treated me.

"I need to fetch the mail," I said, untying my apron. "Mrs. Patterson said there might be a catalog from that supplier in Denver."

Then I turned to my son.

"Be good for Papa while I'm gone," I instructed him, pressing a quick kiss to the top of his head. His hair smelled of the lavender soap I used for his baths.

"Yes, Mama." He held up a particularly large pearl button. "I'll save the prettiest one for you."

"That's so sweet. That's why I call you sugar," I said, tapping my finger on the tip of his cute nose. My heart swelled with affection for this precious child who always thought of others first.

The walk to the post office took only five minutes, but I savored the brief respite. Holbrook's main street bustled with the typical afternoon activity of ranchers heading home, wives finishing their shopping, and children playing in the dust. I nodded to Mrs. Garrett as she swept her porch, exchanged pleasantries with the blacksmith's wife, and waved to old Mr. Patterson dozing in his chair outside the barbershop.

This was the life I'd built for us. Respectable. Safe. Peaceful. Far from my sins of the past, always wrapped in Papa's gracious love and protection. He'd never once questioned my choices or made me feel lesser for the mistakes that had brought Beau into our lives.

The post office smelled of ink and paper, with undertones of the tobacco Mr. Hewitt always chewed. He looked up from sorting letters, his weathered face creasing into a smile.

"Afternoon, Miss Lavinia. Got some mail for your father." He handed me a small stack of envelopes and papers. "And the catalog you were expectin' came in."

"Much obliged." I tucked the mail into my reticule, then paused as my gaze caught something on the wall behind him. Posted among the usual notices and advertisements hung a collection of wanted posters. Rough sketches and photographs of various criminals.

And there, clear as day, was Papa's face.

The world tilted sideways. My stomach lurched violently, and I gripped the counter to keep from swaying. The room felt suddenly airless, and I struggled to draw a proper breath. This couldn't be real. It had to be some sort of horrible dream. The likeness was unmistakable. Papa's kind eyes, his neatly trimmed mustache, even the small scar on his left temple from the war. But the words beneath made no sense at all.

WANTED FOR FEDERAL CRIMES
AVERY CORNELIUS BEAUMONT
LAND FRAUD AND RAILROAD THEFT
$500 REWARD

"Something wrong, Miss Lavinia?" Mr. Hewitt's voice seemed to come from very far away. "You look a mite peaked."

I blinked rapidly, forcing my expression into what I hoped resembled normalcy. The nausea still churned in my stomach, threatening to embarrass me right there in the post office.

"Just the heat, I reckon," I managed, my voice sounding strained. "Makes a body feel poorly sometimes."

I stumbled outside, the afternoon heat hitting me like

a physical blow. My vision wavered, and I pressed a hand to my mouth, certain I was about to lose my dinner right there on Main Street.

"Easy there, ma'am. You need to sit down?"

A deep voice, concerned and gentle, cut through my distress. I looked up to see a tall man in a dusty hat, his blue eyes filled with what appeared to be genuine worry. He'd dismounted from a fine black horse and taken a step toward me.

"I'm... I'm fine," I managed, though my voice sounded shaky even to my own ears.

"You sure don't look it. Maybe you should sit down for a spell." He gestured toward a bench outside the post office. "Heat can be mighty unforgiving."

His kindness nearly undid me. Here was a stranger showing more concern than I'd seen from anyone in months, and all I wanted was to accept his help. But I couldn't. Not now. Not when Papa was in such terrible danger.

"Thank you kindly, but I need to get back." I straightened, drawing on reserves of strength I didn't know I possessed. "My family's expecting me."

The man nodded, though concern still shadowed his features. "All right then. You take care now."

As I walked away from his concerned gaze, the awful truth pressed down on me, thick as desert heat. That was definitely Papa on the poster.

The walk back to the store blurred around me. My breath came too fast, too shallow. The mail trembled in my grip, the edges of the envelopes cutting into my palms.

Land fraud? Railroad theft?

The words tumbled through my mind, refusing to make sense. Papa wouldn't. He couldn't. He was the most honest man I knew. He wouldn't even keep an extra penny if someone miscounted their change. Just last week, Mrs. Garrett had overpaid by a dime, and Papa had practically run down the street to return it to the forgetful woman.

"Honesty isn't just good business," he'd told me afterward, slightly winded from his chase. "It's the foundation of character."

I pressed one hand against the rough wood of a storefront to steady myself. How could anyone accuse him of fraud? Of theft?

There had to be some terrible, terrible error.

The bell above the mercantile door chimed my return, the familiar sound now seeming ominous rather than welcoming. Papa looked up from where Beau was rolling a small wooden horse across the floor behind the counter, making quiet neighing sounds for his imaginary adventures.

"Back already? That was quick—" He stopped mid-sentence, his eyes focusing on my face. "Lavinia, what's wrong? You look like you've seen a ghost."

I glanced meaningfully at Beau, still lost in his make-believe world, then moved closer to Papa. "I need to... I need to speak with you," I whispered, my voice catching. "Privately. Please."

His brow furrowed with deep lines, but he nodded. "Beau, why don't you take your horse to the back and see if you can find some of those empty crates to make a proper stable?"

"Can I use little boxes, too?" Beau asked hopefully, still clutching his wooden toy.

"Of course, son. Build whatever you like."

I led Papa toward the back of the store, near his office, my heart hammering against my ribs. How did one even begin such a conversation?

"Papa," I breathed, struggling to find enough air in my lungs. "There's a... There's a wanted poster at the post office. With your name. Your face." The words came out in broken whispers, each one harder to speak than the last.

The color drained from his cheeks. "What?"

"Federal crimes," I whispered urgently, my voice still unsteady. "Land fraud and railroad theft. Five-hundred-dollar reward."

He stared at me as if I'd spoken in a foreign language. "That's... That's impossible. I've never... Lavinia, I don't understand. I've never committed any crime, let alone federal—"

"I know that," I interrupted softly but fiercely. "Of course I know that. But your picture is right there for everyone to see. Someone could walk in here any minute and recognize you."

Papa sank against the doorframe of his office, suddenly looking every one of his fifty-two years. "Land fraud? Railroad theft? I've never even seen a railroad contract, much less stolen anything from—"

The bell above the front door chimed.

We froze, staring at each other in panic. Booted footfalls echoed across the wooden floor, spurs jangling with each step, the sound marking out our subterfuge with every metallic ring. The footsteps were definitely masculine, definitely unfamiliar, and moving with the measured pace of someone accustomed to command. Papa's eyes widened, and I could see the fear he was trying to hide for my sake.

My head pounded, and my throat felt as dry as dust. Without thinking, I placed both hands flat against his chest and guided him quickly backward. He opened his mouth to speak, but I shook my head sharply. "Don't move," I mouthed, then drew the curtains tight across the entrance to the hall, sealing him from view. I prayed he'd return to the safety of his office down the hall.

My heart felt like a wild bird trapped in my chest as I smoothed my skirts and took a steadying breath. For Beau's sake, I had to appear calm. Normal. I plastered on what I hoped was a welcoming smile and walked toward the front of the store.

"Good afternoon," I called out, pleased that my voice sounded steady. "Welcome to Beaumont's Mercantile."

The man standing near my carefully arranged display

of canned goods was tall, well over six feet, with the lean, dangerous build of someone accustomed to hard living. Wild blue eyes swept the store with the intensity of a predator assessing territory, and reddish-brown hair showed beneath a well-worn hat. His clothes were travel-dusty but well-made, and he carried himself with unmistakable authority.

And violence.

Yet something else lurked there too. Something that made my pulse quicken for reasons beyond fear. He was undeniably handsome in a rugged, untamed sort of way that spoke to some buried part of my soul I'd thought long dead. The realization sent a flush of shame through me. How could I possibly be noticing such things when Papa's life hung in the balance?

"Ma'am." He touched the brim of his hat politely, and I caught a glimpse of those same concerned blue eyes that had offered help outside the post office. Recognition dawned with a sickening jolt. The kind stranger who'd shown concern for my welfare. Now he stood in my store, and every instinct screamed that he was far more dangerous than any casual passerby. "Afternoon."

I moved to stand near Beau, one hand automatically dropping to rest on his small shoulder. He looked up at me with trusting brown eyes, and I forced a smile for his benefit.

"Is there somethin' particular I can help you find?" I asked, pleased that my voice remained steady. He studied the layout of the store, then the doorways, and finally the position of the windows. My pulse quickened. Why was he cataloging every detail? Then my traitorous gaze caught on the firm line of his jaw, the way his shirt stretched across broad shoulders. Heat crept up my neck. This was hardly the time.

"Actually, yes." His voice carried a slight drawl, confident and measured. "I'm looking for the owner of this establishment. A.C. Beaumont."

Every muscle in my body went rigid. Behind me, I heard a faint creak from Papa's office. Whether from his shifting position or the old wood settling, I couldn't tell. Either way, I prayed this stranger hadn't noticed.

"I'm afraid Mr. Beaumont isn't available at the moment," I replied carefully. "Perhaps I could help you instead? I manage most of the day-to-day operations."

Those piercing blue eyes locked onto mine. My throat tightened. The careful composure I'd built threatened to crack under the weight of that stare, as if he could see straight through to the fear I barely kept contained. "And you would be?"

"Miss Lavinia Beaumont." I lifted my chin slightly. "Is this regarding a business matter?"

"You could say that." He moved closer, and I caught the scents of leather, horse, and sage as if the Arizona desert clung to him. My heart stuttered. I stepped back, putting the counter between us. "When do you expect Mr. Beaumont to return?"

"I'm uncertain." I lifted my chin, meeting his gaze despite every instinct screaming at me to look away. "He had business to attend to. Out of town."

It wasn't technically a lie. Papa was definitely unavailable, and you could consider his location in the back office to be out of town in terms of accessibility. Especially for this man neither of us knew.

The stranger nodded slowly, those keen eyes never leaving my face. "I see. And this business... would it involve travel to Denver, by any chance?"

My stomach dropped. How could he possibly know about our supplier in Denver? Unless... unless this had something to do with the wanted poster. With whatever terrible mistake had put Papa's face on that wall.

"I wouldn't know the details of his business arrangements," I said coolly, though my palms were growing damp with perspiration. "As I mentioned, I handle the store operations. Would you like to leave a message?"

"Mama?" Beau's small voice piped up from behind the counter. "Who's the man?"

My son's innocent curiosity cut through my fear like sunshine through storm clouds. Whatever was happening, I wouldn't let it touch him. Not if I could help it.

"Just a customer, sugar," I whispered, stroking his hair. "Keep playing with your horse now."

"Can I make him jump over things?"

"Of course, sugar. Build whatever you like back there."

Beau beamed and returned to his imaginary adventures, making soft galloping sounds as his wooden horse explored the space behind the counter. I waited until he was absorbed in his play again before turning my attention back to the stranger.

"Cute boy," the man observed, and something in his tone made me bristle with protective instinct. He hooked a thumb in his belt loop. That's when I noticed his scraped knuckles and healing cuts sending prickles up my spine. I wondered what kind of violence had caused them.

"Yes, he is." My voice carried a warning that any sensible person would heed. "Was there anything else you needed?"

"Actually, there was." He reached into his vest pocket, and for one terrifying moment, I thought he might draw a weapon. Instead, he produced a folded paper. "I'd like Mr. Beaumont to look at this when he returns. Tell him it's regarding some property transactions that need... clarification."

I accepted the paper with fingers that only trembled slightly, careful not to let our hands touch. The document felt heavy with unspoken threats.

"I'll be sure he receives it," I promised.

"Much obliged." He touched his hat brim again, but his eyes remained watchful. "I'll be staying at the hotel for a few days. Name's Flynn Harper. Your father—" He paused, studying my face. "Mr. Beaumont can find me there when he's ready to discuss those business matters."

Flynn Harper. I committed the name to memory, though something about it nagged at me. It sounded familiar, though I couldn't place where I might have heard it.

"I'll let him know," I said.

He turned to leave, then paused at the door. "Nice establishment you have here, Miss Beaumont. Be a real shame if anything disrupted such a... peaceful business."

The words were spoken mildly, but the implied threat was unmistakable. I straightened my spine, drawing on every ounce of Southern grit Papa had taught me.

"Good day, Mr. Harper."

He tipped his hat and walked out, the bell chiming his departure with deceptive cheerfulness. I waited until his footsteps faded completely before allowing my carefully maintained composure to crack.

My legs felt unsteady as I moved to the window and peered through the glass. Flynn Harper mounted his black gelding. He sat in the saddle with easy confidence, and even from this distance, I could see the gun on his hip.

A lawman. It had to be. Everything about him screamed authority and danger.

"Mama?" Beau's voice made me jump as he peeked around the counter. "Is Papa coming out now? I want to show him my stable."

"In a moment." I forced another smile, though my heart still raced. "Let Mama talk to him first."

I hurried to the back office and slipped inside, closing the door behind me. Papa sat in his chair, hands folded in his lap, looking older than I'd ever seen him.

"Did you hear?" I whispered.

He nodded grimly. "Every word. Flynn Harper." He rubbed his forehead wearily. "I've never heard that name before in my life, Lavinia. I don't understand any of this."

I unfolded the paper Flynn Harper had given me. It was a warrant—official, imposing, bearing federal seals. The words seemed to swim before my eyes: "...suspected of fraudulent land transactions involving Atlantic & Pacific Railroad properties... conspiracy to commit federal theft..."

"Papa, this is serious. Federal charges. They think you've been stealing from the railroad."

"But I haven't!" His voice carried a desperate edge I'd never heard before. "I've never even been to half the places mentioned in these accusations. Denver, Phoenix, Flagstaff. For business maybe, but I've never—"

"I know." I reached out and clasped his hands, which trembled slightly. "I know you haven't. But someone wants people to think you have. The question is why."

We sat in silence for a moment, the weight of our new reality settling over us like dust after a storm—quiet, but heavy in the air. Outside, I could hear the normal sounds of Holbrook going about its afternoon business. Horses' hooves, wagon wheels, distant conversations. Everything the same, except our world had just turned upside down.

"What do we do?" Papa asked quietly.

I thought of Flynn Harper's sharp gaze, his careful assessment of our store, and the subtle threat in his parting words. I thought of Beau's innocent trust, of the life we'd built here, of the respectability that had taken years to establish.

"We'll figure out how to protect ourselves," I said firmly. "And we pray that whoever's behind this makes a mistake before Mr. Harper decides to stop asking polite questions."

Papa nodded slowly, then glanced toward the door. "Beau's waiting to show me his horse's stable."

"Yes." I squeezed his hands once more. "We maintain normalcy as much as possible. For his sake."

"And if Harper comes back?"

I met his gaze, seeing my determination reflected there. I refused to dwell on the stranger who'd made my traitorous heart race at the worst possible moment. "Then we deal with it. Together. Like we always have."

The bell chimed again at the store's front, announcing another customer, normal business continuing despite the turmoil that had just entered our lives. I smoothed my skirts and prepared to greet whoever needed our services, while Papa composed himself to admire his grandson's careful work.

But underneath the veneer of normalcy, my mind was racing. Flynn Harper would be back. Of that, I was certain. And when he returned, we needed to be ready.

The question was: ready for what?

3 - Dangerous Territory

Flynn

I STEPPED BACK into the afternoon heat, the mercantile's shade giving way to the relentless Arizona sun that turned the dusty street into a shimmering mirage. My mind spun with questions and possibilities, but it wasn't just the case that had my thoughts scattered like spooked cattle.

Lavinia Beaumont.

The woman was beautiful in a way that caught a man off guard. Like a desert sunrise, quiet and sudden, stealing the breath right out of his lungs. Her blond hair had caught the morning light spilling through that mercantile window, glinting like sun-bleached wheat against the backdrop of neat shelves lined with dry goods and bolts of fabric. And those eyes—deep brown like strong trail coffee—had fixed on me with a look that made me straighten my spine and check my badge without thinking.

When I'd first seen her outside the post office, looking pale and unsteady in the heat, I'd thought she was just another pretty woman having a hard day. But watching her in her own element, standing her ground in that mercantile, had shown me something else entirely. The fierce loyalty in her voice when she'd called her father a good man. The way she'd positioned herself between me and that boy, ready to take on the whole federal government to protect her family. The steel underneath that honeyed Southern drawl when she'd made it clear I wasn't welcome.

The memory of her defiant stance stirred something deep within me that had nothing to do with official duty. I'd faced down armed outlaws who'd shown me less backbone than that slip of a woman in her plain calico dress. She'd made me question everything I thought I knew about this case, and she'd done it without raising her voice or losing that quiet grace that seemed to follow her every movement.

But even as I admired her spirit, my professional instincts cataloged the details that didn't quite fit together. She'd been nervous as a long-tailed cat in a room full of rocking chairs. Her hands had trembled slightly when she'd taken that warrant from me, and she'd kept glancing toward the back of the store like she expected someone to appear. When I'd asked about her father's business dealings, her pupils had dilated slightly—a sure sign of stress that most people wouldn't notice, but I'd been trained to read such tells.

She'd placed herself in front of the boy, but also deliberately between me and what I now suspected was her father's office. Every movement had been measured, despite the nerves she tried to hide.

And then there was the boy himself. Beau, she'd called him. Dark-haired, maybe five years old, with intelligent eyes that had studied me with the wariness of a child who'd been taught to be careful around strangers. He'd called her Mama clear as day, yet she'd introduced herself as Miss Beaumont.

That raised some interesting questions about the family structure. Was she an unwed mother? A widow? Or was there something else going on that she didn't want a federal marshal to know about?

Most women would have crumbled under the weight of a federal warrant. Lavinia Beaumont had challenged me to prove I was worthy of wielding it, all the while hiding secrets that made her hands shake. When I'd mentioned her father's business dealings, something had shifted in her expression. A wariness that ran bone-deep, like an animal that had been trapped before and barely escaped.

Someone had hurt her, betrayed her trust, and now she was protecting more than just her father. She was protecting herself and that boy, and probably secrets that went deeper than I could imagine.

Seeing that wariness in her eyes hit me harder than it should have. Made me want to hunt down whoever had put it there and show him what real justice looked like. The urge to prove myself different from whatever man had failed her before was pulling at something deep inside me, something I'd spent years keeping locked away.

Getting personally involved was exactly how good marshals ended up dead.

Whatever I might feel for the woman, my professional instincts were telling me there was more to this story than a simple case of mistaken identity. A.C. Beaumont might well be innocent of the charges against him, but his daughter was definitely hiding something. And in my experience, people who had nothing to hide didn't act like spooked horses every time a lawman asked a simple question.

I untied my horse from the hitching post and swung into the saddle, the leather creaking under my weight. Tracker stamped once in the dust, eager to move after standing in the heat. I positioned myself where I could observe the mercantile without being obvious about it, using the natural cover of a water trough and a couple of hitching posts to break up my silhouette.

The afternoon sun cast long shadows across the dusty street. A few tumbleweeds rolled past, propelled by the constant desert wind that carried the scent of creosote. The wooden sidewalks baked beneath the relentless sun, their boards warped and split from years of scorching summers.

The mercantile's front entrance sat in clear view from here, along with the large display windows flanking it. Two stories, well-constructed, with what looked like storage or office space behind it. When I'd ridden into town, I'd spotted a narrow alley behind these buildings barely wide enough for a wagon to squeeze through. The back entrance, though, was a blind spot from this position.

I pulled out my pocket watch, the gold case warm from the heat. Three-thirty in the afternoon. Most mercantiles in towns this size closed around six or seven, depending on the season and the owner's preferences. That gave me time to do some reconnaissance and sniff out the truth before making my next move.

My plan was straightforward. Gather information from multiple sources, cross-reference their stories, and identify the inconsistencies that would point me toward the truth. In my experience, everyone had something to hide, and the people who claimed to know nothing usually knew the most.

I guided my horse down the dusty street, watching the townspeople go about their daily business. A couple of old-timers sat on chairs outside the barbershop, their weathered faces creased with deep lines carved by decades of desert sun. They watched me with casual interest. Word of my arrival had already spread through town like wildfire.

Perfect. Local gossips were often a lawman's best source of information. The trick was knowing how to ask the right questions.

I dismounted and approached the pair, dust swirling around my boots. My gloves hid the worst of the cuts from my encounter with the Canyon Diablo bridge. I was grateful for that. The wooden sidewalk creaked under my weight. "Afternoon, gentlemen."

"Afternoon," the older of the two replied, a grizzled man with tobacco-stained whiskers who squinted as if he'd spent a lifetime looking into the sun. "You'd be the marshal we heard about."

"Deputy U.S. Marshal Flynn Harper," I confirmed, noting how both men's postures shifted slightly at the mention of my title. Nothing dramatic, but enough to tell me they were suddenly more alert. "Word travels fast in a town this size."

"Faster than wildfire in dry grass." The second man chuckled. He was younger, maybe sixty, with the calloused hands and sun-darkened forearms of someone who worked outside. "Name's Pete Morrison. This here's Obadiah Cain. We been watching this town grow for nigh on twenty years."

"Then you gentlemen know the townsfolk pretty well," I said, settling into the conversational tone that had served me well in dozens of similar situations. Keep it friendly, let them think they're helping, and listen for the things they don't say as much as the things they do. "I'm looking into some business dealings involving A.C. Beaumont. What can you tell me about him?"

The two men exchanged glances, and I caught the slight tightening around Morrison's eyes. Body language that said they'd discussed this topic before. Probably within the last hour. In a town this size, news of a federal marshal's arrival would have spread to every front porch and business within minutes.

"A.C.'s a good man." Morrison paused, as if measuring his next words. "Honest in his dealings, fair with his prices. Been here maybe six years now, him and his daughter."

"And the boy?"

Another exchanged look, this one lasting a fraction longer. Morrison's left hand slipped into his pants pocket. Whatever they weren't telling me had him on edge. "Beau? Sweet kid. Polite as they come. Lavinia's done a fine job raising him."

"Her husband around?"

"Ain't no husband," Cain said quickly, then caught Morrison's warning look. The older man's jaw tightened, and I saw him give the slightest shake of his head. "I mean, she's never been married, far as we know. Came here with the boy when he was just a baby. A.C. said he was adopting the child, giving him the family name and all."

Interesting. That explained the "Miss Beaumont" designation, but it also raised more questions. Why would a single woman with a baby flee to Arizona Territory? And why would A.C. Beaumont be so willing to take on that responsibility? In my experience, men didn't usually uproot their lives to help unmarried daughters unless there was a compelling reason.

"They seem close," I observed.

"Thick as thieves," Morrison agreed, but there was something in his tone that suggested he was holding back. "A.C. dotes on that boy like he was his own grandson. And Lavinia... well, she's protective of her family. Fierce protective."

The way he said it made me think he'd seen that protectiveness in action. "Any idea why someone might want to cause trouble for A.C.?"

The silence stretched long enough to be uncomfortable. Both men shifted in their chairs, Morrison's hand moving to his pocket again while Cain suddenly became very interested in a loose thread on his shirt cuff. Finally, Cain spoke up.

"A.C. ain't the kind to make enemies. Minds his own business, helps folks when he can. If someone's got a beef with him, it ain't nothing that started in Holbrook."

That was telling. These men clearly knew something, but they weren't talking. Whether from loyalty or fear, I couldn't tell yet, but the defensive posture of both men suggested they were protecting more than just a neighbor's reputation.

"Much obliged," I said, touching my hat brim. "I'll be around for a few days if anything comes to mind."

I mounted up and continued my circuit of the town, making mental notes of the layout. The main street ran roughly east-west, with cross streets branching off toward the residential areas. The business district was compact, maybe a dozen buildings including the mercantile, a saloon, the hotel, a barbershop, and a few other establishments. In a town where everyone knew everyone else's business, the silence around A.C. Beaumont's troubles was telling.

The saloon was quiet this time of day, but I could see movement through the batwing doors and smell the familiar combination of whiskey, tobacco, and sawdust that marked every frontier drinking establishment. The bartender might be another source of information. Men talked when they drank, and bartenders heard everything. I'd save that for the evening when tongues would be looser.

Across the street, a woman in a faded calico dress swept her front porch, stealing glances in my direction. When she caught me looking, she quickly averted her eyes and hurried inside. More potential information, but I'd need to approach her carefully. Women in small towns were often more observant than men, but also more protective of their neighbors' secrets.

I'd get my answers. And I had a feeling that before this was over, I'd need every piece of information I could gather. Because something told me that A.C. Beaumont's troubles were just the beginning.

I reined Tracker to a halt near the alley behind the mercantile, letting the horse settle while I studied the building's layout. Two rear windows, both shuttered. One door, reinforced with iron hinges and a newer lock—likely Lavinia's doing. A rain barrel sat beneath the eaves, half full despite the dry spell. No crates, no discarded freight. Clean. Controlled. Like someone had gone out of their way to erase any trace of recent deliveries.

I dismounted and ran a gloved hand along the edge of the doorframe. No scuff marks. No signs of forced entry. But the lock was new. Expensive. Not the kind most shopkeepers used unless they had something worth protecting.

I stepped back and scanned the alley. Narrow, boxed in by adobe and timber. A perfect funnel for anyone trying to corner someone or escape unseen.

I wished Shane were here. He had a way of seeing the angles I missed, of weighing evidence without letting emotion cloud the facts. He'd remind me to look at the paper trail, not just the people. To trust the process, even when the people involved stirred up things I didn't want to feel.

Because Lavinia Beaumont stirred up plenty.

I'd seen guilt before. Guilt that made men twitch when they heard their name. She didn't have that. She had fear. Protective fear that came from knowing too much and saying too little.

And the more I thought about it, the less the evidence against A.C. Beaumont made sense. The warrant was clean, with specific charges. But the timing, the source, the sudden appearance of forged documents. It all felt too convenient. Like someone had built a case designed to hold just long enough to ruin a man's reputation.

Taking Tracker's reins, I led him down the main street, briefly glancing over my shoulder toward the mercantile, where Lavinia's silhouette moved behind the curtains. She was watching the street. Watching me.

I adjusted my hat and turned away. I wasn't ready to confront her again. Not until I had more facts. Not until I could separate duty from instinct, and justice from whatever it was I felt when she looked at me like that.

4 - Shadows and Secrets

Flynn

THE HOTEL WAS a two-story affair with a wraparound porch and windows that had seen better days. Paint peeled from the shutters, and the porch sagged slightly where the desert sun had warped the wood. But it perfectly positioned me with a clear view of the mercantile's front entrance and most of the main street. I tied my horse to the rail and pushed through the front door, the bell above it announcing my arrival with a cheerful chime that seemed out of place in a town where tension hung in the air like the heat itself.

Though cooler than outside, the interior still held a dry heat that made a man's throat feel like sandpaper. Open windows offered no relief. No breeze stirred the stifling air. Behind the desk, a clerk looked up from his newspaper and fixed on my badge with the wariness I had expected.

"Help you?"

"Need a room for a few days. Something with a view of the street, if you have it."

"Dollar a night, meals extra." He pushed the register

across the desk with fingers that shook slightly. "Name?"

"Flynn Harper. Deputy U.S. Marshal."

If my title surprised him, he didn't show it. Just nodded and handed me a key. "Room six, upstairs. Front corner. You'll have a good view of Main Street from there."

Perfect. "Much obliged. Anything else I should know about the town?"

The clerk, a thin man with prematurely gray hair and a pale complexion that suggested he spent most of his time indoors, studied me for a moment. "Depends on what you're looking for, I reckon."

"Just trying to get a feel for the place. Understand A.C. Beaumont runs the mercantile."

"He and his daughter, yeah. Good folks. Pay their bills, don't cause trouble." The same carefully neutral response I'd gotten from everyone else.

"Known them long?"

"Since they came to town. Maybe six years now. Came from back east somewhere. Georgia, I think. Set up shop and been here ever since."

"They live above the store?"

The clerk shook his head. "Nah, got themselves a nice little house over on Coronado Street. Residential section, about a five-minute walk from the store. Safer neighborhood, better for the boy."

Now that was useful information. "Family man, is he?"

The clerk's expression grew more guarded, and his hand moved unconsciously toward the drawer behind the desk. "Like I said, good folks. Don't cause trouble."

The same neutral phrasing again, delivered with body language that suggested the whole town had discussed what to say to the federal marshal. Either A.C. Beaumont was genuinely well-liked, and the town was protecting him, or people were afraid to say otherwise. In my experience, it was usually one or the other, and the fear option often proved more interesting.

I headed upstairs, my boots echoing on the solid floorboards. Good construction. The windows offered clear sight lines too. The stairs creaked under my weight, and the sound of my spurs rang softly with each step. Room six was small but clean, with a commanding view of Main Street, clean as a rifle barrel.

From this position, the mercantile sat clearly visible, as well as the movement of people and horses along the thoroughfare. The afternoon sun slanted through the glass, heating the room like a cookstove left too long, but the view was worth the discomfort.

I pulled the documents from Kellerman's satchel and spread them across the small table by the window. Bills of sale, shipping manifests, land deeds, all bearing what appeared to be A.C. Beaumont's signature. The evidence that had seemed so straightforward when I'd first examined it now felt less certain.

Something about the whole situation bothered me. Here was a man with a solid reputation, respected by everyone I'd talked to, yet accused of sophisticated federal crimes that would require connections and resources far beyond what a small-town shopkeeper would possess. The documents looked legitimate enough with quality paper, proper ink, and official language. But the disconnect between the man's reputation and the charges against him gnawed at me like a splinter under the skin.

Maybe the problem wasn't with the evidence itself, but with my understanding of the situation. Maybe A.C. Beaumont wasn't the simple shopkeeper he appeared to be. Or maybe someone else was involved, someone who'd implicated an innocent man for reasons I hadn't uncovered yet.

I needed to see a sample of A.C.'s actual handwriting before I could make any real judgments about these documents. Until then, I had been working with assumptions that might be completely wrong.

I leaned back in the chair and considered the tactical

situation. If this were a set up, someone had gone to considerable trouble to make it look legitimate. That suggested planning, resources, and a specific motive. Random criminals rarely targeted small-town merchants unless there was something to gain.

Maybe A.C. had seen something he shouldn't have. Maybe he'd refused to take part in something illegal. Or maybe he was just a convenient patsy, a respectable man whose identity could be stolen to cover someone else's crimes.

The townspeople's consistent defense of A.C. Beaumont, his daughter's fierce protectiveness, the disconnect between his reputation and the charges all pointed to a puzzle I hadn't solved yet.

I glanced at my pocket watch. Four-fifteen. Still plenty of time before the mercantile closed.

I positioned myself at the window and began a systematic observation of the building across the street. The front entrance was clearly visible, as was the large display window that showed the store's interior. Movement inside revealed Lavinia arranging merchandise, with the boy playing behind the counter. No sign of A.C. Beaumont. But then again, he wouldn't be working in the store if he were trying to stay hidden.

After an hour of watching, I'd learned several things. First, the mercantile did steady business. People came and went regularly, most carrying packages or bundles. The town was clearly prosperous enough to support a thriving general store. Second, Lavinia clearly managed it. She handled customers, managed inventory, and kept a close eye on the boy, all with the practiced efficiency that suggested she'd been doing it for years.

Third, and most interestingly, she was definitely on edge. Her movements, the frequent glances toward the back of the store, the way she positioned herself to keep watch on both the front entrance and the building's rear all revealed a woman watching for something. Or someone.

At five-thirty, she began closing procedures. The boy helped her bring in some outdoor displays, and she pulled down the shade on the front window. A few minutes later, she flipped the sign on the door and locked it from the inside.

But they didn't come out the front.

I waited another ten minutes, then made my way downstairs and around to the back of the hotel. The evening air was slightly cooler but still warm, and the smell of cooking food drifted from the hotel's kitchen. From this new position, the rear of the mercantile stood clearly visible.

Sure enough, a few minutes later, Lavinia emerged from the back door with Beau in tow. She locked the door behind them with careful attention to the mechanism, then set off down the alley at a brisk pace. The boy chattered as they walked, his voice carrying on the still air, though I couldn't make out the words.

Time to see where they lived.

I followed at a distance, keeping to the shadows and using buildings and parked wagons to mask my movements. The sun was setting, painting the sky in shades of orange and purple that seemed to set the desert landscape on fire. Lavinia had good instincts. She glanced back twice, her movements quick and alert like a deer sensing a predator. But she didn't seem to spot me.

They turned onto Coronado Street, just like the hotel clerk said. I kept my distance. This part of town felt quieter, more refined. Houses stood back from the road behind neat front yards. Cottonwoods lined the street, their leaves whispering in the breeze, casting long shadows that cooled the leftover heat. The entire neighborhood carried a kind of quiet dignity. Nothing like the grit and noise of Main Street.

Lavinia stopped in front of a two-story house halfway down the block. Modest, but cared for. Fresh white paint brightened the shutters. A small porch framed the entrance. A picket fence enclosed a tidy yard, where someone had coaxed roses and desert marigolds into bloom with defiant little bursts of color thriving in the dry soil. The perfect picture of respectable frontier domesticity.

I slipped behind a wide cottonwood, its trunk rough against my back. From here, I had a clean view of the front of the house, shielded by shade and distance. Dust mingled with the fresh scent of torn leaves. Through the branches, I could see the parlor window and part of the kitchen just enough to watch without being seen.

Lavinia and Beau went inside, and within minutes, movement stirred in the parlor. Oil lamps were lit, casting a warm yellow light through the windows. The boy ran from room to room, his tiny figure darting past the windows like a moth drawn to light. Lavinia moved more slowly, going about evening routines.

I stayed put for another hour, watching as the sun slipped behind the mountains and the desert began to cool. Stars spilled across the sky, and the air shifted, carrying the scent of cooling earth and night-blooming cereus. Through the parlor window, Lavinia helped Beau with a puzzle, her movements easy to track.

Still no sign of the man.

Either A.C. wasn't there, or he kept to the parts of the house I couldn't see from where I sat.

The smart tactical move would be to circle the house, find a position where I could see the back rooms and the second story. But that would mean moving closer, risking discovery if someone looked out at the wrong moment. And something told me that Lavinia Beaumont would notice a shadow where no shadow should be.

I studied the house layout from my position. The back corner and side entrance remained out of view. The kitchen extended further back than I could observe, and there was an entire second story that remained hidden from my view. A.C. could be anywhere in that house, or he might not be there at all.

Was he hiding in his own home while his daughter managed the store and took care of the boy? Or was he somewhere else entirely, leaving them to face the danger alone?

Lavinia moved through the parlor, tidying up, then disappeared toward the kitchen. A few minutes later, she reappeared with the boy, leading him toward the staircase. She took his hand, her movements gentle and unhurried.

Bedtime routines.

I couldn't see the second floor from my position, but I could imagine it. Lavinia seemed like a woman who would take her time with the routine. Read him a bedtime story. Tuck him in tight. Press her lips to his forehead and murmur something that made him feel safe.

Something punched me in the gut at the image.

I'd never had that. Lilian and Shane did their best to get us through—to survive Galen's abandonment and losing our mama. But they were only twelve and thirteen. Just kids themselves, trying to keep six children alive. There'd been no bedtime stories. No gentle tucking in. Just the exhausted collapse after another day of scraping by.

I wondered what it would have been like. To have a mother who kissed your forehead and made you believe the world was safe. To drift off to sleep without the constant gnaw of hunger or fear.

I adjusted my stance behind the cottonwood, shifting just enough to relieve the pressure on my left knee without breaking line of sight. Years of following criminals had taught me how to blend into the landscape and how to become part of the scenery until even the most watchful eyes passed over me. I counted windows, tracked light sources, and noted the rhythm of movement inside the house. Lavinia moved with purpose, but not panic. Her routine was practiced, deliberate. She wasn't hiding, at least not in the way guilty people did.

But something still didn't sit right.

I'd seen families under pressure before. Seen how

fear twisted their habits, how guilt made them sloppy. This wasn't that. Lavinia wasn't covering for a criminal. She was protecting something—or someone—with a quiet ferocity that made me question everything I thought I knew about this case.

The warrant said A.C. Beaumont had signed fraudulent land deals and shipping manifests. But the man hadn't shown his face once since I arrived. And the daughter he'd supposedly raised was running the store, raising the boy, and keeping watch like a soldier guarding a fort.

I'd bet my badge she knew more than she'd said. But I'd also bet she wasn't the one orchestrating this mess.

I exhaled slowly, letting the desert air settle in my lungs. This was the part Shane would handle differently. He'd take his time, ask the right questions, wait for people to reveal themselves. I preferred the direct approach. Follow the lead, verify the story, and find the truth. If she were hiding her father, I'd know soon enough.

I shifted again, eyes fixed on the second-story window. If A.C. Beaumont was in that house, I'd find out. But I'd do it by the book.

Even if that meant watching an innocent woman's house all night.

I waited until the house was completely dark before making my move. Keeping to the shadows, I circled the property. Front and back doors. Three windows facing the street, two on each side. A cellar entrance opened on the east wall, and a six-foot fence enclosed the backyard.

The house was secure but not impregnable. A determined man could get in if he wanted to. More importantly, a desperate man could get out if he needed to. There were multiple exits, suitable cover from the neighboring houses, and easy access to the maze of alleys that would allow someone to disappear into the desert if necessary.

As I made my way back to the hotel, my mind churned with new information. The night air was finally cooling, and the distant call of a coyote echoed somewhere in the desert beyond the town. A.C. Beaumont might be in that house, hiding. Or he might be elsewhere entirely, leaving his daughter to maintain the facade of normal life while he stayed out of sight.

The answer, I suspected, lay in discovering who had reason to want A.C. Beaumont out of the way. Whether this was a case of mistaken identity or something more deliberate, someone had gone to considerable trouble to put his name on those documents.

I settled back in my hotel room, checking my revolver and ensuring it was loaded before placing it within easy reach. The desert night was quiet except for the distant sound of music from the saloon and the soft whisper of wind through the cottonwoods.

Tomorrow, I'd need to press harder, ask more pointed questions. Someone in this town knew something about who might want to frame A.C. Beaumont. And the woman who had gotten under my skin with nothing more than a challenging look and a fierce devotion to her family was right in the middle of it all.

Whatever was coming, I'd be ready for it. I'd pinned on this badge to protect the innocent.

Even if one of those innocents made it mighty hard to keep my mind on the job.

5 - Hold the Line

Lavinia

THE SCRAPE OF seasoned pine against pine echoed through our kitchen as Papa and I worked to pry up the floorboards near the back wall. The sharp scent of sawdust mixed with the earthy smell of the root cellar below. Sweat beaded on his weathered forehead despite the cool morning air, and I noticed how his hands trembled as he positioned the loose planks. Hands that had once been steady enough to thread a needle or count out exact change.

From the front room, I could hear Beau's cheerful voice as he played with his wooden horses, creating elaborate adventures that involved brave stallions and daring rescues. The sound was a balm to my frayed nerves, a reminder of why we were doing this.

"This oughta do," Papa said, easing himself partway into the root cellar. His voice echoed faintly in the tight space. "Deep enough to hide a man. And if we slide the table over…" He nodded toward our dining table, its oak top worn smooth by six years of meals. "No one would be the wiser."

I kneeled beside the opening, pine floor biting into

my knees. The scent of earth and old vegetables drifted up, mingling with the iron tang of the cellar hinges. "It's awfully tight."

"Better tight than swinging from a rope." His voice came out low, bitter. He climbed back up, brushing dirt from his vest. "Truth be told, I've been wondering if I oughta just light outta here. Spare you and Beau the trouble."

The words stung like a slap in the face. My stomach clenched, and I swallowed against the lump rising in my throat. "You're not going anywhere." I stood, arms crossed. "We're family. We don't run from each other."

"Lavinia-girl…" He sank into a kitchen chair, the wood groaning beneath him. "That's a mighty heavy thing you're asking. If they catch me here, you'll be charged the same as me. What happens to Beau then?"

"What happens to him if you run?" I snapped sharper than I meant to. "Who's gonna help me keep food on the table? Who's gonna teach him what a good man looks like?"

Papa's shoulders sagged. "I've been thinking about that. You're capable, darling. More than most women twice your age. You've been helping with the store since we opened."

"And you've been running this house since Mama passed." I moved to the stove, checking the coffee pot just to keep my hands busy. The rich aroma couldn't quite cut through the tension. "Twelve years of cooking, cleaning, patching clothes, tending scraped knees. You think I forgot?"

A ghost of a smile tugged at his mouth. "You were a handful back then. Still are."

"So we switch." I turned to face him, skirts rustling. "You mind the house—cooking, cleaning, watching Beau. I'll run the store. Folks are used to seeing me there anyhow."

"It isn't that simple." He stood, pacing to the window

that overlooked the alley. Morning light caught the silver in his hair. "I can't just vanish. Folks'll talk."

"Not if we're smart." I joined him, voice low so Beau wouldn't hear. I pushed aside the gingham curtain, the glass cool under my fingers. "We say you're feeling poorly. Lung trouble, maybe. Doctor's orders for you to rest in bed."

Papa drummed his fingers on the windowsill, calloused and steady. "And when folks ask to see me?"

"I'll handle it." I touched his arm, familiar with the rough weave of his shirt. "You raised me to be strong. Let me be strong now."

He turned, eyes glistening. "I never wanted this for you, baby girl. You oughta be thinking about a husband, a life of your own. Not hiding your old man from the law."

"I have a life." I nodded toward the front room, where Beau's laughter rang out. "You and Beau are all I need."

"Are we?" His voice softened, but it held weight. "That marshal yesterday. I saw the way he looked at you. And the way you looked back."

Heat rushed to my cheeks. I turned away, fussing with the already-neat counter. The memory of Marshal Harper's blue eyes stirred something I didn't want to name. "I don't know what you mean."

"Don't you?" He stepped closer, his tone gentle. "Lavinia, I may be old, but I am not blind. And I'm not fool enough to think a girl like you oughta spend her days raising your boy and tending to her daddy."

Warmth bloomed in my chest. Your boy. Even when we had to pretend otherwise, Papa never forgot Beau was mine.

"Beau's my responsibility," I whispered. "And so are you. That's the end of it."

He studied me a long moment, then nodded. "All right. We'll try it your way. But if things get too dangerous…"

"They won't."

"If they do," he said, voice firm, "you let me go. Promise me, Lavinia. Don't you sacrifice yourself or Beau for my sake."

My protest died on my lips. "I promise."

He reached out, squeezed my hand. "Now let's run it again. If someone knocks on that door, I need to be down there and gone in under a minute."

We spent the next hour fine-tuning the system. Papa had built the hiding spot with the precision only a soldier could manage. The boards lifted smoothly on hidden hinges he'd set just right, and the table slid quietly as a whisper over strips of canvas he'd nailed underneath. The root cellar ran deeper than I'd realized, braced with old beams that carved out a narrow but workable space for one man to vanish.

"Picked this up during the war," Papa said as we reset the boards for the third time. "Sometimes staying alive came down to how fast you could disappear."

I brushed sawdust from my palms. "What about supplies? Food, water… chamber pot?"

"Already handled." He opened the pantry and pulled out a small wicker basket packed tight with jerky, hardtack, a water jug, and a few other essentials. "This goes down with me. And there's a tunnel that leads out to the alley. Dug it myself when we moved in. Old habits die hard."

I blinked. "You never told me about a tunnel."

"Didn't need to." He slid the basket back onto the shelf. "But if things go sideways, I can slip out with no one on the street being the wiser."

A chill crept up my spine, despite the warmth of the kitchen. We were planning escape routes. That's how bad things had gotten.

"Papa—" I started, but he raised a hand, head tilted toward the front of the house.

"Someone's coming up the steps."

My heart hammered against my ribs as I moved to the

front window. Through the delicate lace curtains, I saw the familiar tall figure of Marshal Harper approaching our door. He moved with that same confident stride I'd noticed yesterday, but something about his expression seemed different. More determined. More focused.

"It's the marshal," I whispered, my voice barely audible.

Papa was already moving toward the kitchen. "How long do I have?"

"Maybe thirty seconds."

He grabbed the supply basket and dropped into the root cellar with surprising agility for a man his age. I replaced the boards, my hands steady despite my racing pulse, and slid the table back into position. The canvas on the feet did its job perfectly. Not a sound. By the time Marshal Harper's firm knock echoed through the house, I was smoothing my skirts and checking my reflection in the hallway mirror.

"Miss Beaumont?" His voice carried clearly through the door, deep and resonant. "I'd like to speak with you, if you have a moment."

I opened the door, chin lifted. "Marshal Harper. What can I do for you?"

Up close, he looked even more imposing than I remembered. Tall and lean, with those sharp blue eyes that missed nothing. His dark hair sat slightly tousled from the ride, and the scent of leather and horse clung to him along with something cleaner, masculine, that made my pulse skip despite my better judgment.

"May I come in?" He removed his hat, revealing more of that thick reddish-brown hair. "I've got a few questions I'm hoping you can help me with."

"Of course." I stepped aside, motioning him in. The room seemed to shrink around him. "Though I'm not sure what more I can tell you. Papa's still away on business."

He scanned the front room with slow, deliberate focus. I watched his eyes take in the mended curtains, the worn but polished furniture, Beau's toys scattered near the hearth where he sat playing with his favorite horse.

"Mama?" Beau's voice piped up. "Is that the marshal man?"

My breath caught. "Yes, sugar. The marshal just has a few questions for me. You keep playing with your horses."

Marshal Harper's expression softened as he glanced at Beau, then back to me. "Fine boy you have there."

"Thank you." I moved toward the kitchen, needing to put some distance between us and my racing thoughts. "Coffee?"

"That's kind, thank you." He followed me into the kitchen, and my stomach tightened as his gaze swept over the floor. Those sharp eyes missed nothing. Was he looking for something specific? Any sign of our recent work?

I reached for the coffeepot, grateful that my hands remained steady. Marshal Harper settled into one chair—thankfully not the one directly over the hidden entrance. He kept his back to the wall, positioned where he could see both the front door and the back exit.

"Miss Beaumont, I need to ask you some questions about your father's business." He accepted the cup I poured with a nod of thanks. His fingers were long and capable-looking, marked with small cuts. "The charges against him involve land transactions and railroad dealings. Sizeable sums of money. Has he ever mentioned anything like that to you?"

I sat across from him, wrapping my hands around my coffee cup to hide their slight trembling. The warmth seeped through the ceramic. "No, Marshal. Papa's business is simple. He orders supplies from wholesalers and sells them to local folks. He's never talked about land deals or railroad investments."

"What about travel? Has he been to Phoenix or Flagstaff recently? Denver?"

"Flagstaff once or twice for supplies, but that was months ago. Never Denver." I met his gaze, letting him see the truth in my eyes. "Marshal, my father runs a mercantile. Imported tea is probably the most exotic thing in his store."

A slight smile tugged at the corner of his mouth, transforming his stern features. The expression made him look younger, more approachable. "And yet the evidence suggests he's been involved in fraudulent land deals worth thousands of dollars."

"Then your evidence is wrong." The words came out sharper than I had intended. I took a breath, forcing myself to remain calm. "I mean no disrespect, Marshal, but I know my father. He's the most honest man I've ever known."

Marshal Harper leaned back in his chair, the wood creaking softly. His expression was thoughtful. "That's what everyone tells me. Your father has quite a reputation for integrity."

"Because he's earned it." I held his gaze, refusing to back down. "Every day for the past six years, through honest work and fair dealing."

"Six years." He nodded slowly. "That's when you moved here from Georgia?"

My breath caught. How did he know about Georgia? "Yes. After my mother passed."

The half-truth tasted bitter on my tongue. The marshal didn't need to know Mama had passed many years before we left. Or that I was the reason for our relocation.

"I'm sorry for your loss." His voice carried genuine sympathy, and something in his tone made me look up. There was understanding in those blue eyes, as if he'd known loss himself. "It must have been difficult moving so far from everything familiar."

"It was." I stared into my coffee, the steam curling up in delicate wisps. Those first months in Arizona had been brutal as my fear pressed in from all sides, my secrets piling until I could barely breathe. "But sometimes a fresh start's the only way forward."

He didn't answer right away. When I looked up, his eyes tracked my every movement, and his expression remained unreadable.

"Miss Beaumont," he said, voice low and deliberate, "I didn't come here to pin this on the wrong man. If someone's setting up your father, I aim to find out who."

The sincerity in his voice sent pleasant tingles through me. Part of me wanted to believe him, wanted to trust that this lawman was different from others who'd abused their power. But I'd learned too well the cost of such trust.

"I appreciate that, Marshal." I kept my voice level. "But you'll forgive me if I put little faith in the justice system. In my experience, it favors those with money and influence over ordinary folks like us."

Something flickered in his eyes. Surprise, maybe, or recognition. "You sound like you've had personal experience with that."

"Haven't we all?" My pulse quickened. The last thing I needed was to reveal too much about my past. "It's easy to see how the world works, even from a small town like this."

A soft thud thumped from the kitchen floor.

Marshal Harper froze, coffee cup suspended midair. His gaze snapped toward the sound, sweeping the floor with critical precision. I caught the slight clench of his jaw, the shift in his breathing. Slower now, measured. When his eyes met mine again, they held a new edge. Sharper. Suspicious.

"Just the house settling," I said too quickly. I crossed to the stove, forcing my steps to stay even. My pulse hammered, but I kept my tone light. "These old buildings creak and groan something fierce when the temperature swings. More coffee?"

"No, thank you." He rose, smooth and deliberate, every movement coiled with readiness. "I'll let you get back to your day. But Miss Beaumont, if anything comes to mind that might explain these charges… enemies your father's made, changes in his business—anything at all, I'd appreciate hearing about it."

"Of course." I walked him to the door, aware of his presence beside me. He was tall enough that I had to tilt my head back to meet his eyes, and close enough that I could smell the clean scent of his shaving soap mixed with leather.

He paused on the threshold, turning back to face me. "I hope you find whoever's really responsible," I said.

"So do I." His gaze held mine for a moment longer than necessary, and I felt that unwelcome flutter in my chest again. "I'll be in touch if I have more questions."

I watched him descend the front steps with that sure, deliberate stride, every movement measured and unhurried. When he mounted his horse, he took the reins with practiced ease, settling into the saddle like he'd been born to it. Then he was gone, disappearing around the corner. But the memory of him lingered, subtle and persistent, like his scent hanging in the air.

I shut the door and leaned against it, knees threatening to buckle. My heart still raced, but not just from fear. Flynn Harper's steadiness had unsettled me in a way I didn't expect. He made me want to trust him, even after everything I'd learned about powerful men and the broken promises they left behind.

"Papa?" I called softly, stepping back into the kitchen.

A moment later, the boards scraped aside. "Is he gone?"

"Yes." I rushed to help him climb out of the hiding space. "What was that noise?"

"Dropped the water jug." He looked sheepish, brushing dirt from his vest. "Think he heard?"

"I think so, but I covered it." I sank into a chair, my legs heavy. "This is harder than I thought."

"He wasn't what I expected." Papa settled beside me, his weathered face drawn. "Asked good questions. Didn't act like he'd already made up his mind."

"Don't." I shook my head. "Don't start thinking he's on our side. He's a lawman. His job is to bring you in."

"Maybe so." Papa rubbed his jaw. "But what if he's actually after the truth? What if he could help us figure out who's behind this?"

My pulse jumped at the thought, and I had to tamp down my rising hope. "We can't afford that kind of trust. Even if he believes you're innocent, there are folks who want you to hang for something you didn't do. Until we know who they are and why they're after you, we keep our guard up."

Papa nodded slowly. "You're right. I just hate that this is how you have to live. Watching your back, lying to neighbors, hiding your own father."

"I hate it too." I reached for his hand, squeezed it tight. "But I'd rather live like this than bury you."

"Lavinia…"

"No, Papa. We'll see this through. You, me, and Beau. That's all that matters right now."

He squeezed back, his hand warm and familiar. "All right. But I want you to be careful around that marshal. He's sharp, and he's already sniffing around."

"I know." I thought about the way Marshal Harper had looked at me, the questions he'd asked, the quiet concern in his voice. "Suspicious doesn't always mean dangerous."

"Maybe not," Papa said, voice low. "But it doesn't mean safe either. Men with badges get dangerous when they think they're right."

The words settled over me like a heavy blanket. Papa knew about Thurston Blackwell and the full extent of what a man with power and authority could do to someone like me.

"Come on," I said, standing and smoothing my skirts. "I need to get to the store, and you need to practice disappearing faster. That was too close."

Papa stood as well, but his expression remained troubled. I moved toward the front door, checking to make sure the street was empty. Seeing it was, I grabbed my reticule.

"Beau, sugar," I called toward the front room. "Time to go to the store."

"Coming, Mama!" His cheerful voice drifted back, followed by the sound of wooden toys being gathered.

A moment later, Beau appeared clutching his favorite horse to his chest, ready for another day of adventures behind the mercantile counter. Papa reached over and ruffled Beau's hair, his touch gentle. But his eyes told a different story, fixed on that carefree smile, shadowed with worry he couldn't hide.

As we stepped out into the morning sunshine, Beau chattering about his plans for the wooden animal, I breathed in the dry desert air mixed with the scent of sage and dust. The weight of secrets pressed down on my shoulders, but I straightened my spine and kept walking. We had a store to run, a life to maintain, and a father to protect.

And somewhere in the back of my mind, Flynn Harper's blue eyes and steady voice lingered. Not quite a promise. Not quite a threat. Just a presence I couldn't seem to shake, no matter how hard I tried.

6 - Unexpected Reunion

Flynn

THE MORNING SUN cast long shadows across Holbrook's main street as I made my way back to the mercantile. Dust motes danced in the golden light streaming through the store's front windows. Lavinia moved behind the glass, arranging merchandise with practiced efficiency. Even from across the street, her graceful movements captured my attention and wouldn't let go.

All night I'd studied Kellerman's documents, comparing signatures and dates, searching for inconsistencies that might point toward the truth. The more I examined the evidence, the clearer the pattern became. Someone had gone to considerable trouble to implicate A.C. Beaumont. The forgeries were too perfect, and the timing too convenient. But proving it demanded evidence. Evidence I hadn't uncovered. Yet.

The bell above the mercantile door chimed at my entrance. Lavinia looked up from the crate of canned goods she was unpacking. Her wary brown eyes met mine, but something else flickered beneath the caution. We both knew what stood between us. I wore the badge, and she protected the man I'd come to arrest.

"Marshal Harper." She straightened, smoothing her blue calico skirt with hands that betrayed the slightest tremor. The morning light caught the gold threads in her hair as she moved. "Back so soon?"

"Ma'am." I touched my hat brim, stepping closer to the counter. The scent of coffee and cinnamon drifted from somewhere in the back of the store. "I was hoping to speak with your father again. Has he returned from his business trip?"

A shadow crossed her features, gone before I could read its meaning. "I'm afraid not. Papa's still away, and I'm not sure when he'll be back." She moved behind the counter, but as she did, her sleeve caught the edge of a small glass jar.

We both reached for it at the same time as it teetered on the counter's edge. My fingers brushed hers as we steadied the jar together, and the warmth of her skin against mine sent a jolt through me. For a heartbeat, we stood close enough that the tiny flecks of gold in her brown eyes were visible, and the faint scent of lavender soap from her hair filled the space between us.

She pulled back quickly, color rising in her cheeks. "Clumsy of me."

"No harm done." I kept my voice steady despite my racing pulse. The solid oak counter now stood between us like a barrier. She stood where she could watch both doors.

"Is there something I can help you with?" she asked, her voice slightly breathless. "Perhaps more shaving soap? A new pair of gloves?"

I studied her face and posture. Careful. Guarded. Her shoulders carried tension she couldn't quite hide. Everything about her posture suggested she was prepared for a fight she hoped to avoid. "I've been reviewing the documents in my possession, Miss Beaumont. There are some discrepancies I need to discuss with him."

"What kind of discrepancies?"

Before I could answer, the sound of approaching hoofbeats caught my attention through the open windows. The rhythmic clip-clop on packed earth followed by the creak of leather and the jangle of spurs. I glanced toward the front window and felt my stomach drop like a stone thrown into a well. A familiar figure dismounted from a paint gelding, moving with the serene confidence I'd known all my life.

Shane.

My older brother tied his horse to the hitching post with the methodical care that marked everything he did, then turned toward the mercantile. Even at this distance, I recognized the silver star pinned to his vest and the careful way his eyes swept the street. Habits ingrained through years of tracking outlaws.

What in blazes was he doing in Holbrook?

The bell chimed again as Shane pushed through the door, his tall frame filling the entrance. His dark hair was dusty from travel, and the familiar scents of leather, horse, and desert air clung to him. When his gaze found mine, surprise flickered across his features.

"Flynn?" His voice carried the same steady authority I remembered from childhood, tinged now with confusion. "What are you doing here?"

Shane glanced at the healing cuts on my hands but saved his questions for later.

"I could ask you the same question." I moved closer, aware of how Lavinia watched our exchange. The family resemblance between Shane and me was unmistakable. We shared the same blue eyes, the same stubborn jawline, though Shane carried himself with a patience I'd never cultivated.

"Livestock investigation." Shane's gaze shifted to Lavinia, and he assessed her with the same professional eye he applied to everything. "Ma'am. Shane Harper, Territorial Livestock Detective."

"Lavinia Beaumont." She offered a polite nod, but her hands gripped the counter's edge until her knuckles turned white. "Welcome to our store, Mr. Harper."

Shane's attention returned to me, questions forming behind his careful expression. "Federal case?"

"Land fraud. Railroad theft." I kept my voice neutral, though inside I calculated the implications of Shane's unexpected arrival. "You said livestock investigation?"

"Cattle rustling. Been tracking a pattern of thefts from ranches between here and Canyon Diablo." Shane removed his hat, running a hand through his hair. "The brands have been altered. Someone with skill is behind this operation."

A chill ran down my spine as the pieces began clicking together in my mind. Professional brand alteration. Land fraud. Document forgery. The connection was too obvious to ignore, yet too circumstantial to prove.

"Interesting timing," I murmured.

Shane's eyes sharpened. "How so?"

I glanced at Lavinia, who listened to our conversation with obvious interest. Her gaze flicked between Shane and me like she was trying to solve a puzzle, and I wondered what she made of the sudden appearance of another Harper lawman in her carefully ordered world.

"Perhaps we could discuss this outside," I suggested.

"Of course." Shane settled his hat back on his head. "Miss Beaumont, pleasure meeting you. Fine establishment you have here."

"Thank you." Her voice remained carefully polite, but she watched us through the window as we stepped onto the wooden sidewalk.

The morning air was already warming under the desert sun, and dust devils spun lazily in the distance. Somewhere down the street, a hammer rang against an anvil in steady rhythm. Shane positioned himself where he could keep an eye on both the street and the mercantile's entrance. Then he slid the metal holder from his vest pocket, retrieved a toothpick, and clamped it between his teeth.

"So," he said. "Want to tell me what's really going on here?"

I studied my brother's face. Lines that hadn't been there the last time we'd met now creased his forehead and bracketed his mouth. Shane had always been the steady one, the anchor that kept the Harper family from completely falling apart after our father's abandonment. His presence here complicated everything, but it also offered possibilities I hadn't considered.

"Got a warrant out for A.C. Beaumont."

"The shopkeeper's husband?"

Heat warmed my face, and I glanced inside the building, shaking my head. "Her father."

Shane grinned and bobbed on his heels, rolling the toothpick to the other side of his mouth. I narrowed my eyes, not sure what the cocky smile meant. So I continued.

"He's supposedly involved in fraudulent land deals involving railroad property. But everyone in town swears he's honest as the day is long." I kept my voice low, though no one was close enough to overhear. "The evidence looks solid, but something doesn't feel right about this case."

Shane nodded slowly. "And the rustling operation I'm tracking involves altered brands and forged shipping documents. Someone's been moving stolen cattle through legitimate channels, making the thefts look like legal sales. We're talking about hundreds of head, Flynn. Maybe thousands. This isn't some small-time outfit."

"Forged documents," I repeated, feeling another piece of the puzzle slide into place. "The same skill set required for land fraud."

"Exactly." Shane leaned against the hitching post, his expression thoughtful. "What if we're chasing different parts of the same operation? These aren't ordinary rustlers. They've got connections with railroad officials, land office clerks, maybe even territorial politicians."

The possibility settled in, sharp and sudden, like biting down on a bad tooth. If Shane was right, then A.C. Beaumont might not be a criminal at all. He might be a victim. Someone stole his identity to cover an outlaw ring.

"The daughter seems protective of him," I observed, glancing back toward the mercantile where Lavinia stood visible through the window.

"Can't say I blame her." Shane followed my gaze, and a slight smile touched his lips. "She's a handsome woman with a backbone of iron. Watch how she carries herself."

Heat crept up my neck at Shane's casual observation. "This is official duty. Nothing more."

"Is it?" Shane's tone remained mild, but I knew that look. He'd worn the same expression when we were children and he'd tried to coax the truth out of me about some minor transgression. "Because from where I was standing, you looked at her like she was a lot more than just a witness."

"You're imagining things."

"Am I?" Shane straightened, crossing his arms. "How long since you've taken any time for yourself? Any time that didn't involve chasing criminals across the territory?"

"That's not relevant to the case."

"Maybe not. But it's relevant to you." Shane's voice carried the same gentle authority he'd used to talk sense into me countless times over the years. "You can't live your whole life trying to prove you're different from him."

The words hit closer to home than I wanted to admit. "This isn't about Galen Harper."

"Isn't it?" Shane studied my face with uncomfortable intensity. "Every case you take, every criminal you chase... You're still trying to wash the stain off our family name. At some point you have to realize you've already proven yourself."

I started to speak, but the truth had already drawn first. How many criminals had I tracked across this territory? How many times had I pushed myself harder, taken greater risks, simply to prove that a Harper could stand on the right side of the law? To live up to the creed Shane had given us: When justice is executed, it is a joy to the righteous but a terror to evildoers.

"The case still needs to be solved," I said finally.

"Agreed. And we'll solve it." Shane pushed away from the hitching post. "But we'll do it right. Thorough investigation, proper evidence, no shortcuts."

"I don't take shortcuts."

"No," Shane said, voice steady but edged. "Though you do let anger steer the reins."

He didn't blink. "Prescott ring a bell? You rode in so set on the chase, you near forgot your own skin."

The memory stung because it was accurate. I'd cornered a suspected murderer in an abandoned mine shaft, so focused on making the arrest that I'd walked straight into an ambush. Only God and Shane's timely arrival had kept me breathing.

"This is different," I insisted.

"Is it? Because from what I can see, you're already emotionally invested in proving A.C. Beaumont's innocence. And that investment might have more to do with his daughter than the evidence."

Before I could respond, the mercantile door opened, and Lavinia stepped onto the sidewalk. She moved with purpose, her blue skirts swishing around her ankles. The morning light brought out the gold in her hair, and the wooden boards creaked softly under her feet as she approached.

"Marshal Harper," she addressed me, then included Shane with a polite nod. "Mr. Harper. I couldn't help but notice your serious discussion. If it concerns my father, I'd appreciate being included."

Shane glanced at me, one eyebrow raised in a silent question. I studied Lavinia's face. The determined set of her jaw. The way she held herself ready for whatever we might tell her. She had a right to know what we suspected, even if it meant revealing more than I'd originally intended.

"Miss Beaumont," I began carefully. "Looks like someone might be using your father's name to hide their own wrongdoings. If that's the case, he's being set up to take the fall."

Relief flickered across her features so quickly I almost missed it, followed immediately by anger that brought color to her cheeks. "You mean someone's been deliberately framing him?"

"It's a possibility we're investigating," Shane said smoothly. "But we'll need more evidence before we can prove anything."

"What kind of evidence?" Lavinia stepped closer. The scent of lavender soap drifted from her hair, and my pulse kicked harder. "What can I do to help?"

"We need a sample of your father's actual handwriting," I explained. "Something we can compare to the signatures on the fraudulent documents."

A shadow crossed her face. "That might be difficult, given that Papa's still away on business."

Shane studied her with the same careful attention he applied to analyzing cattle brands. "Miss Beaumont, with respect, your father's absence is mighty convenient timing. When the law's closing in, some men'd rather ride into the hills than stand tall in a courtroom or swing from a tree."

"My father is not running from anything." Lavinia's voice carried a sharp edge that reminded me of that quiet grit I'd glimpsed yesterday. "He's an honest man who's never broken a law in his life."

"We believe you," I blurted. "But we need his cooperation to prove his innocence. The longer he stays away, the more it looks like he's guilty."

Lavinia's hands clenched into fists at her sides. "What are you suggesting?"

"We need to speak with him," I said. "Get his side of the story. Obtain handwriting samples. Find out if he has any idea who might want to frame him."

"And if we can connect his case to the rustling operation I'm investigating," Shane continued, "we might be able to expose the entire criminal network."

I watched Lavinia's face as she processed this information. Her brown eyes flitted between Shane and me. She was weighing options, trying to decide how much she could trust us.

"When Papa returns," she said finally, "I'll ask him to speak with you. But I won't have him arrested on trumped-up charges while you're still investigating."

"That's fair," Shane agreed before I could speak. "We're not looking to arrest an innocent man. We want the truth."

"And what if the truth is inconvenient for your careers?" The question came out sharper than she'd probably intended, and she winced slightly. "What if proving Papa's innocence means admitting the federal government made a mistake?"

The pain in her voice suggested men with power had hurt her before. Betrayed her. Someone who should have protected her. The realization stirred something in my chest, a desire to hunt down whoever put that wariness in her eyes.

"Miss Beaumont," I said, "I took an oath to uphold justice, not to defend the government's reputation. If your father's innocent, I'll move heaven and earth to prove it."

She studied my face for a long moment, like she saw straight through to my soul. Whatever she found there must have satisfied her, because some of the tension left her shoulders.

"I believe you mean that," she breathed.

"He does." Shane's voice carried conviction. "Flynn's many things—stubborn, impulsive, too quick to anger—but he's never compromised his integrity for convenience."

Heat crept up my neck at Shane's casual inventory of

my flaws, but I couldn't dispute the assessment. "We should get back to work. The longer this drags out, the more danger your family might be in."

Lavinia's eyes widened. "Danger?"

"If someone's gone to this much trouble to frame your father, they won't want him around to tell his side of the story," Shane explained. "Professional criminals rarely leave loose ends. And if this operation is as big as I think it is, they've got resources and connections we're only beginning to understand."

The color drained from Lavinia's face, and her hand moved unconsciously toward her throat. "You think they might try to hurt him?"

"It's possible." I kept my voice steady, though I silently cursed myself for not considering this angle sooner. "Which is another reason we need to find the real criminals quickly."

"I'll talk to Papa when he returns," Lavinia promised. "But please be careful. If these people are as dangerous as you suggest, you could walk into more than you bargained for."

The concern in her voice sent unexpected warmth through my chest. When was the last time someone worried about my safety? Shane did, of course, but that was different. Family obligation. This felt personal in a way that both thrilled and terrified me.

"We'll be careful," Shane assured her. "And Miss Beaumont? If you notice anything unusual—strangers asking questions, anyone watching your house or the store—let us know immediately."

She nodded, though fear shadowed her face. "I should get back to work. Beau will wonder where I've gone."

"Beau?" Shane asked.

"My son," Lavinia explained, and I caught the slight hesitation before the word son. "He's five years old."

Shane nodded politely, but the quick glance he shot in

my direction spoke volumes. Another rope to untangle in a knot that was already plenty snarled.

"Take care, Miss Beaumont," I said, touching my hat brim.

"You too, Marshal Harper. Both of you."

We watched her disappear back into the mercantile, and Shane studied my face with obvious amusement.

"Don't," I warned.

"Don't what?"

"Don't say whatever you're thinking."

Shane chuckled, the sound carrying warmth. "I was just thinking that this case keeps getting more interesting."

"It's about justice," I repeated.

"'Course it is." Shane's tone was completely innocent, which made it even more suspicious. "Just remember, she's part of your investigation. Getting too close to witnesses makes it harder to see them clearly."

Heat crept up the back of my neck. "I'm not getting too close."

"Good. Keep it that way." Shane's expression returned to business. "So, what's our next move?"

I forced myself to focus on the investigation, though part of my mind remained fixed on brown eyes and a voice that carried the music of home. "We need to compare our evidence. If the same people are behind both the land fraud and the rustling, there should be connections we can trace."

"Agreed. And Flynn?" Shane's expression grew serious. "Whatever your feelings about Miss Beaumont, don't let them cloud your judgment. She's hiding something. Saw it in the way she answered our questions."

It caught me off guard, clean and sudden, like wind through a broken window. Shane was right again. Lavinia was definitely concealing something, and her careful responses suggested it was more significant than simply not knowing where her father was.

"I know," I admitted.

"Do you? Because from where I was standing, you looked ready to take her word as gospel truth."

The accuracy of Shane's assessment stung. "She's protecting her family. That doesn't make her a criminal."

"No, but it might make her an obstacle to finding the truth. Promise me you'll keep your objectivity."

The urge to argue rose in me, to tell him he was wrong about my feelings affecting my judgment. But the truth was, every instinct I possessed screamed that Lavinia Beaumont was exactly what she appeared to be. A devoted daughter trying to protect her family from forces beyond her control.

"I'll keep my objectivity," I promised, though the words felt like a lie.

"Good." Shane mounted his horse with easy grace. "I'm going to ride out and check some ranches that have reported rustling. See if I can find any connection to your land fraud case."

"I'll ask around town, see if anyone remembers strangers asking questions about A.C. Beaumont."

"Meet back here this evening?"

"Agreed."

Shane rode off, disappearing around the corner in a cloud of dust. I stood alone on the wooden sidewalk. Through the mercantile window, Lavinia moved between the shelves, her graceful form a constant distraction from the questions that needed answering.

Shane was right about one thing. My emotional investment in this case had nothing to do with official duty. The problem was, I wasn't sure I cared enough to change that fact.

Because for the first time in my life, I'd found something worth fighting for that had nothing to do with badges or justice or proving myself different from the man who'd abandoned us.

I'd found a woman whose courage and devotion made me want to be better than I'd ever imagined possible.

The question was whether she'd ever trust me enough to let me try.

7 - Unwelcome Guest

Lavinia

THE BELL ABOVE the mercantile door chimed my return, but instead of bringing its familiar comfort, today the sound sent a chill down my spine. My hands still trembled slightly from the conversation with the Harper brothers, and my mind raced with everything they'd revealed. Professional criminals. Dangerous connections. The possibility that Papa was being deliberately framed.

I hurried toward the back of the store, my calico skirts rustling against the wooden counters. "Beau, sugar, where are you?"

"Back here, Mama!" His cheerful voice drifted from behind the main counter where he'd built an elaborate city from empty wooden crates and bolts of fabric. "Mama, look! I made a jail for the bad horses!"

Despite everything weighing on my mind, I couldn't help but smile at his innocent play. "That's wonderful, sugar. You keep building while Mama checks on something."

I pushed through the curtain that separated the main room from the back office and storage area, expecting to find the space empty. Instead, I nearly collided with Papa, who was crouched behind a stack of flour barrels, peering through a gap in the curtain toward the front of the store.

"Papa!" I hissed, my voice sharp with panic and anger. "What in heaven's name are you doing here?"

He straightened, his weathered face creased with concern. "I was worried about the marshal showing up. I thought if something went wrong—"

"Something could have gone very wrong!" I stepped closer, keeping my voice low but letting my fury show. "Do you have any idea how dangerous this was? Marshal Harper notices everything—if he'd seen you, if he'd heard something—"

"I was careful," Papa insisted. "I came through the back alley, making sure no one saw me."

"That's not the point!" My hands shook as I gestured toward the front of the store. "Papa, they just told me we're dealing with a gang of outlaws. People who don't leave loose ends. And here you are, exposing yourself in broad daylight!"

His shoulders sagged, and the fight went out of him, leaving him looking frail and worn. "I'm sorry, darling. I just... I couldn't stand the thought of you facing this alone."

The genuine remorse in his voice softened my anger, though the fear remained sharp as a knife blade. "I know. I know you were trying to protect me. But Papa, we have to be smarter than this."

I quickly filled him in on everything the Harper brothers had told me. They suspected someone was using his identity to cover larger crimes. The connection to cattle rustling. The possibility of exposing an entire criminal network. With each word, I watched hope and fear war across his features.

"They really think I'm innocent?" he asked.

"They do. Marshal Harper said he'd move heaven and earth to prove it if you're being framed." The memory of

Flynn's intense blue eyes and the conviction in his voice touched my heart. "They also said these criminals won't want you around to tell your side of the story."

The color drained from his face. "You mean they might try to—"

"Yes." I reached out and gripped his hands, feeling how they trembled slightly. "Which is why your taking risks like this terrifies me. We need to be more careful than ever."

Before Papa could respond, the bell at the front of the store chimed again. We both froze, listening to measured footsteps moving through the store.

"Stay hidden," I whispered, adjusting the curtain to conceal him completely. "I'll handle whoever it is."

I smoothed my skirts and checked my reflection in the small mirror Papa kept for customers trying on hats. My face was pale but composed, though my brown eyes still held traces of the fear that had been my constant companion since seeing that wanted poster. Taking a deep breath, I pushed through the curtain and stepped into the main room.

"Good afternoon," I called out, forcing brightness into my voice. "Welcome to Beaumont's Mercantile."

The man standing near my display of canned goods was tall and distinguished, with dark hair silvered at the temples and an expensive suit that marked him as someone of means. A gold pocket watch chain glinted across his vest, and his perfectly polished boots had never seen a day of honest work. He carried himself with an air of authority that commanded attention and respect.

Years of careful distance unraveled, thread by thread, as he met my gaze.

Thurston Blackwell.

Six years. Six years since I'd last seen that handsome face, those calculating dark eyes. Six years since he'd whispered sweet promises in my ear and painted pictures of the life we'd build together. Six years since he'd taken my virtue and my trust, then disappeared like morning mist when I'd told him about the baby.

He stood there, and something in me buckled quietly, like a porch beam giving way. My stomach lurched violently, and I gripped the edge of the counter to keep from swaying. I was as exposed as I had been at sixteen.

"Miss Beaumont." His voice was exactly as I remembered, smooth as aged whiskey, cultured and confident. He smiled, and I saw the same charm that had once swept me off my feet. "Or should I say, Miss Lavinia Beaumont of Holbrook, Arizona?"

I opened my mouth to speak, but no words came. My throat closed, and my heart hammered against my ribs so loudly I was certain he must hear it too.

"You look well," he continued, moving closer, his poise and veiled tone too familiar. "Frontier life agrees with you."

"I..." The word came out as barely a whisper. I cleared my throat and tried again. "I'm sorry, but I don't believe we've been introduced."

The lie tasted like ash in my mouth, but what else could I say? The truth was impossible. He was here in our store, with Papa hidden mere feet away and Beau playing innocently behind the counter.

Thurston's smile widened, and I saw the flash of amusement in his dark eyes. He was enjoying my obvious distress.

"Of course not," he said smoothly. "How thoughtless of me. Thurston Blackwell, at your service." He removed his hat with a flourish, revealing more of that silver-touched hair. "I'm here on business. Railroad investments and land speculation. I was told this was the finest mercantile in town."

Railroad investments. Land speculation. The words echoed in my mind as pieces began clicking together with horrible clarity. The charges against Papa. The fraudulent documents. The sophisticated criminal network the Harper brothers had described.

Sweet merciful heaven. Could Thurston be behind it all?

"Mr. Blackwell," I managed, proud that my voice sounded steadier than I felt. "What can I help you find?"

"Actually, I was hoping to speak with the owner. A.C. Beaumont, I believe?" His gaze swept the store with casual interest, but his eyes lingered on the curtained doorway to the back office. "Is he available?"

Terror shot through me like lightning. Papa was back there, probably listening to every word. If Thurston discovered him...

"I'm afraid my father is away on business," I said. "I manage the store operations. Perhaps I could assist you instead?"

"Your father." Something cold flickered in his expression. "I've heard so much about his... ventures. And you've been running things here for how long?"

The innocent question carried a hidden meaning that made my skin crawl. How much did he know about our life here? How long had he been watching, planning, waiting?

"Several years," I replied carefully. "Is there something specific you're looking for, Mr. Blackwell?"

Before he could answer, Beau's voice piped up from behind the counter. "Mama, look! I made a church for the good horses!"

A chill settled in my bones as Thurston's gaze sharpened, focusing on the area where my son's voice had come from. Those calculating dark eyes took on a predatory gleam that made my skin crawl.

"You have a child?" he asked, moving toward the counter with deliberate steps.

"Yes." I hurried to intercept him, positioning myself between Thurston and Beau. "My son. He's five years old."

Beau popped his head up from his play area, dark hair

tousled and brown eyes bright with curiosity. "Hello, mister!"

I watched Thurston's face as he took in Beau's features—the dark hair, the intelligent eyes, the distinct jaw that would someday mirror his own. For a moment, something flickered in his expression. Surprise? Recognition? Or did I imagine connections that weren't there?

"Hello there, young man," Thurston said, his voice carrying the same false warmth I remembered from our courtship. "What's your name?"

"Beauregard Beaumont. But everyone calls me Beau. Mama says it's 'cause I'm beautiful."

I saw Thurston's slight smile at the introduction, and rage mixed with my terror. Here was Beau's natural father, the man who'd abandoned us both, now threatening to destroy the only family my son had ever known.

"Beau is a fine name for a fine boy," Thurston observed. "He has your eyes, Miss Beaumont. But other features... must favor his father."

The comment found its mark, like a needle through worn cloth. I knew what he was thinking, what he was calculating. The timing would be right. The age would match. And if he'd been keeping track of me...

"Beau, sugar," I said, my voice tight with the effort to remain calm. "Why don't you take your horses to the office and set up your stable there? Mama needs to help this gentleman."

Beau gathered his wooden animals and disappeared through the curtain, his cheerful chatter fading as he moved deeper into the store. I prayed Papa would keep him occupied and quiet.

Thurston watched this exchange with obvious interest, then turned his attention back to me. "Charming boy. You've done well for yourself here, Lavinia."

My skin crawled at the familiar intimacy in his voice. "I prefer Miss Beaumont, if you please."

"Of course. How proper of you." His smile never

wavered, but something cold flickered in his eyes. "It's remarkable, really. A young unmarried woman building such a respectable life in a place like this. Most people would ask questions about... circumstances."

The threat was subtle, but unmistakable. He knew my secrets, knew how precarious my position was. One word from him about my past, about Beau's parentage, and everything I'd built would crumble like dust.

"Was there something you needed to purchase, Mr. Blackwell?" I asked, lifting my chin despite the terror clawing at my throat.

"Actually, I was hoping to discuss some business opportunities with your father. Land investments, railroad contracts. Ventures that could be quite profitable for a man with the right... connections."

He was taunting me, letting me know exactly what he was doing to Papa while standing here in our store, threatening everything we'd built.

"Papa doesn't involve himself in land speculation," I said firmly. "He's a simple merchant."

"Is he?" Thurston moved closer. I caught the scent of his expensive cologne—the same one he'd worn in Georgia, the one that had once made my foolish young heart race. Nausea rolled through me. "Because I have some documents that suggest otherwise. Contracts bearing his signature. Business dealings worth considerable sums."

My hands clenched into fists at my sides. "I don't know what you're talking about."

"Don't you?" He stepped closer, close enough to murmur. "Lavinia, surely you don't believe this is all just coincidence. My business brought me here, to this charming little town, to this particular store?"

The possessiveness and familiarity in his voice turned my stomach. This wasn't coincidence. He'd found me deliberately, had been planning this encounter. But why now? What did he want?

"I think you should leave," I said, proud that my

voice remained steady.

"Should I? But I haven't made my purchase yet." He moved to the display of goods near the window, picking up items at random. "Beautiful little town you have here. Safe. Peaceful. A place where people mind their own business, and don't ask too many questions about a person's past."

Each word reminded me how vulnerable we were. Our reputation, our business, our safety—all of it hung by a thread he could cut whenever he chose.

"It would be a shame," he continued, examining a bolt of brown fabric with apparent interest, "if something were to disrupt such a peaceful community. If, say, certain revelations about respected citizens came to light. Revelations that might force a family to... relocate again."

Rage mixed with terror until my vision blurred. How dare he stand here in our store, enjoying my helplessness? How dare he destroy Papa's life to cover his own crimes, then come here to gloat about it?

But underneath the anger ran something deeper and more corrosive—shame. I'd been naïve enough to trust him. My stupidity had given him this power over us. My past sins now endangered the two people I loved most in the world.

"Five dollars should cover this fabric," Thurston said, placing money on the counter. "And Miss Beaumont? I'll be staying in town for a few days. Perhaps we'll have another chance to... renew our acquaintance."

He tipped his hat and strolled toward the door, taking his time like a man savoring his victory. At the threshold, he turned back.

"Give my regards to your father when he returns from his business trip. I do hope we'll meet soon."

The bell chimed his departure, leaving me alone with the echo of his threats and the devastating knowledge of what I'd done to my family.

My legs gave out. I sank onto the stool behind the

counter, trembling like a leaf in a windstorm. All those nights I'd lain awake, wondering if he'd ever come looking for me, if he'd ever want to claim Beau or destroy what I'd built. I'd thought we were safe here, thought the distance and time had protected us.

But I'd been wrong. So terribly, foolishly wrong.

"Lavinia?" Papa's voice drifted through the curtain, thick with concern. "Who was that man?"

I couldn't answer. Couldn't find the words to explain that our past had finally caught up with us, that the monster from my nightmares had walked back into our lives.

Behind the curtain, I could hear Beau's merry chatter as he played with his wooden horses, innocent of the danger that had just darkened our doorstep. My beautiful, sweet boy, who would never know his real father was a devil in expensive clothes.

The irony was bitter as poison. Just hours ago, I'd begun to hope that Flynn Harper might be different from other powerful men, that his promise to help Papa might be genuine. I'd actually started to believe that someone with a badge and authority might be trustworthy.

And now Thurston was here, reminding me why trusting any powerful man was the most dangerous mistake a woman could make.

I sat there in the afternoon sunlight streaming through the windows, surrounded by the familiar comfort of the store we'd built together, and watched my carefully constructed world begin to collapse.

The past never really stayed buried. My sins would follow me no matter how far I ran.

I closed my eyes and tried to find the peace that prayer usually brought, but the words wouldn't come. How could I ask God for protection when my own sins had brought this danger to our door? Yet somewhere in the darkness of my despair, I remembered Papa's gentle words from years ago. *God's grace covers even our worst mistakes, darling. Don't let shame keep you from His love.*

I knew it was true. Had preached it to myself countless times. But knowing and feeling were different things entirely. Grace felt distant as the stars in this moment, crushed as I was by the weight of my shame.

8 - Buried Ghosts

Flynn

THE HOTEL DINING room smelled of fried beef and strong coffee, with undertones of tobacco smoke drifting in from the adjacent smoking lounge. Oil lamps cast flickering shadows across the rough-hewn walls, and the murmur of conversation from other patrons created a backdrop for private discussion. I claimed a corner table with a clear view of both the front entrance and the staircase leading to the guest rooms upstairs.

Shane entered the hotel at precisely seven o'clock, dust still clinging to his boots and his shoulders sagging from a long day in the saddle. He was always punctual. Some habits never changed.

"Find anything interesting?" I asked as he settled into the chair across from me, positioning himself so he could watch the room's other occupants.

"More than I bargained for." Shane signaled the waitress, a tired-looking woman with graying hair pulled back in a practical bun. "Coffee, ma'am, and whatever's hot."

"Same for me," I added, though I'd barely touched food since this morning's conversation with Lavinia. Her carefully controlled responses nagged at me like a splinter I couldn't quite locate.

Shane waited until the waitress moved out of earshot before dropping his voice to the low murmur we learned during childhood when discussing matters our father shouldn't overhear. "Visited three ranches today. Each one reported cattle missing over the past six months. Professional job, Flynn. Brands altered so cleanly you'd think they were original if you didn't know better."

I nodded, expecting as much. Shane had been slowly unraveling a territory-wide network of rustlers ever since we helped Hayley with that job at the Aztec Land & Cattle Company. Capturing their outlaw leader had been only the beginning.

"What about the paperwork?"

"That's where it gets interesting." Shane pulled a folded document from his vest pocket, keeping it below table level. "Found this bill of sale at the Morrison ranch. Looks legitimate—proper stamps, official language, even the right paper. But the signature—" He shook his head grimly. "Morrison swears he never signed it."

"Wait, Morrison?" I set down my coffee cup, remembering the grizzled face and tobacco-stained whiskers. "Pete Morrison? Older fellow hangs around the barbershop?"

"That's him. Son runs the ranch now. You know him?"

"Talked to him yesterday when I was asking around about A.C. Beaumont. He and another old-timer named Cain were sitting outside the barbershop." I leaned forward as understanding dawned. "He defended A.C.'s character, said he was honest in his dealings. But now that I think about it, he seemed nervous. Kept fidgeting, wouldn't quite meet my eyes."

"Nervous about what?"

"I figured he was just being cautious around a federal marshal. But what if he was worried about his family's troubles? Stolen cattle, forged paperwork." I rubbed my jaw thoughtfully. "What if Morrison didn't want to mention the rustling problems because he was afraid it would somehow connect to A.C.'s legal troubles?"

"Or because he knows more about both situations than he's letting on." Shane's expression turned thoughtful. "Small town like this, everybody knows everybody's business. If there's a connection between the land fraud and the cattle theft, the locals might have noticed patterns we're missing."

The waitress returned with steaming mugs of coffee and bowls of beef stew that smelled downright tantalizing. My stomach growled. I waited until she'd departed again before examining the document Shane slid across the table.

The handwriting was confident, flowing. The work of someone educated and practiced. Too practiced, maybe. Just like the signatures on the documents from Kellerman's satchel.

"Same quality as the land fraud evidence," I observed, comparing the paper to my mental image of A.C. Beaumont's supposed contracts. "Whoever's behind this has resources. Professional forgers and inside connections."

"And patience." Shane took a cautious sip of coffee, testing the temperature. "This isn't some spur-of-the-moment operation. Someone's been planning this for months, maybe years."

I thought about my conversations with the townspeople today, the careful way they defended A.C. Beaumont while revealing as little as possible about their own observations. Most had been genuinely protective, but one exchange stuck in my mind like a burr.

"Talked to the postmaster after you left," I said. "Interesting fellow. Loves to gossip, but he mentioned something odd. Said a wealthy Southern gentleman had been asking questions about land deals in the area. Recent visitor, maybe three weeks ago."

Shane's spoon paused halfway to his mouth. "Describe him."

"Well-dressed, expensive clothes. Cultured accent, polite manners. Claimed to be interested in railroad investments." I stirred my stew absently, my mind working through the implications. "At first I wondered if he meant A.C., but nobody else described him as particularly wealthy. Just a shopkeeper making an honest living."

"Three weeks ago would fit the timeline." Shane's brow furrowed. "Most of the altered bills of sale are dated within the last month. And," He drew closer, dropping his voice even further. "The cattle that were stolen? They've been shipped east on the Atlantic & Pacific. Someone with railroad connections is moving them through legitimate channels."

The picture was becoming clearer, and it made my stomach churn. Skilled forgery. Railroad connections. A wealthy Southern gentleman asking pointed questions about local land deals. This wasn't a random crime. It was deliberate, organized, and backed by someone with serious resources.

"There's something else," I said, remembering Kellerman's last words with a familiar surge of anger. "Right before he fell, Kellerman said something about how our family name is connected to these documents."

"That where you got those?" Shane examined the wounds on my palms.

"Yup."

His face hardened. "What do you think he meant?"

"Could be nothing. The ravings of a desperate man trying to rattle me." I took a bite of stew, barely tasting it. "But what if he meant something specific? What if whoever's behind this has some connection to our past?"

"You mean to him." Shane didn't need to specify who he meant. Galen Harper's shadow followed us our entire lives, coloring every choice we made and every badge we pinned on.

"Maybe." I stared into my coffee, seeing my wretched father's face reflected in the dark surface. "Or maybe Kellerman was just trying to get under my skin. He knew my reputation, knew how to push my buttons."

Shane watched my face with careful attention. "You don't believe that."

"No," I admitted. "I don't. Something about this whole situation feels personal. Too targeted, too specific. Why frame A.C. Beaumont? Why choose a small-town shopkeeper with no political connections?"

"Unless he's not as powerless as he appears." Shane's tone carried a warning. "Have you considered the possibility that A.C. Beaumont might not be entirely innocent?"

The suggestion hit me harder than it should have. "Everyone in town vouches for his character."

"Everyone in town might be wrong. Or they might have reasons to protect him that have nothing to do with his actual guilt or innocence." Shane remained patient, but I caught the underlying concern. "I know you want to believe the best about this family, but we can't let personal feelings cloud our judgment."

Heat crept up my neck at his implication. "This isn't about personal feelings."

"Isn't it?" Shane studied me with uncomfortable intensity. "You've talked to his daughter a few times, and you're already convinced he's being framed. That's not like you."

I bit back a protest. Every instinct I possessed screamed that Lavinia Beaumont was exactly what she appeared to be—a devoted daughter protecting her family from forces beyond her control. And that instinct had nothing to do with evidence or judgment.

"She's hiding something," I admitted reluctantly. "But hiding something doesn't make her father guilty of federal crimes."

"No, but it makes her information unreliable." Shane sipped his coffee. "Promise me you'll keep an open mind about this case. All the possibilities, not just the ones that make her father innocent."

I nodded, though the words felt like swallowing glass. "I'll consider all the evidence."

"Good. Because tomorrow we need to—" Shane stopped mid-sentence, his gaze shifting to something beyond my shoulder. His hand moved instinctively toward his holster.

A crash of breaking glass and raised voices erupted from across the street. I turned toward the commotion. A brawl spilled out of the saloon, two cowhands grappling on the boardwalk while others shouted encouragement.

Then my attention snagged on something else entirely.

A man stepped into the pool of light cast by the mercantile's front window, well away from the saloon fight.

My chest tightened. The air in the room seemed to thin.

Tall. Lean build with broad shoulders that carried themselves with casual arrogance. The way he moved—confident, predatory, like a man who'd never met an obstacle he couldn't overcome or eliminate. Even from this distance, even in the waning light, something about the angle of his head, the particular set of his jaw, the way his hands hung loose at his sides but ready...

Cold sweat broke across my shoulders. My right hand drifted toward my holster before I caught myself.

It couldn't be him. The rational part of my mind knew it was impossible. Galen Harper was locked up in Yuma Territorial Prison, rotting behind walls three feet thick. We'd put him there ourselves. Watched the judge hand down the sentence. Received confirmation of his transfer.

But the irrational part—the part that had learned to survive by reading danger in shadows and anticipating violence before it arrived—that part screamed recognition.

The figure moved again, turning slightly as if surveying the street. The lamplight caught his profile, and for just a moment I saw the sharp angles of a face I'd spent years trying to forget. The same build I'd watched disappear into the night after another beating, another abandonment, another lesson proving my father was a demon.

My pulse hammered against my throat.

"Flynn?" Shane's voice seemed to come from very far away. He'd dismissed the saloon brawl as nothing serious. "What is it?"

I dragged my focus back to his face, noting the concern creasing his features. "Thought I saw... Never mind. Trick of the light."

But Shane knew me too well to accept such a casual dismissal. His gaze sharpened, and he turned in his chair to glance toward the window. The figure had already moved past, swallowed by the darkness between buildings. "What did you see?"

"Nothing definite." I rubbed my forehead, feeling foolish for letting shadows and lamplight play tricks on my mind. "Just someone walking past who reminded me of..."

I couldn't finish the sentence. Couldn't voice the impossible fear that gripped me when that familiar silhouette crossed my vision.

"Of him?" Shane whispered.

I nodded, still staring toward the window where the empty street now stretched under the stars. "But that's impossible. He's in Yuma, rotting where he belongs."

"'Course he is." Shane's response came too quickly, betraying his own discomfort with the topic. "Territorial prison doesn't exactly have a reputation for letting inmates wander around the Arizona Territory."

"Right." I forced a laugh that sounded hollow even to my own ears. "Must be getting paranoid in my old age."

But Shane didn't laugh. Instead, he watched my face with the same methodical attention he used to examine that forged bill of sale. "When's the last time you checked on his status? Confirmed he was still locked up?"

The question came sharply, with no warning, like a bullet through fog. The last time I'd verified Galen Harper's imprisonment felt like a lifetime ago.

"It's been a while," I admitted.

"How long is a while?"

"Six months. Maybe more." The admission tasted like failure. What kind of lawman stopped tracking the most dangerous criminal he'd ever known? "But if he'd escaped, we would have heard. Every U.S. Marshal in the territory would have received a notification."

"Would they?" Shane's uncertainty chilled me more than any outright fear. "You know how information travels out here. Delays, lost messages, bureaucratic confusion. And if he had help?"

The implications hung between us like smoke from a dying fire. Galen Harper had always been charming, persuasive, capable of turning people to his purposes. If he corrupted someone in the prison system, if he bought or manipulated his way to freedom...

"You don't really think he escaped, do you?" The words came out rougher than I had intended.

Shane was quiet for a long moment, his gaze distant. When he finally spoke, his tone carried all the weight of our shared childhood fears. "I think we need to send a telegram to Yuma first thing tomorrow morning. Confirm his status. Put our minds at ease."

"And if he's not there?"

"Then we deal with it." Shane met my eyes without flinching. "Same way we've dealt with everything else he's thrown at us. Together."

I nodded, grateful for the solid presence of my older brother. Shane had been our anchor during the worst years, the steady voice of reason when our father's abandonment and abuse left us adrift.

I forced myself back to the case at hand. "What if whoever's framing A.C. Beaumont is also behind the cattle rustling? The Southern gentleman, the timing, the railroad connections. It all fits."

"Makes sense." Shane seemed relieved to focus on concrete evidence rather than old nightmares. "Operations this organized usually have multiple schemes running. Land fraud, cattle theft, and other crimes we haven't discovered yet."

"Which means A.C. Beaumont might just be the most visible victim. A convenient fall guy to take the blame while the real criminals operate behind the scenes."

"Or he might be the mastermind of it all." Shane's tone remained carefully neutral, but I caught the warning underneath. "I know you want to believe in this family's innocence, but we can't ignore the possibility that there's more to this story."

I thought about Lavinia's careful responses to my questions, how she positioned herself between me and whatever hid in the back of the store. The fear in her eyes when I mentioned her father's supposed crimes. That fear could mean many things like terror at false accusations, panic about family secrets, or genuine guilt about criminal activity.

"I'll keep an open mind," I promised, though every instinct rebelled against the idea that Lavinia could be involved in anything dishonest.

"Good." Shane pushed his empty plate away and signaled for more coffee. "Because tomorrow we start pulling this thread until we unravel the whole mess. Question the hotel clerk about this Southern gentleman. Check with the railroad about shipping records. Maybe even pay another visit to the mercantile."

The thought of seeing Lavinia again made my pulse quicken. Logic demanded I keep my guard up, but her fierce protectiveness and quiet strength awakened something I'd never had time to consider.

"Shane?"

"Yeah?"

"What if this case turns out to be bigger than we

thought? What if we're not just dealing with organized criminals, but with something big enough to threaten us?"

Shane considered this, his features grave in the lamplight. "Then we do our jobs. Follow the evidence wherever it leads, arrest the guilty parties, and make sure justice is served."

"Even if it means going up against people with political connections? Railroad money? Power that can destroy careers?"

"Especially then." Shane's quiet conviction had sustained our family through the darkest years. "We didn't pin on these badges to take the easy cases. We took them to prove that justice isn't just for the wealthy and connected."

"When justice is executed, it is a joy to the righteous but a terror to evildoers." Shane quoted the verse that set us Harper siblings on the path of justice.

The words settled into my chest, familiar and true. I'd built my career on them, used them to justify every fast decision, every time I chose action over patience.

Shane stood, stretching his back with the weariness of a long day's ride. "Ready to head upstairs?"

"In a minute." I remained seated, staring at the dark street beyond the window. "Think I'll finish my coffee first."

Shane nodded and headed toward the staircase, his spurs ringing softly against the wooden floor. I sat alone in the dining room, nursing lukewarm coffee and wrestling with ghosts I thought were safely buried.

The dining room gradually emptied. A rancher and his wife finished their meal and departed with quiet thanks to the waitress. Two traveling salesmen paid their bill and climbed the stairs, still arguing about railroad stocks. The waitress wiped down empty tables and gave me a look that said she was ready to close up for the night.

I stared out the window at the darkening street, my coffee growing cold. That silhouette earlier and the way the figure had moved through the lamplight. A familiar confidence in his gait. It had shaken something loose in my memory.

I was eleven years old again, standing at a window in that crumbling ranch house. Watching Shane walk toward the barn where Galen and his gang waited in the moonlight. My older brother's head had hung low, but the tension in his shoulders was visible even from a distance.

I'd known Shane had made a bargain with the devil a year and a half earlier, trading his soul to give Ike his one and only real birthday. Now Galen was calling in the debt.

Galen's silhouette had been unmistakable that night—tall, commanding, drawing Shane into his orbit like a moth to a flame. I'd watched them ride out together, my hand pressed against the windowpane, fear colder than any Arizona winter settling in my chest.

I'd been certain I would lose Shane that night. That Galen would corrupt him, claim him, and turn him into another version of himself. Lilian had prayed. I'd just hoped.

Shane had come back before dawn. Different. Harder. The next day, he'd started teaching me how to fight. How to protect myself. How to read danger in a man's posture and respond before violence erupted.

Even at eleven, I'd understood his intent had been to protect me from Galen. To make sure I could defend myself when Shane couldn't be there.

I pulled my gaze from the window and looked down at my cooling coffee. I wasn't a helpless child watching from a distance anymore. Shane had taught me to be a protector. Now I'd found someone vulnerable who needed me to step up and use those skills. A woman and her innocent son, who deserved protection from whatever storm was coming.

I drained the last of my coffee and left a few coins on the table, then made my way upstairs to the small room I'd rented. The floorboards creaked under my boots, and lamplight flickered in the narrow hallway. Somewhere down the corridor, someone snored loudly enough to rattle the walls.

Inside my room, I lit the oil lamp and locked the door. The space was barely large enough for a narrow bed, a washstand, and a single chair pushed against the wall. Functional. Temporary. Like most places I stayed.

I sat on the edge of the bed, unbuckling my gun belt. The oil lamp cast long shadows across the rough walls. Sleep felt impossible. That figure on the street, Shane's words, and the verse about justice churned in my mind like a dust devil picking up speed.

Prayer had never come easy to me. Words seemed inadequate for the tangle of thoughts and fears knotted in my chest. But the verse we'd built our lives around kept echoing in my mind. *When justice is executed, it is a joy to the righteous but a terror to evildoers.*

Executed. The word implied action, finality, swift completion. I'd always believed justice required an immediate response, no hesitation. See a threat, eliminate it. Suspect betrayal, punish it. Someone gets in your way, remove them.

That was exactly how Galen Harper operated.

I closed my eyes, my jaw clenching against the truth I'd been avoiding for years. The line between honest justice and criminality blurred beyond recognition. Swift decisions. Decisive action. Ruthless when necessary. Every choice I'd made, every criminal I'd pursued with relentless determination, looked an awful lot like the patterns Galen had seared into my soul. The same violence, just with a marshal's badge to make it feel more justified.

I opened my eyes, staring at the rough ceiling beams. The silence pressed against my ears, broken only by the creak of the building settling and distant sounds from the street.

What if I'd been focusing on the wrong part of the verse this whole time? What about the joy for the righteous? Was there any joy in the justice I delivered? Or just grim satisfaction that another criminal had been captured, another threat eliminated?

I leaned forward, elbows on my knees, and let my head drop into my hands.

Help me know when to move and when to be still. When to act and when to trust Your timing. Help me be something more than just his anger with a badge pinned on it.

The prayer felt inadequate, raw. But it was honest, and maybe that was enough.

Something in my chest loosened slightly. Not peace, exactly. More like the first crack in a dam that had been holding back too much pressure for too long.

Tomorrow I'd verify A.C. Beaumont's location. Clear his name or execute the warrant. Either way, I'd make sure Lavinia and Beau were protected best I could. But maybe I could do it without becoming the very thing I'd spent my life trying to escape.

Shane had faced the devil once to protect me. Now it was my turn to stand in the gap. Not with Galen's ruthless efficiency, but with something better. Something that might actually bring joy to the righteous instead of just terror to evildoers.

I hung my gun belt on the bedpost within easy reach and stretched out on the narrow bed, still fully dressed except for my boots. The oil lamp flickered, casting dancing shadows across the walls.

Tomorrow would bring answers. About A.C. Beaumont. About Galen. About whether I could be something more than my father's son.

9 - The Devil's Games

Lavinia

THE LATE MORNING sun streamed through the mercantile's front windows, highlighting the dust on jars and sacks. I hummed softly while dusting the shelves near the counter, grateful for the familiar rhythm of normal work. Papa had stayed home today, claiming he felt poorly. Our agreed-upon excuse was becoming easier to maintain as the stress of hiding took its toll on his health.

Behind the counter, Beau played quietly with his carved animals, creating elaborate adventures that involved horses jumping over bolts of fabric and rescuing toy soldiers from imaginary dangers. His cheerful chatter provided a comforting backdrop to the morning's tasks.

"Mama, the brown horse wants to visit the penny candy," he announced, holding up his favorite figure. "Can horses eat peppermints?"

"I don't think peppermints are good for horses, sugar," I replied, smiling at his innocent question. "But maybe the horse could smell how sweet they are."

"Oh! He could smell them and think about eating grass that tastes like peppermints!"

The simple joy in his voice warmed my heart. Despite everything threatening our small world, Beau remained blissfully unaware of the dangers lurking just beyond our carefully maintained facade. I intended to keep it that way for as long as possible.

The bell above the door stayed blessedly silent most of the morning. A few customers had come and gone. Mrs. Patterson picked up thread, the blacksmith's wife purchased coffee beans, and old Mr. Cain bought tobacco. Nothing out of the ordinary. No federal marshals asking pointed questions. No unwelcome visitors from my past.

Maybe Thurston had moved on. Maybe his business in Holbrook was finished, and he'd disappeared back into whatever shadows had concealed him for the past six years. My hope felt as fragile as spun glass, but I clung to it anyway.

I needed to restock the canned goods display near the window. The crate of new inventory sat in the back store-room, heavy enough that I'd been putting off the task until absolutely necessary. Now, with the shelves looking sparse, I could delay no longer.

"Beau, sugar, I need to fetch something from the back room," I called over my shoulder. "Keep playing with your horses. I'll be right back."

"Yes, Mama. Can I make them a parade?"

"Of course. Just don't let them march too close to anything breakable."

I pushed through the curtain, breathing in the familiar scents of coffee beans, leather goods, and the faint musti-ness that clung to the older inventory. The crate of canned peaches sat exactly where the supplier had left it three days ago, slats nailed tight and the contents heavy enough to make my back ache just thinking about lifting it.

I crouched beside the crate and began working the boards loose with a small pry bar, the sharp scent of fresh pine mixing with the earthier smells of the storeroom. The work was harder than I'd expected—whoever had nailed this crate shut had been thorough—and sweat beaded on my forehead despite the cool air.

Finally, the last board came free with a satisfying crack. I lifted several cans at a time, loading them into my apron to carry them more efficiently. The weight pulled at my shoulders, but I'd managed heavier loads. Running a business required strength in more ways than most people realized.

A faint chime from the front barely reached me through the curtain and my own movements. Another customer, probably. Nothing unusual. I gathered the last of the cans and turned toward the front of the store, my arms full and my attention focused on not dropping anything.

I pushed through the curtain with my shoulder and stepped into the main room, already composing my cheerful greeting for whoever had entered. The words died on my tongue.

Thurston Blackwell stood beside the counter where Beau played, his expensive suit and polished boots a jarring contrast to the worn floorboards and shelves of our frontier store. His presence alone would have unsettled me, but the way he studied my son set my nerves on edge. His gaze lingered on Beau with focused attention, as if he recognized something or wanted something. The same man who'd abandoned me when I was pregnant now studied my son like he had some claim to him.

"What a handsome boy," Thurston said, his cultured voice carrying the same smooth charm I remembered. "And so intelligent. You can see it in his eyes."

Beau looked up from his toys, those same eyes that had apparently caught Thurston's attention. "Thank you, mister. Mama says I'm smart like Papa."

"Does she?" Something cold flickered across Thurston's expression, though his smile never wavered. "And where is your papa today?"

"He's sick at home. Mama says he needs rest." Beau held up one of his figures, unaware of the dangerous undercurrents in the conversation. "Wanna see my horse? His name is Thunder."

"Thunder. That's a fine name for a fine horse." Thurston crouched down to Beau's level, bringing his face closer to my son's. The sight froze my blood. "You know, every boy should have a real father. Someone to teach him important things. Help him become the man he's destined to be."

The cans in my arms suddenly felt impossibly heavy. I wanted to rush forward, to snatch Beau away from this monster, but my legs wouldn't obey. Terror had turned my muscles to water.

"I have Papa," Beau said with the simple confidence of a child who'd never known want or abandonment. "He teaches me lots of stuff. About the store and counting money and being a gentleman."

"I'm sure he does his best." Condescension dripped from Thurston's tone, and my hands curled into fists around the cans. "But a boy with your potential deserves more than a simple shopkeeper can provide. Education. Opportunities. A proper place in the world."

"Papa gives me everything," Beau replied, his youthful voice carrying a note of defensiveness that broke my heart. Even at five years old, he could sense criticism of the man who'd been nothing but a loving grandfather to him.

"For now, perhaps." Thurston straightened, his gaze finally shifting from Beau to me. The smile that had charmed me at sixteen now looked predatory, calculating. "But circumstances change, don't they, Miss Beaumont? Sometimes unexpectedly."

I found my voice at last, though it came out rougher than I'd intended. "Mr. Blackwell. I didn't hear you come in."

"I move quietly when the situation calls for it." His eyes swept over me with the same possessive assessment he'd given Beau. "I was just getting acquainted with your son. Remarkable boy. He has such distinctive features."

The threat was subtle, but unmistakable.

"Beau, sugar," I managed, setting the cans on the nearest shelf with hands that trembled only slightly. "Why don't you take your horses to the back and set up that stable we talked about?"

"But Mama, the nice man wanted to see Thunder—"

"Now, please." The sharpness in my voice made Beau's eyes widen with surprise. I softened my tone with effort. "You can show him later. Go on, sugar."

Beau gathered his carved animals, clearly confused by the tension he could feel but not understand. "Yes, Mama."

He disappeared through the curtain, his small footsteps fading toward the storage area. The hush he left behind filled the space, heavy as grief with nowhere to go.

"Protective mother," Thurston observed, moving closer to where I stood. "Admirable quality. Though sometimes misguided."

"What do you want?" I kept my voice low, unwilling to risk Beau overhearing whatever poison Thurston intended to spread.

"Want?" He picked up one can I'd just brought out, examining the label with apparent interest. "Such a direct question. I'm simply conducting business in this charming town. Meeting the local merchants. Getting a sense of the opportunities available."

"Your business here is finished."

"Is it?" He set the can down with deliberate precision, his movements controlled and threatening. "Lavinia—may I call you Lavinia? We do have a history, after all. I think you misunderstand the nature of my business here."

Hearing him speak my name with such familiarity turned my stomach. "I prefer Miss Beaumont."

"Of course you do. How wonderfully respectable." The words dripped with mockery. "It's remarkable, really, what a person can accomplish when they put their mind to it. Building a new life and gaining the community's trust. Creating the impression of virtue and respectability."

Each word cut deep, quiet and precise, like a needle through silk. "I don't know what you're implying—"

"Don't you?" He leaned closer, his voice dropping to a murmur meant for my ears alone. "I'm suggesting that some foundations are less solid than they appear. Even the most carefully constructed facades can crumble with the slightest pressure."

I gripped the counter's edge until my knuckles turned white. "Are you threatening me?"

"Threatening? Goodness, no. I'm simply observing that reputations are fragile things. Especially in small communities where everyone knows everyone else's business." His smile showed all teeth and no warmth. "It would be tragic if someone's past indiscretions came to light. If a respected merchant family suddenly found themselves the subject of unwelcome gossip."

The meaning behind his words soured my stomach. He could destroy everything with a few well-placed words. Our business, our standing in the community, Beau's innocent childhood—all of it balanced on the knife's edge of Thurston's whims.

"The boy seems happy here," he continued, as if we were discussing the weather. "Content with his simple life, his loving papa, his devoted mother. But children are adaptable creatures. They adjust to new circumstances remarkably quickly, especially when those circumstances offer advantages they've never known."

Terror shot through me like lightning. "You stay away from my son."

"Your son?" Something dangerous flickered in his eyes. "How interesting that you should phrase it that way. Almost as if you have an exclusive claim to him."

Before I could respond, the bell above the door chimed again. I looked up to see Marshal Flynn Harper stepping into the store, his tall frame filling the doorway and his blue eyes immediately assessing the situation with the sharp intelligence I'd learned to both fear and admire.

His gaze moved from me to Thurston, and I saw something shift in his expression. Recognition? Suspicion? The careful neutrality of a lawman encountering a potential threat?

"Morning, Miss Beaumont," Flynn said, touching his hat brim in greeting. His voice carried its usual courtesy, but underneath, I caught a note of tension. "Hope I'm not interrupting anything important."

"Not at all, Marshal," I replied, grateful that my voice sounded steadier than I felt. "Mr. Blackwell was just browsing."

Flynn's attention focused on Thurston with uncomfortable intensity. "Blackwell? That wouldn't be Thurston Blackwell, would it? I've heard that name mentioned in town."

Thurston's smile became, if possible, even more menacing. "Marshal Harper, I presume? Your reputation precedes you. I'm flattered that my humble business dealings have attracted a marshal's attention."

"Depends on the nature of those business dealings," Flynn replied evenly. His tone carried a subtle challenge that made the air between them feel charged.

"Railroad investments, primarily. Land speculation. Nothing that should concern a U.S. Marshal." Thurston's voice remained smooth, but I caught the slight tightening around his eyes. "Unless, of course, you're investigating something specific?"

The two men faced each other across my store like gunfighters preparing to draw, and I stood caught between them, terrified of what either might reveal. Flynn represented the law, justice, protection. Everything I'd learned not to trust. But Thurston represented something far worse. My past had come back to haunt me.

"I follow wherever the truth leads," Flynn said. "Amazing how interconnected things can be in a small territory like this. A man thinks he's conducting private business, but it turns out federal interests are involved in ways he never imagined."

"Indeed." Thurston straightened, his posture shifting. "Well, Marshal, I'm sure a man of your capabilities will uncover whatever needs uncovering. The question is whether that benefits everyone involved."

Flynn shifted closer, his shoulder now between me and Thurston. "In my experience, the truth usually benefits honest folks and makes things difficult for those with something to hide."

"How wonderfully idealistic." Thurston moved toward the door. "I do hope your investigation yields results, Marshal. Though sometimes the truth proves more complicated than it first appears."

He tipped his hat to me with mock courtesy. "Miss Beaumont, always a pleasure. I'll need to speak with your father when he has a moment. And do take special care of that precious boy of yours. Children can be so vulnerable in uncertain times."

The threat was so blatant that I felt Flynn stiffen beside me. But Thurston was already moving toward the door, his expensive boots clicking against the floor with the confidence of a man who believed himself untouchable.

The bell chimed his departure, leaving Flynn and me alone in the sudden quiet. I realized I was shaking, gripping the counter so tightly that my fingers had gone numb.

"Miss Beaumont?" Flynn's voice was gentle but concerned. "Are you all right?"

I looked up into those intense blue eyes and saw genuine worry there. For a moment, I wanted nothing more than to tell him everything—about Thurston, about the past, about the danger that had just walked out of my store wearing an expensive suit and a predator's smile.

But the habit of hiding, of protecting my secrets, was too strong to break so easily.

"I'm fine," I managed. "He makes me nervous. Something about him isn't right."

Flynn nodded slowly, his gaze still fixed on the door where Thurston had disappeared. "No, there isn't. Miss Beaumont, that man matches the description of someone I've been looking for. Someone who might be connected to criminal activity in the territory."

My blood turned cold. Could there be some connection between Thurston's presence and Papa's troubles? The timing seemed too coincidental, but then again, Thurston had always been drawn to schemes that benefited him at others' expense.

"What kind of criminal activity?" I whispered.

"I'm not certain yet. But I intend to find out." Flynn's voice held an edge that reminded me why criminals feared him. "In the meantime, Miss Beaumont, I think you and your family should be very careful. Lock your doors at night. Don't let the boy wander alone. And if that man approaches you again."

"Yes?"

"Send for me immediately." His blue eyes met mine with an intensity that made my breath catch. "I meant what I said before. I won't let anything happen to innocent people. Not on my watch."

The sincerity in his voice nearly undid me. Here was a man offering protection, promising to stand between my family and whatever danger threatened us. Part of me wanted to trust him, to believe that someone with a badge could actually help rather than hurt.

But trust was a luxury I couldn't afford. Not when Beau's safety hung in the balance.

"Thank you, Marshal," I said quietly. "I'll remember that."

He studied my face for a moment longer, and I wondered what he saw there. Fear, certainly. Desperation, probably. But also the stubborn determination that had carried me through years of building a new life from the ashes of the old.

"I'll be back tomorrow," he said finally. "To check on things. Make sure everything's quiet."

I nodded, not trusting my voice to remain steady. Flynn touched his hat brim once more and headed for the door, his spurs ringing softly against the floor. He paused on the threshold, looking back.

"Miss Beaumont? That man is dangerous. More dangerous than he appears. Please be careful."

Then he was gone, leaving me alone with my fear and the echo of Thurston's threats. I sank onto the stool behind the counter, my whole body trembling like a leaf in a windstorm.

From the back room, I could hear Beau's cheerful voice as he played with his carved animals, creating stories of brave horses and daring rescues. The innocent sound broke my heart. He had no idea that a monster from my past had just walked through our door, making veiled claims about his future.

I closed my eyes and tried to find the strength to face whatever came next. Two separate nightmares were converging on my family—Papa's legal troubles and Thurston's return. Whether they were connected or a terrible coincidence, I wasn't certain that love and determination would be enough to protect the people I held most dear.

Because Thurston Blackwell had found us. And something told me he wasn't planning to leave empty-handed.

10 - Brothers Divided

Flynn

I WAS STILL thinking about Blackwell's thinly veiled threats at the mercantile when I spotted Shane waiting on the courthouse steps. The way that snake had looked at Lavinia, the fear in her eyes. It all pointed to dangers I hadn't anticipated. But first, we had court records to examine.

The morning sun cast long shadows across Holbrook's courthouse steps as Shane and I approached the solid brick building that housed Navajo County's legal proceedings. The structure stood two stories tall, with white-painted trim that gleamed against the red brick, a testament to territorial ambition in this dusty frontier town.

"You sure about this approach?" Shane asked, adjusting his badge to catch the light. "Court clerks can be touchy about federal marshals questioning their records."

"We need to verify the authenticity of these documents," I replied, checking my pocket watch. Eight-thirty in the morning. Early enough so that we'd catch the clerk before the day's business got hectic. "If someone's been forging A.C. Beaumont's signature, there might be other fraudulent papers filed here."

Shane nodded, but I caught the way his eyes swept the street behind us. He'd been more watchful since yesterday evening, when I'd mentioned that glimpse of a familiar silhouette outside the hotel. Neither of us had spoken Galen Harper's name aloud, but the specter of our father hung between us like smoke from a dying fire.

The courthouse interior smelled of ink, aged paper, and the lemon oil used to polish the wooden railings. Our boot heels thudded against the polished floors as we made our way to the clerk's office, where a thin man with wire-rimmed spectacles looked up from a ledger with the expression of someone whose morning routine had just been disrupted.

"Gentlemen? The court doesn't convene until ten o'clock."

"Morning," Shane said, producing his badge with practiced ease. "Shane Harper, Territorial Livestock Detective. This is Deputy U.S. Marshal Flynn Harper. We're hoping you could help us with some questions about document authenticity."

The clerk's name was Emerson Hartwell, according to the nameplate on his desk. His eyes darted between our badges. "Document authenticity? What sort of documents?"

I pulled the papers from Kellerman's satchel, spreading them across his desk. "These land deeds and shipping manifests. We need to verify whether they match any official records you might have on file."

Hartwell leaned forward, studying the documents through his spectacles. His ink-stained fingers traced the edges of the papers.

"The signatures appear legitimate," he said after several minutes of examination. "Quality paper, proper language, official seals. But I'd need to check our files to see if we have corresponding records."

"We'd appreciate that," Shane said smoothly. "Take your time."

Hartwell disappeared into the back room, leaving us alone with the musty scent of legal documents and the tick of a grandfather clock that marked time with solemnity. Shane moved to the window, positioning himself where he could watch both the street and the clerk's office.

"Nervous fellow," I observed.

"Nervous about something," Shane agreed. "Question is whether it's us or the documents."

Twenty minutes later, Hartwell returned with an armload of files and ledgers. Sweat beaded on his forehead despite the cool morning air.

"I found some interesting discrepancies," he said, setting the materials on his desk with shaking hands. "These documents you've shown me don't match our official records. The land parcels mentioned here were sold two years ago to different buyers entirely."

My pulse quickened. "So these are forgeries?"

"Sophisticated ones," Hartwell admitted. "Someone with considerable skill created these. The paper, the ink, even the official language seems carefully crafted to appear legitimate."

Shane leaned forward. "Mr. Hartwell, have you seen documents like these before? Other forgeries that might be connected?"

The clerk's gaze flicked toward the door. "There have been irregularities. Documents filed with signatures that don't quite match our usual standards. Always involving valuable land parcels or railroad property."

"What kind of irregularities?" I pressed.

Hartwell swallowed hard. "About a month ago, we started seeing questionable documents. Business papers and shipping manifests. Always legitimate on the surface, but something about them felt wrong."

"Did you raise concerns about them?"

"I did." His voice dropped. "I brought them to my

supervisor's attention."

Shane's posture shifted. "And?"

"And I was told not to worry about it. Specifically, they instructed me that higher authorities had reviewed and approved the filings. That questioning them further would be inappropriate."

A cold weight settled in my stomach. "Which authorities?"

"I wasn't given names. Just told that the proper people had signed off on the transactions." His fingers trembled as he touched the ledger. "When documents come with that backing, a clerk doesn't ask questions. Not if he wants to keep his position."

The implications hung heavily between us. Someone with power had shut down questions about fraudulent documents either through direct corruption or by lending their authority without proper examination.

"These questionable documents," I said. "Who signed them?"

"They came through a secretary for an attorney in Flagstaff." Hartwell opened his ledger, flipping through pages with agitated movements. "Business documents, contracts, that sort of thing. The signature was always the same."

My pulse quickened. "What name?"

"B. Irving." Hartwell tapped the entry in his ledger.

It hit like truth often does—quiet, sharp, and hard to shake. My breath caught, and the room seemed to tilt. B. Irving. One of Galen Harper's favorite aliases, used during his gang's reign of terror across the territory. I heard Shane draw a sharp breath beside me. He recognized it too.

I forced my voice to remain steady. "Can you describe this B. Irving?"

"Never met him personally. He always sent representatives with the documents." Hartwell studied his ledger. "But I understand he's an older gentleman. Well-dressed, dignified. Someone who knows how to handle legal documents."

The description was vague enough to fit dozens of men, but the timing made my blood run cold. If Galen had somehow escaped from prison, if he was operating under his old alias three hundred miles from where he should be locked behind bars...

Shane drew a slow breath before speaking, his voice steady. "Mr. Hartwell, have you noticed anyone new around your office recently? Someone asking questions about document procedures?"

The clerk's face went pale. "I... well, there was someone who came by a few weeks ago. Very polite, very dignified. Said he was interested in learning about territorial record-keeping procedures. Educational purposes, he claimed."

My hands clenched into fists at my sides. "Can you describe him?"

"Older gentleman, maybe fifty or fifty-five. Gray hair, distinguished bearing. Expensive clothes, educated speech. He seemed genuinely interested in how we verify document authenticity." Hartwell's voice dropped to barely above a whisper. "I showed him our procedures. Let him examine sample documents. I thought I was being helpful."

The description still didn't match Galen Harper's appearance from six years ago, but prison could change a man considerably. More importantly, the approach was pure Galen—charming, seemingly innocent, gathering information for later criminal use.

Shane leaned forward slightly. "Did he give you a name?"

"I..." Hartwell's brow furrowed. "I should remember. He had credentials, business cards. Everything appeared legitimate." He removed his spectacles, cleaning them with shaking hands. "But I can't quite recall—"

"Could it have been B. Irving? Using a false name?" I asked quietly.

Hartwell froze. His spectacles slipped from his fingers and clattered against the desk. When he looked up, his face had gone white as fresh snow.

"Dear Lord." His voice came out as barely a whisper. "What have I done?"

Shane placed a reassuring hand on the clerk's shoulder. "Mr. Hartwell, a professional criminal manipulated you. This isn't your fault."

But I could see the guilt and fear warring in the man's eyes. If B. Irving was indeed our father, then Hartwell had unknowingly armed an outlaw with sophisticated forgeries. Framing innocent men and destroying lives.

"We'll need a list of any documents bearing B. Irving's signature," Shane said. "And descriptions of anyone who brought documents to file on his behalf."

Hartwell nodded eagerly, grateful for concrete tasks that might help undo whatever damage had been done. As he bustled around gathering materials, Shane pulled me aside toward the window.

"This is bigger than we thought," he muttered, his voice pitched for my ears only.

I kept my expression neutral, but my pulse hammered in my throat. "Could be someone else using the alias. A coincidence."

Shane's eyes bored into mine. The look said he knew better. That we both knew better. The timing, the sophistication, and the approach all pointed to one man. But neither of us would speak Galen Harper's name aloud in this office.

"We need to be careful about how we proceed," Shane said.

I gave a slight nod. We'd talk about this later, away from witnesses. For now, we had evidence to gather and an innocent man to protect. Whatever else Galen Harper might be, he'd made A.C. Beaumont his target. And that meant Lavinia and Beau were in danger too.

We spent another hour with Hartwell, examining

documents and compiling evidence. The scope of the operation became clearer with each revelation. Forged contracts worth thousands of dollars, fraudulent land deals involving railroad property, and shipping manifests that allowed stolen goods to move as legitimate freight.

By the time we left the courthouse, my head pounded with the implications of what we'd discovered. This wasn't just about A.C. Beaumont's innocence anymore. If Galen Harper was involved, then our family's past had collided with our present in the worst possible way.

"We need to talk to Thurston Blackwell," Shane said as we walked toward the hotel. "Find out more about his connection to these land deals."

"Agreed. But we need to be careful. If he's working with whoever's behind this, we can't tip our hand too early."

Shane's boots scuffed the dusty boardwalk as we turned the corner toward the hotel. He was quiet for a stretch, gaze fixed ahead, jaw set in that way he got when his mind was working through a problem.

"You ever think about how justice works?" he asked.

I glanced at him. "You mean the law?"

"No. I mean justice. The kind that doesn't always show up in courtrooms." He paused. "The kind that takes patience. Stewardship."

I snorted. "You sound like Pastor Whitmore."

"Maybe. But I've been thinking about what we're walking into. If Galen's behind this, it's not just about catching a criminal. It's about protecting people from a lie that's been dressed up to look like truth."

I nodded slowly. "You think Lavinia knows more than she's saying?"

"I think she's scared. And I think Blackwell's sniffing around because he knows she's the key to unraveling something bigger." Shane's voice dropped. "I asked around about his business dealings. He's got ties to a freight company that's been rerouting shipments through private land—land that changed hands under questionable deeds."

My pulse quickened. "So he's part of the network."

"Looks that way. And if Galen's pulling strings, Blackwell's one of the puppets."

We reached the hotel, but Shane paused at the base of the steps.

"You rush this, Flynn, and we might miss the real rot. I know you want to protect Lavinia. I do too. But justice isn't just about speed. It's about truth. And truth takes time."

I looked at him, the brother who'd always been slower to act, who mapped out every angle before making a move. "You think I'm too impatient."

"I think you're afraid of what waiting might reveal."

I didn't answer. Couldn't. Because part of me wanted vengeance. Wanted Galen stopped, exposed, and punished. But Shane's words settled like dust in my chest, gritty and impossible to ignore.

We climbed the hotel steps and made our way to my room on the second floor. The documents needed another review, and we needed privacy to discuss the Galen Harper connection without anyone overhearing.

Inside my room, Shane settled into the chair by the window while I spread the papers across the small table. The afternoon sun slanted through the glass, illuminating the forged signatures and fraudulent seals with harsh clarity.

"Earlier this morning, I asked around town about Blackwell's activities," Shane said, his voice carrying a note of concern. "That man's been asking specific questions about Lavinia Beaumont."

I felt my shoulders tense. "What kind of questions?"

"Personal ones. About her past, about the boy's father, about how long she's been in Holbrook. Questions a man asks when he's looking for leverage." Shane studied my face. "The hotel clerk overheard him asking someone whether Miss Beaumont had any prior association that might be worth knowing about."

Heat flooded my face, followed immediately by an icy rage. "He's investigating her?"

"Looks like it." Shane paused. "I think A.C. Beaumont might have stumbled onto evidence, and someone discredited him before he could report what he'd seen. And I think Miss Beaumont might know more about her father's discoveries than she's admitted."

"That doesn't make her guilty of anything."

"No, but it makes her a target." Shane's expression grew grim. "If they framed her father to keep him quiet, what do you think they'll do to her if she asks the wrong questions?"

The thought of Lavinia in danger sent cold fear shooting through my veins, but before I could respond, a knock sounded at the door.

I opened it to find the hotel clerk standing in the hallway, slightly out of breath.

"Marshal Harper? I've been looking for you. You've got a telegram. Came in about an hour ago." He handed me a folded yellow paper. "Marked urgent. I checked your room earlier, but you weren't in, so I've been watching for you."

"Thank you." I pressed a coin into his hand and closed the door.

Shane stood, his expression alert. "What is it?"

I unfolded the telegram, scanning the brief message. The words seemed to jump off the page, each one hitting me like a separate blow:

GALEN FREE. ESCAPED YUMA THREE WEEKS PAST. DANGEROUS. BE CAREFUL. - H

The paper trembled in my hands as the full implications crashed over me. Hayley's warning from Phoenix confirmed our worst fears. Three weeks. The same timeframe when B. Irving had first appeared in the court records. The same period when sophisticated document forgeries started showing up across the territory.

"Flynn?" Shane moved closer, concern etching lines around his eyes.

I handed him the telegram, then moved to the window. The afternoon sun cast long shadows across Holbrook's dusty streets, and somewhere out there, Galen Harper might be watching. Planning. Destroying innocent lives to build his criminal empire.

Shane read the message, his face hardening. "So it really is him."

"Looks that way." My voice came out rougher than intended.

"We need to verify A.C. Beaumont's whereabouts," Shane said. "Execute that warrant or clear his name. Either way, we can't let this drag on while Galen's running loose."

"I know." The words tasted bitter. "Tomorrow. I'll verify his location tomorrow."

Shane studied me for a long moment. "Be careful, Flynn. However this plays out, don't let your feelings cloud your judgment."

After Shane left, I remained at the window, watching the street below. The telegram lay on the table behind me, Hayley's warning a physical weight in the room.

Three weeks. Galen had been free for three weeks, and in that time he'd built a network of forgeries and corruption sophisticated enough to fool court clerks and frame innocent men. Whatever he was planning, it was big. Bigger than anything I'd faced before.

And somehow, A.C. Beaumont had gotten caught in the middle of it. Which meant Lavinia was in danger whether she knew it or not.

I thought about the way she'd looked at me in the mercantile the day we met. Guarded, but not cold. Like someone who'd seen danger dressed as kindness before. There was something about Lavinia Beaumont that stirred parts of me I'd long kept locked away. Her courage, her devotion to her family, and the steel beneath that gentle voice spoke to something old and quiet in me—something I hadn't trusted in years.

But Shane was right. I couldn't let those feelings compromise my duty. Not when so much was at stake.

Tomorrow, I'd verify whether A.C. Beaumont was in Holbrook or truly away on business. I'd face whatever truth emerged, no matter how it complicated my growing feelings for his daughter. And I'd figure out how to protect an innocent family from a criminal mastermind who happened to be my father.

The irony wasn't lost on me. I'd spent years trying to prove that a Harper could stand on the right side of justice. Now I had to stop another Harper from destroying everything I'd worked to build.

Some time later, a soft knock interrupted my thoughts. I spun toward the door, hand instinctively reaching for my Colt.

"Who's there?"

Silence answered. I crossed the room in three strides and jerked the door open.

The hallway stood empty. Lengthening shadows pooled in the corners, and distant piano music drifted up from the saloon across the street. The other guest room doors remained closed, undisturbed.

My jaw clenched. Either I was jumping at phantoms, or someone wanted me to know I was being watched.

I scanned the hallway once more, then locked the door and wedged the chair under the handle. Shane would call me paranoid. Maybe I was. But Galen Harper had three weeks to plan, to position his pieces, and to turn this town into his hunting ground.

And I'd just become his primary obstacle.

I returned to the window. Darkness crept across Holbrook's streets like spilled ink. Somewhere out there, my father was planning his next move. And somewhere in this town, Lavinia Beaumont was trusting me to keep her family safe, trusting a man whose own blood ran thick with criminal intent.

My reflection stared back at me from the darkened window. Same jaw as my father, same eyes, same stubborn set to my shoulders. The resemblance had always haunted me. Now it felt like a prophecy I was desperate to outrun.

I'd be careful, like Hayley warned. But I'd also be relentless.

Because that's what separated me from the man who sired me. I protected the innocent and brought the guilty to justice, even when the guilty shared my blood.

Especially then.

11 - The Reckoning

Flynn

THE COTTONWOOD TREE'S rough bark pressed against my back as I shifted position for what felt like the hundredth time in the past hour. My legs ached from crouching behind the thick trunk, and sweat trickled down my spine despite the shade the broad leaves provided. I could see the Beaumont house from here. Porch, windows, all of it. The waiting scraped at me like a file on iron.

I confirmed Lavinia was at the mercantile two hours ago, watching through the store's front window as she arranged displays with her usual graceful efficiency. Beau had been there too, playing behind the counter with his wooden horses. Normal family life continued while I lurked in the shadows, preparing to shatter their peace.

Shane's words from this morning before breakfast echoed in my mind like the persistent buzz of a hornet that wouldn't leave me be. *You still have a warrant to execute, Flynn. Stop letting your feelings for that woman cloud your judgment.* The conversation had started civil enough, but by the end we'd been standing toe to toe in my hotel room, voices raised despite the thin walls.

"You've been here three days," Shane had said, his patience finally fraying around the edges. "Three days, and you still haven't verified whether A.C. Beaumont is actually in town or not."

I wished I could tell him he was wrong about my motivations. Truth was, I had avoided when I had to choose between the woman I was growing to care about and the duty I swore to uphold.

Duty. The word tasted bitter as sawdust in my mouth.

Shane had paced the small room like a caged wolf, his frustration clear in every sharp movement. "If Galen's really behind this criminal network, if he's using his old aliases to corrupt officials and frame innocent men, then we can't afford to waste time protecting your feelings."

"This isn't about my feelings."

"Isn't it?" Shane had stopped pacing to fix me with his steady gaze. "When's the last time you took three days to execute a simple warrant? When's the last time you accepted a suspect's family's word without verification?"

The questions stung because they were fair. I had tracked killers across hundreds of miles of desert without hesitation. I had arrested men twice my size and twice my age. But the thought of walking up to Lavinia's front door and demanding to search her home made my stomach turn like bad beef.

"Today," I finally promised. "I'll verify A.C.'s whereabouts today."

"See that you do," Shane replied, but his tone softened slightly. "Flynn, I know you care about her family. But if you're right about their innocence, then the best way to protect them is to get to the truth."

Now, crouched behind this tree with the afternoon sun beating down and my duty as clear as creek water, I couldn't delay any longer. Shane was right—he was always right, curse his hide. The not knowing was eating at me worse than any certainty could.

I checked my pocket watch. Two-fifteen. Lavinia

would be at the store for at least another three hours, giving me time to approach the house without her interference. Time to finally do what I should have done days ago.

Rising from my cramped position, I worked the stiffness from my legs and adjusted my gun belt. My Colt settled against my hip, its familiar presence a cold comfort as I considered what I was about to do. If A.C. was innocent as his daughter claimed, this conversation might clear his name.

I pushed that thought away. Whatever the truth, it was time to face it.

Instead of approaching the front door like a welcomed guest, I circled around to the back of the house. If A.C. was indeed hiding, he'd be more likely to use the rear entrance, away from the street's prying eyes. The narrow alley behind the row of houses was empty except for a few chickens pecking at scattered grain and a wooden wagon with one broken wheel leaning against a neighbor's fence.

The Beaumont property was well-maintained even from the back, with a small garden plot lined with neat rows of vegetables, a chicken coop that looked recently repaired, and clotheslines strung between sturdy posts. Normal signs of a family making their home in this frontier town.

That's when I saw him.

A man stood with his back to me, hanging a damp shirt on the clothesline. Gray hair caught the afternoon light, and his build matched the general description of A.C. Beaumont. He wore a simple cotton shirt and dark trousers. Practical clothes a shopkeeper might favor for domestic work.

My heart hammered against my ribs as three days of speculation crystallized into certainty. A.C. Beaumont was definitely not out of town on business. He was here, hanging laundry in his own backyard while his daughter lied to me about his whereabouts.

The betrayal hit harder than it should have. I wanted

to believe Lavinia, wanted to trust that her guarded responses came from protective instincts rather than deliberate deception. But here was proof that she had lied to my face since the moment we met.

Shane's voice echoed in my memory. *Your judgment's compromised.*

Anger at myself surged through me for being played for a fool, at Lavinia for her deception, at the whole situation that forced me to choose between my heart and my badge. I stepped forward, my boots crunching on the dry grass, and drew myself up to my full height.

"A.C. Beaumont," I called out, my voice carrying the authority of my badge. "Deputy U.S. Marshal Flynn Harper. I need to speak with you."

The man's shoulders stiffened, but he didn't turn around immediately. For a moment, he remained motionless with the wet shirt clutched in his hands, as if hoping I might disappear if he wished hard enough. Then, with the slow deliberation of a man who'd been expecting this moment, he turned to face me.

The resemblance on the wanted poster was unmistakable. This was definitely A.C. Beaumont, despite the deeper lines around his eyes and the additional gray in his hair. But his expression surprised me. Not panic or guilt, but a weary resignation that seemed to age him before my eyes.

"Marshal Harper," he said, setting the shirt back in the laundry basket. "I recognize you from the store. I wondered when you'd finally come."

The admission confirmed what I suspected. Lavinia had told him about our encounters and had been reporting our conversations while maintaining her tale about his absence. The knowledge twisted in my gut like a knife blade.

"Sir, I have a federal warrant for your arrest on charges of land fraud and railroad theft." I kept my voice level despite the chaos of emotions churning beneath the surface. "You're going to need to come with me."

A.C. studied my face for a long moment, and I caught

something unexpected in his gray eyes. Not fear, but a desperate hope that made me shift uncomfortably. "Marshal, before you arrest me, would you be willing to hear me out? Just for a few minutes?"

Everything in my training said to refuse. A warrant was a warrant, and suspects didn't get to negotiate the terms of their arrest. But his tone and dignified bearing made me hesitate.

"I can listen while I escort you to jail," I said finally.

"Please." A.C. gestured toward the back door of the house. "Just a few minutes. In private. There are things you need to know about this situation that go far beyond what's written in your warrant."

Against my better judgment, I nodded. "Five minutes. But I'm armed, and I will arrest you if you try to run."

"I wouldn't dream of running, Marshal. I've been waiting for someone like you to arrive for weeks."

I followed him through the back door into a kitchen that smelled of coffee and cinnamon, with the lingering warmth of fresh baking. Sunlight streamed through gingham curtains, illuminating the well-kept room. Hard to reconcile this peaceful setting with the serious federal crimes listed in my warrant.

I leaned against the wall near the door, one hand resting casually near my sidearm. A.C. moved to the stove and poured two cups of coffee without asking if I wanted any, his movements unhurried.

"Marshal," he began, settling into a chair at the small wooden table, "I need you to understand something. I am not the criminal described in your warrant."

"The evidence suggests otherwise, Mr. Beaumont."

"Does it? Or does the evidence suggest that someone wants you to believe I'm guilty?" A.C. wrapped his weathered hands around his coffee cup, and I noticed how they trembled slightly. "Someone's been using my name, my signature, and my reputation to cover their own crimes. When I refused to cooperate further, they framed me for everything."

The words hit me like cold water. "What do you mean, refused to cooperate further?"

A.C. looked up at me with eyes that held more pain than any man should have to carry. "Three weeks ago, a man came to see me. Called himself B. Irving. Said he had some business documents from Georgia. Records that could destroy everything I've built here in Holbrook."

My gut went cold.

B. Irving.

The same alias we found in the court records. The same name stamped on forged documents from Tucson to Prescott. The same name Galen Harper used every time he slipped the noose.

"What kind of records?" I asked.

"From the Reconstruction years. Times when a man had to make hard choices to keep his family fed." A.C.'s voice carried old shame. "After the war, after my wife died, I was desperate. Banks wouldn't lend to Southerners. Legitimate suppliers wouldn't sell on credit. So I... I had falsified some business records. Bought and sold goods without proper documentation. Small-scale survival, but he could make it look like deliberate fraud."

The confession hung between us like smoke in the still air. I sank into the chair across from him, the rigid formality of arrest procedures forgotten in the face of this revelation.

"This B. Irving had proof of your Georgia activities?"

"Documents. Correspondence. Even witnesses who could testify about my irregular business practices." A.C. stared into his coffee as if searching for answers in its dark depths. "He said he could make it all disappear, or he could make sure it reached the territorial authorities. My choice."

"What did he want in return?"

"At first, just small favors. My signature on a few harmless business documents. Use of my mercantile's letterhead for what he claimed were legitimate shipping arrangements." A.C.'s mouth formed a thin line. "But the requests kept escalating. Soon he demanded access to my shipping accounts, pressuring me to sign contracts without reading them."

The picture was becoming clearer, and it made my stomach churn with rage. Someone manipulated this man, using his past mistakes and his love for his family as leverage to force his cooperation.

"When did you refuse?"

"Last week. When he brought the documents, I knew they would implicate me in serious federal crimes. Land deeds for property I'd never seen, shipping manifests for goods I'd never handled." A.C. met my eyes directly. "I told him I wouldn't sign another paper, no matter what he threatened to expose."

"And that's when the warrant was issued."

"Two days later. Suddenly I'm wanted for crimes I never committed, using documents they forced me to provide." The bitterness in his voice was palpable. "Marshal, I've made mistakes in my life. Survival mistakes during desperate times. But I am not the criminal you're looking for."

I stared at the man across from me, seeing a father and grandfather caught in a web of manipulation and blackmail, not the criminal I had expected. Everything made sense now. His genuine confusion about the charges, Lavinia's fierce protectiveness, and the family's desperate efforts to keep him hidden.

"Can you describe this B. Irving?"

"Older gentleman, maybe fifty-five. Well-dressed, educated speech. Gray hair, distinguished bearing. A man you'd trust with your life savings." A.C. paused, studying my face. "He knew things about my past that only someone with extensive resources could have discovered. And Marshal, a few days ago a man came to the store. Expensive clothes, Southern accent. He threatened my daughter and grandson in ways that made my blood run cold."

Thurston Blackwell. The pieces were clicking together with horrible clarity. If Blackwell and B. Irving were connected, if they were part of the same criminal network operating across the territory...

"Mr. Beaumont, I think you and your family are in more danger than you realize."

Before A.C. could respond, the sound of the front door opening echoed through the house. Footsteps moved across the wooden floor toward the kitchen, accompanied by the cheerful chatter of a boy telling his mother about his day.

A.C.'s face went white as fresh snow. "She's early," he whispered. "She wasn't supposed to be home for hours."

The kitchen door swung open, and Lavinia stepped inside with Beau at her side, her arms full of parcels from the store. She was talking to her son about something involving wooden horses and penny candy, her voice warm with the affection I recognized.

Then she saw us.

The parcels fell from her arms, hitting the floor with sounds that seemed unnaturally loud in the sudden silence. Her brown eyes went wide with shock, moving from my face to her father's and back again. The color drained from her cheeks until she looked like a woman who'd seen her own death warrant.

"Papa?" Her voice came out as barely a whisper, thick with terror and confusion.

Beau looked between the adults, his young mind trying to process the tension that suddenly filled the room. "Mama? Why is the marshal man here?"

Lavinia's hands moved instinctively to her son's shoulders, pulling him closer to her side in a protective gesture that twisted my gut. This was what my investigation did to this family. It turned their home and business into places of fear instead of safety.

"Marshal Harper," she managed, her voice steadier than I would have expected given the circumstances. "I... I can explain..."

But I could see in her eyes that she expected the worst. Expected me to arrest her father and drag him away while her son watched. Expected the law to destroy her family.

The fear radiating from both mother and child twisted something in my chest. I'd watched Lavinia protect her son with quiet dignity ever since I'd arrived in Holbrook. And now I was the threat at their kitchen table, the badge that reminded them justice didn't always protect the innocent, despite my promises.

In that moment, my duty as a federal marshal crystallized into something entirely different from what I expected. These people weren't criminals. They were victims of a sophisticated gang of outlaws that had manipulated and threatened them into compliance.

And if B. Irving was indeed Galen Harper, if my father was behind the destruction of this family's peace, then my oath to uphold justice demanded something far different from an arrest.

I stood slowly, keeping my movements unthreatening. "Miss Beaumont," I said, "I think it's time we had a completely honest conversation. All of us."

The fear in her eyes didn't diminish, but I caught a flicker of something else—hope, maybe, or at least the possibility that this confrontation might not end the way she feared.

"Beau, sugar," she said, never taking her eyes off my face, "why don't you go to your room and play with your horses? Papa and I need to talk to the marshal."

"But Mama—"

"Now, please."

Beau looked between us once more, then obediently gathered his wooden animals and headed toward the stairs.

Lavinia remained standing, her hands clasped so

tightly her knuckles had gone white. She was braced for whatever blow was coming, ready to fight for her family even against impossible odds.

That courage, that fierce devotion to the people she loved, decided everything for me. They needed my protection. And if that meant taking on a gang of outlaws that might include my father, so be it.

Justice, I was beginning to understand, wasn't always about arrests and convictions. Sometimes it was about standing between decent people and the forces that would destroy them.

"Miss Beaumont," I said, settling back into my chair and gesturing for her to join us, "your father has been telling me about a man named B. Irving. I think it's time you told me everything you know about the people who've been threatening your family."

Cautious relief quickly replaced the surprise that flickered across her face. She moved to the table with deliberate steps, as if she couldn't quite believe this conversation was really happening.

But as she sank into the chair beside her father, I saw her reach for his hand with the desperate grip of someone who thought they were about to lose everything.

Whatever came next, whatever truths emerged from this kitchen table, I was no longer here to arrest A.C. Beaumont.

I was here to protect him. To protect all of them.

12 - Cornered

Lavinia

THE SIGHT OF Flynn Harper sitting at our kitchen table with Papa stopped me in the doorway. Everything we'd worked so carefully to hide, every secret we'd protected, lay exposed in the warm lamplight between them. My worst nightmare had come to pass. Marshal Harper had found Papa.

But he wasn't arresting him.

My pulse stuttered, then raced. Instead of handcuffs and harsh words, I saw two men deep in serious conversation, empty coffee cups between them, Papa's ledger books spread across the table. Marshal Harper's hat rested on the chair beside him. His posture relaxed rather than threatening.

"Beau, sugar," I said, steadier than I expected. "Why don't you take your horses upstairs to your room? You can build that big stable we talked about."

"But Mama, I want to stay with you and Papa and the marshal."

"Upstairs, please." I softened my tone, ruffling his dark hair. "I'll call you down for supper real soon. Promise."

Beau looked between the three adults, sensing the tension he couldn't understand. But he gathered his wooden animals obediently. "Yes, Mama. Can I use the extra blankets for horse stalls?"

"Of course, sugar. Whatever you like."

His footsteps disappeared up the stairs. I heard his door close with a soft click. Only then did I allow myself to fully take in the scene before me. The packages I'd dropped lay scattered across the floor: coffee beans, fabric, the few supplies I'd purchased before my world had turned upside down.

I kneeled and began gathering them, my hands trembling. Flynn rose immediately, moving to help without being asked.

"Miss Beaumont." He crouched beside me to collect the spilled coffee beans. "Your father and I have been having an enlightening conversation."

The beans rattled as I poured them back into their brown paper sack. "So I see."

His hands were careful as he helped. I noticed again the healing cuts across his hands. Whatever dangers he'd faced recently had left their mark. "He's told me about the blackmail. About B. Irving and the documents they forced him to sign."

I glanced up at Papa, who sat watching us with weary relief etched in every line of his weathered face. "You told him everything?"

"Most everything," Papa replied. "Marshal Harper believes we're dealing with something bigger. An organized gang responsible for cattle rustling across the territory."

Flynn gathered the last of the scattered items, his movements efficient but unhurried. "The evidence suggests they framed your father to cover someone else's crimes. Whoever is behind this has serious resources and political pull."

I stood clutching the packages as if they could keep

me safe. “And you believe him? Just like that?”

“The handwriting analysis alone proves the documents are forgeries.” Flynn’s blue eyes met mine with steady conviction. “Your father’s been trapped in a conspiracy he had no part in creating.”

Relief flooded through me so intensely my knees weakened. For days I’d lived with the terror that Papa might truly be guilty, that somehow the man who’d raised me had secrets darker than I could imagine. To hear Flynn’s certainty about his innocence... I could breathe freely for the first time in weeks.

“But there’s something else.” Papa folded his hands on the table. “Something you need to tell the marshal, Lavinia.”

My stomach clenched. I knew exactly what he meant, and the thought of speaking those words aloud to Flynn sent heat flooding my cheeks. “Papa.”

“The man who visited the store the other day. Thurston Blackwell.” Papa’s tone left no room for argument. “Marshal Harper needs to know about your connection to him.”

Flynn’s attention sharpened like a hawk spotting prey. “Connection?”

I couldn’t look at him. The packages in my arms pressed against my ribs until breathing became difficult. “Mr. Blackwell and I... we knew each other. Before. In Georgia.”

“Knew each other how?”

The question came quietly, but I heard the lawman’s instincts underneath. Shame rose like bile in my throat. “He courted me. When I was sixteen. He led me to believe we would have a more permanent relationship.”

The silence stretched so long I forced myself to glance up. Flynn’s expression remained carefully controlled, but something dangerous flickered in his blue eyes. “And?”

“And when I told him about Beau, he disappeared.”

The words rushed out, each one harder to speak than the last. "Left Georgia without a word. I never saw him again until this week."

"Beau is his son."

It wasn't a question. Flynn had put the pieces together. The certainty in his voice made my shame complete.

"Yes." The admission was barely a whisper.

I couldn't bear to see the judgment written on Flynn's face. Instead, I turned away, setting the packages on the counter. My hands shook despite my efforts to appear calm. Cooking would help. The familiar routine of preparing a meal would give me something to focus on besides the crushing weight of my exposed secrets.

"Lavinia." Flynn's voice followed me, softer than I deserved. "Look at me."

I kept my attention fixed on the salt pork, unwrapping it from its butcher paper with unnecessary care. "I need to start supper. Beau will be hungry soon."

"This changes everything." His boots crossed the kitchen floor, stopping close enough that I could smell leather and something clean and masculine. "If Thurston Blackwell is Beau's father, and he's connected to the men framing your father—"

"Then we're all in danger." Papa's voice was grim. "He's not just trying to destroy me. He's trying to control Lavinia through the boy."

The salt pork slipped from my numb fingers. Flynn caught it before it hit the floor, his quick reflexes saving us from waste we couldn't afford. When I finally looked up, his blue eyes held none of the disgust or dismissal I'd expected. Instead, I saw protective fury blazing there.

"He threatened me." The words tumbled out before I could stop them. "Said circumstances could change unexpectedly. That reputations were fragile things in communities like this."

Flynn's jaw tightened. "Lavinia, you and your family are in more danger than you realize. Thurston Blackwell isn't just some smooth-talking scoundrel. He's connected to serious crimes across multiple territories. Federal crimes."

I sliced the salt pork, letting the familiar task steady my nerves. "What are you saying?"

"I'm saying you need to let me move you somewhere safe. All of you. Tonight."

The knife stilled in my hand. "Leave Holbrook?"

"Temporarily. Until we can arrest Blackwell and whoever else is involved in this operation." Flynn moved closer. Every movement he made drew my attention despite my efforts to focus on cooking. "There are safe houses. Places where we can protect you."

"No." The refusal came instinctively. "I won't run again. This is our home. Our life."

"Lavinia-girl," Papa said. "Maybe we should consider..."

"No, Papa." I turned to face them both, gripping the knife handle for strength. "I ran once before, and look where it got us. Thurston found us anyway. But you should go. Let Marshal Harper take you somewhere safe while he investigates. You're the one with the federal warrant. You're the one they want to arrest. If you disappear, Thurston's entire scheme falls apart."

"And what about Blackwell's interest in Beau?" Flynn asked.

The question struck sharply and suddenly, like a chilly wind through a cracked window. I tried not to dwell on the way Thurston's eyes had lingered on my son, cold and measuring, as if sizing up livestock. "Beau is my responsibility. I'll protect him."

"How?" Flynn's voice remained steady, but his point was sharp as a blade. "Against a man with resources, connections, and a criminal network at his disposal?"

I had no answer to that. The helplessness was familiar, a ghost from that summer when I was sixteen, pregnant and abandoned in a hostile world. But this time, I had more to lose than just my future.

"Find somewhere safe for Papa," I repeated. "That's the most important thing right now."

Flynn studied my face for a long moment, and I wondered what he saw there. Stubborn determination, probably.

"All right," he said finally. "I can get your father to safety tonight. But this isn't over, Lavinia. I'm not abandoning you to face this alone."

The certainty in his voice sent an unwelcome flutter in my middle. When was the last time a man had made such a promise? When was the last time I'd even wanted to believe such words?

I turned back to the stove, lighting the fire under the bean pot. My hands were steadier now. "I should get supper ready. Beau will wonder what's taking so long."

The next hour passed in a strange mixture of domestic normalcy and underlying tension. I warmed the beans Papa had cooked yesterday, fried the salt pork until it was crispy and golden, and set out the leftover biscuits I'd baked that morning. Flynn watched my movements.

When the simple meal was ready, I called upstairs for Beau. He appeared with his hair mussed from play and his wooden horse clutched in one hand.

"Can Thunder eat with us?" he asked hopefully. "He's been working really hard building fences."

"Thunder can sit beside your plate," I agreed, grateful for his innocent chatter to fill the heavy silence.

We gathered around the table like a normal family sharing supper. But nothing about this meal was normal. Papa's face showed the strain of the past few weeks, Flynn's presence reminded us that everything was about to change, and I could barely taste the food I'd prepared.

"Beau," Papa said when he had finished most of his beans. "I need to tell you something important."

My son looked up with those trusting brown eyes that broke my heart. "What, Papa?"

"I have to go away for a little while. On business. Like when Mama goes to town, but longer."

Beau's face crumpled with confusion. "How long?"

"I don't know exactly, son. But I promise we won't be apart forever. And while I'm gone, you need to take extra good care of your mama. Can you do that for me?"

"Yes, sir." Beau's voice was quiet, but he straightened his shoulders with unconscious dignity. "Will you write me letters?"

"If I can." Papa's voice roughened with emotion he was trying to hide. "And I'll think about you every single day."

"Me too, Papa. Thunder will miss you too."

Flynn cleared his throat softly. "Your papa's going to be helping me with something very important, Beau. Something that will help keep your family safe."

Beau nodded solemnly, and my heart squeezed. He believed Papa completely because Papa had never broken a promise to him.

After supper, Flynn offered to help with the dishes, but I shook my head firmly. "You need to get Papa to safety. The sun's already going down."

"Lavinia's right," Papa agreed, rising from the table. "Dark enough now. We should go."

"You have supplies?" Flynn asked. "Food, clothes?"

"Already packed." Papa gestured toward the leather bag sitting by the back door. "Been ready since this morning."

The three of us moved toward the kitchen's back wall, where Papa lifted the loose floorboards to reveal the root cellar below. In the lamplight, I could see the narrow tunnel that led toward the alley behind our house.

"You dug this yourself?" Flynn asked with obvious admiration.

"Old habits from the war," Papa replied. "Sometimes the difference between living and dying is having a way out nobody knows about."

Flynn nodded with understanding. "I'll go through first to make sure the way is clear."

He disappeared into the tunnel's darkness, moving with the quiet confidence of a man accustomed to dangerous situations. After several minutes, we heard his soft whistle. The all-clear signal Papa had taught him.

"Time to go." Papa turned to embrace me.

His arms were fragile around my shoulders, and I realized how much the stress of recent weeks had aged him. "Papa."

"Take care of yourself, darling. And take care of that precious boy." His voice thickened with unshed tears. "Do nothing foolish. Don't face Thurston alone."

"I won't." The lie came easily, though we both knew I'd do whatever was necessary to protect Beau.

"I love you, Lavinia. Whatever happens, remember that."

"I love you too, Papa."

He kissed my forehead, then disappeared into the tunnel with his leather bag. I replaced the floorboards carefully to hide any sign of the entrance.

Beau had fallen asleep at the table, his head pillowed on his arms and Thunder still clutched in one hand. I carried him upstairs to his room, tucking him into bed with the routine that usually brought us both comfort.

"Good night, sugar," I whispered, pressing a kiss to his forehead. "Sweet dreams."

"Night, Mama. Tell Papa good night for me when he comes home."

The innocent words nearly broke my heart. "I will, sugar. I will."

I closed his door softly and returned to the kitchen, where the dirty dishes waited. The simple task of washing plates and cups had always been soothing, a way to mark the end of each day with accomplishment. Tonight, it was like trying to hold back a flood with bare hands.

The first tears came as I scrubbed the bean pot. Then

the sobs I'd been holding back for hours finally broke free, shaking my shoulders until I had to grip the edge of the washbasin to keep from collapsing. Everything I'd built, everyone I loved, hung in the balance, threatened by forces beyond my control.

Thurston had found us. Papa was gone. Flynn Harper, a man I barely knew but trusted despite my fear, had disappeared into the night with the only family I had left besides Beau.

The soapy water grew cold as I wept, releasing weeks of fear and months of carefully controlled anxiety. When the tears finally stopped, I dried my hands on my apron and kneeled beside the kitchen window, where the moonlight streamed across the worn wooden floor. For the first time in longer than I could remember, I folded my hands and bowed my head in earnest prayer.

"Lord," I whispered, "I know I haven't been faithful in coming to You. I know I've tried to handle everything myself, thinking I could protect my family through my strength. But I can't do this alone anymore."

The words came haltingly at first, then with growing confidence. "Please keep Papa safe wherever Flynn takes him. Please watch over Beau and help me be strong enough to protect him from whatever's coming. And Lord, if You could help me trust Flynn Harper the way Papa seems to, I'd be grateful. I'm afraid of trusting any man again, but Papa believes he's different."

I paused, listening to the night sounds outside. Wind through the cottonwoods, the distant call of a coyote, and the soft settling of our house around me.

"Give me wisdom to know what to do. Give me strength to face whatever Thurston throws at us. And please, Lord, let Papa's promise to Beau be true. Let us be a family again when this is over."

The prayer didn't remove the fear or solve the problems that would face us tomorrow. But it settled something deep in my soul, a peace I hadn't known since this nightmare began.

I rose from my knees and checked the locks on both doors, then climbed the stairs to my room. Tomorrow would bring new challenges, new fears, new tests of the fragile trust I'd placed in Flynn Harper.

But tonight, Papa was safe. Beau was sleeping peacefully in his own bed. And somewhere in the darkness, a federal marshal was working to prove that justice still existed for people like us.

It would have to be enough.

13 - Badge and Honor

Flynn

THE TUNNEL EXIT opened behind a stack of hay bales near Carson's livery stable, the earthy scent of horses and leather mixing with the cool desert air. I pushed aside the wooden covering A.C. had disguised as part of the livery's foundation, then helped him climb out into the gathering darkness. His hands shook as he brushed dirt from his clothes, and he kept glancing over his shoulder like he expected more federal marshals to appear at any moment.

"Easy," I murmured, positioning myself between him and the main street. "We're clear for now."

A.C. nodded, but his breathing remained shallow and quick. Being hunted for crimes you didn't commit would rattle anyone, especially a shopkeeper who'd never broken a law in his life.

"Where are we going?" he whispered, his voice barely audible above the distant sounds of evening. Horses snorted in their stalls. Music drifted from the saloon.

"Somewhere safe. But first, I need to find my brother." I checked the street and marked the positions of the few people still moving about town. "Can you wait here?

Stay behind those hay bales, and keep quiet?"

"I... yes. Yes, I can do that." The strain in A.C.'s voice told me the man was near his breaking point. "Marshal, I want you to know how much this means to me. What you're doing for my family..."

"Don't thank me yet. We've got a long road ahead before this is over."

I left him crouched behind the hay bales and made my way toward the hotel, sticking to the shadows and avoiding the pools of light spilling from windows and doorways. The wooden sidewalks creaked softly under my boots, and lingering heat radiated from sun-baked boards.

Shane was exactly where I expected to find him on the hotel's front porch, positioned where he could observe the entire main street while appearing to enjoy the evening air. He glanced up as I approached, and his expression shifted from casual alertness to sharp concern.

"Flynn. Where have you been? I've been looking for you for the past hour." He stood, moving closer so we could speak without being overheard. "And why do you look like you've been crawling through a mineshaft?"

I brushed at the dirt clinging to my shirt, realizing I probably looked exactly like a man who'd just emerged from an underground tunnel. "We need to talk. Privately."

Shane studied my appearance and the tension in my voice. "What's going on?"

"Not here." I glanced around. Half a dozen men scattered across the porch, most absorbed in their own conversations. "My room."

We climbed the stairs in silence, Shane's spurs ringing softly against the wooden steps. Once inside my room, he closed the door and turned to face me with that patient expression that said he was prepared to talk sense into me, no matter how long it took.

"All right." He settled into a chair. "Let's have it."

"A.C. Beaumont is innocent."

Shane's eyebrows rose slightly. "That's not exactly

news, Flynn. We suspected as much yesterday. What I want to know is why you look like you've been digging graves and why you disappeared without telling me where you were going."

Heat crept up my neck. "I was protecting a witness."

"What witness?"

"A.C. Beaumont himself."

The silence that followed was deafening. Shane leaned back in his chair, studying my face with an expression I couldn't quite read. When he finally spoke, his voice carried a dangerous calm.

"Flynn. Please tell me you didn't just admit to harboring a federal fugitive."

"I kept an innocent man safe from people who want to see him hang for crimes he didn't commit." I began pacing the small room, my boots drumming against the floorboards. "Shane, this whole thing is a setup. A.C.'s being blackmailed. Has been for months."

"When did you first make contact with Beaumont?"

"This afternoon. Watched Lavinia's house for hours." The name slipped out more easily than Miss Beaumont would have, and Shane's sharp look told me he'd caught it. "He's been hiding there, terrified to show his face."

"As he should be. There's a federal warrant—"

"Based on forged evidence!" I stopped pacing. "Look at these forgeries again. The legal language, the knowledge of territorial filing requirements. Whoever created these understood the system inside and out."

Shane picked up one of the land deeds, his experienced eyes scanning the document. After a moment, he went absolutely still.

"This level of sophistication suggests someone with legal training."

"Exactly. And remember what Hartwell told us? When he raised concerns about irregular documents, they instructed him that judicial authorities had reviewed and approved them." I moved closer to the table. "Shane, the same system that let Galen Harper terrorize half of the Arizona Territory before we finally brought him down. The system that's so corrupt criminals can buy their way out of territorial prison. You really think I should trust that with an innocent man's life?"

Shane set the document down carefully, weighing what I'd said. When he looked up, I saw the shift in his expression—that protective determination I'd seen when our family faced threats we couldn't handle alone.

"What specific evidence did you uncover about the blackmail?"

Relief flooded through me. He was listening.

"Someone calling himself B. Irving has been threatening him for months. Forcing him to sign documents he wasn't allowed to read. Using his business as cover for criminal activities." I faced Shane directly. "When A.C. finally refused to cooperate, suddenly there's a federal warrant with forged documents bearing his signature."

"B. Irving?" Shane straightened. "That's Galen's old alias."

"Exactly. Three weeks since Galen escaped, three weeks since B. Irving started this operation." The connections crystallized as I spoke. "This isn't coincidence."

"So we're looking at a network. Galen provides the aliases and forgery expertise..."

"And Blackwell handles the intimidation and political connections. With A.C. as the perfect fall guy." I clenched my fists. "And possibly with someone in the judicial system providing cover."

Shane moved to the window, staring out at the darkened street below. I could see him weighing options, calculating risks.

"You're right." His voice was quiet but firm. "We can't take A.C. through official channels. Not until we know who's compromised."

"Thank you."

He turned from the window. "But Flynn, you understand what we're doing? If we hide a federal fugitive, we're both risking our careers. Possibly facing criminal charges ourselves."

"I know. But what's the alternative? Follow procedures that might get an innocent man hanged?"

"No alternative I can live with."

Shane's agreement settled something in my chest. He was making this choice based on evidence and duty to protect an innocent man from a corrupt system.

But my conviction ran deeper.

This wasn't just about A.C. being innocent. It was about choosing what was right over what was legal when the two diverged. Like Daniel in the Bible when he refused the king's unjust decree. Or Peter telling the authorities he had to obey God rather than men.

I could lose my badge over this. My career. Everything I'd worked for since pinning on the star.

The weight pressed against my ribs.

Some things mattered more than a badge.

Shane was quiet for a moment, studying my face. "Are you making tactical decisions based on evidence, or are you being manipulated by that family?"

"What's that supposed to mean?"

"It means you've known Miss Beaumont for a few days, and you're already risking your career to protect her father." His tone remained patient. "You keep calling her Lavinia. That level of personal involvement concerns me."

Heat flooded my face. "She asked me to keep her father safe. I gave my word."

"Your word as a federal marshal, or your word as a man who's attracted to her?"

The accuracy stung because I couldn't deny it. Yes, I was attracted to Lavinia Beaumont. Yes, seeing her fierce devotion to her family had awakened something in me that had nothing to do with my badge. But that didn't make A.C.'s innocence any less real.

"Both. I've seen the evidence. A.C. told me everything. For months, a man has been blackmailing him, forcing him to sign documents, using his business as cover. The man's a victim, not a criminal."

"What kind of blackmail?"

"Threatened to expose some questionable business practices from his Georgia days. Survival decisions during Reconstruction, when half the South was breaking the law just to keep food on the table." I faced Shane directly. "Nothing that justified federal charges, but enough to destroy his reputation here."

"And you believe him?"

"I've seen the man. Talked to him. He's terrified and desperate to protect his family. If he were really the head of a gang, would he be hiding in his own house, dependent on his daughter to bring him food?"

Shane rubbed his forehead, then nodded slowly. "All right. Where is he?"

"Carson's livery. Hidden behind the hay bales near the back entrance."

Shane grabbed his hat and gun belt. "Then let's go get him before someone else does."

I followed him toward the door, then paused. "Shane? I appreciate you backing my call on this."

He stopped, one hand on the doorframe. "You're the Deputy U.S. Marshal. It's your jurisdiction, your case." His expression softened slightly. "I just want to make sure you're thinking clearly. Personal feelings can cloud judgment."

"They can. But they can also sharpen it." I met his eyes. "Sometimes caring about people helps you see the truth."

"Maybe." He settled his hat. "Just don't let it get you killed. Or hanged."

We made our way through the darkened streets, moving with the practiced silence of men who'd learned to hunt dangerous prey. The livery stable was quiet except for the soft sounds of horses settling in for the night. Hay, leather, and the earthy scent of animals filled the air.

A.C. emerged from behind the hay bales like a ghost, his face pale and drawn in the dim light. He looked worn down by fear and circumstances beyond his control.

"A.C., this is my brother Shane," I whispered. "Shane Harper, Territorial Livestock Detective."

A.C. nodded nervously. "Mr. Harper. Flynn says you might help me."

Shane studied the older man. "Are you willing to co-operate fully with our investigation? Answer questions honestly, provide any evidence you have?"

"Of course. Anything that might clear my name and protect my family."

"Good." Shane gestured toward his horse. "We're taking you somewhere safe. Somewhere Blackwell and his associates won't think to look."

"Where?" A.C. asked.

"The Aztec Land and Cattle Company. About an hour's ride north of town." Shane's voice carried quiet authority. "The foreman there owes me a favor, and he's not fond of criminals who prey on honest ranchers."

I nodded in approval of the plan. We'd helped Hayley investigate a big rustling operation at the massive cattle ranch last year. They employed nearly a hundred cowboys and covered a million acres. If there was anywhere A.C. could disappear for a few days while we built our case, that would be it.

"Will my family be safe?" A.C. asked as we prepared to mount up.

"Safer than if you're caught and hanged for crimes you didn't commit." The grim truth of my words hung in the air. "But A.C., this is just buying time. We still need to prove who's really behind this conspiracy."

"I understand." A.C. accepted the reins Shane offered him, his hands steadier now that he had a plan. "What do you need from me?"

"Everything," I said. "Every detail about this B. Irving character. Every document you were forced to sign. Every threat that was made. We're going to build a case so solid that not even Blackwell's political connections can protect him."

We rode out of Holbrook under a canopy of stars, three men united by the pursuit of justice but traveling different paths to reach it. The desert air was cool against my face, carrying the scents of sage and creosote, and I could hear the distant call of a coyote.

Beside me, A.C. rode with determination, hope restored. Shane led the way with his characteristic calm efficiency, navigating by landmarks invisible to less experienced eyes. And I brought up the rear, constantly scanning for pursuit, ready to fight anyone who tried to stop us.

The Aztec Land and Cattle Company's headquarters appeared as a cluster of lights against the dark landscape, lanterns burning in windows and the glow of a campfire where night riders gathered between patrols. Shane led us directly to the main house, a sprawling wooden structure.

Burton Mossman emerged onto the front porch before we'd even dismounted, a tall man with reddish hair, light eyes, alert and commanding.

"Shane Harper." Mossman's voice carried a note of wariness. "Wasn't expecting to see you back so soon. Everything all right?"

"Depends on how you define all right." Shane dismounted and approached the porch. "Burton, I need a favor. A big one."

Mossman's gaze shifted to A.C. and me, taking in our travel-dusty appearance and the tension that clung to us. "What kind of favor?"

"The kind that involves hiding an innocent man from people who want to frame him for federal crimes."

Mossman was quiet for a moment, considering this. I could see him weighing the request against his own responsibilities, his own safety. Finally, he nodded.

"Come inside. Let's talk."

The main house was comfortable but practical, furnished with heavy wooden furniture that could withstand the rough handling of ranch life. Mossman gestured us toward chairs arranged around a large stone fireplace, then poured coffee from a pot that had been keeping warm on the hearth.

"All right." He settled into his own chair. "What's the story?"

Shane outlined the situation quickly and efficiently—the forged documents, the framing of A.C., the connection to Blackwell and possibly Galen Harper. Throughout the explanation, Mossman listened without interruption, his experienced eyes studying A.C.'s face as if reading the truth written there.

"You're asking me to harbor a federal fugitive," Mossman said when Shane finished.

"We're asking you to protect an innocent man while we expose the real criminals," I corrected.

"Same thing, legally speaking." Mossman took a sip of coffee, considering. "After you Harpers helped us clean up the rustling operation, I figure I owe you one."

Relief flickered across A.C.'s features. "Mr. Mossman, I can't tell you how much this means to me. My daughter, my grandson... they're all I have left in this world."

Mossman set down his coffee cup and leaned forward. "Here's what I can do. You can stay in the old foreman's cabin, about a mile from here. It's isolated, well-supplied, and nobody goes there unless I send them. But I want your word that you won't bring trouble to my operation."

"You have it," A.C. said immediately.

"And I want regular updates from you two." Mossman looked at Shane and me. "If this situation goes bad, if marshals start sniffing around asking questions, I need to know immediately."

"Understood," Shane agreed. "How long can you keep him?"

"Few days, maybe a week if you're lucky. After that, people start noticing when the foreman disappears for mysterious errands."

I nodded, understanding the limitations. A week would have to be enough time to unravel the conspiracy and expose the real criminals.

"Thank you," I said.

Mossman stood, signaling the end of the discussion. "Don't thank me yet. Just make sure this doesn't blow up in all our faces."

As we prepared to leave A.C. in Mossman's capable hands, the older man pulled me aside.

"Flynn," he said quietly. "Take care of my family. Lavinia and little Beau. They're everything to me."

"I will. We're going to end this, A.C. All of it."

He nodded, tears gathering in his eyes. "I know you will. I see your strength, son. The same strength that brought you this far."

The ride back to Holbrook passed in thoughtful silence, both Shane and I lost in our own plans and concerns. The stars provided enough light to navigate by, brilliant pinpoints against the black canvas overhead. Cool desert air carried the scent of sage and dust.

I brought up the rear, constantly scanning the darkness for pursuit. Old habits. My hand rested near my revolver, ready.

But my thoughts weren't on tactics tonight.

A.C.'s face kept appearing in my mind—that desperate hope when I'd promised to protect his family. The trust Lavinia had placed in me despite every reason not to. Little Beau's innocent smile.

I'd made promises. Given my word.

And now I'd crossed a line that couldn't be uncrossed.

Lord, I hope I'm doing the right thing here.

The prayer came unbidden, not formal or practiced. Just honest. I wasn't much for regular churchgoing. Had seen too much evil in the world to trust easy answers.

But watching A.C.'s quiet faith, seeing how Lavinia turned to prayer when everything fell apart... something in that struck deeper than I wanted to admit.

They believed God cared about justice. Real justice, not just the corrupted version men twisted to serve themselves.

I studied Shane's silhouette ahead of me, steady and sure in the saddle. He'd agreed to help because the evidence demanded it. Protecting innocent people was part of the job, even when a federal warrant said otherwise.

Shane didn't need faith to do the right thing. He just did it.

But I needed... something. Some assurance that choosing righteousness over rules wouldn't destroy everything.

If this went wrong, I'd lose the badge. Maybe worse.

My career had been my identity since the day I had pinned a marshal star on my vest. The law had given me purpose, direction, a way to fight the darkness Galen Harper represented.

What would I be without it?

The question haunted me as my horse's hooves struck a steady rhythm against the hard-packed trail.

The stars stretched overhead, eternal and uncaring. Maybe not uncaring. Maybe just patient in ways I couldn't comprehend.

A.C. had said something earlier about trusting God's timing even when it made no sense. About faith being the substance of things hoped for, the evidence of things not seen.

I didn't have that kind of faith. Wasn't sure I ever would.

But maybe I could trust the conviction pressing against my chest, the certainty that protecting A.C. was right, even if it cost me everything. Do the job smart, do it right, and trust that righteousness mattered more.

The rest I'd have to leave in hands bigger than mine.

"Flynn," Shane said as the lights of town appeared ahead of us.

"Yeah?"

"Tomorrow we pull this thread until we unravel the whole mess. Just promise me you'll talk things through before making any more decisions that could end both our careers."

I thought about Lavinia waiting at home, wondering if her father was safe. Thought about little Beau playing with his wooden horses, unaware that monsters were circling his family. Thought about justice and duty and the sometimes impossible balance between the two.

"You have my word. But Shane? If it comes down to a choice between following procedures and protecting innocent people..."

"I know. When the time comes, we'll face it together. Like always."

The lights of Holbrook grew brighter as we approached, and I thought about the next phase of our investigation. Tomorrow would bring new challenges, new revelations, and hopefully the beginning of the end for whoever was behind this conspiracy.

But tonight, A.C. was safe. And sometimes, that was enough to build justice on.

14 - Shifting Ground

Lavinia

THE LATE AFTERNOON sun slanted through the mercantile's windows as I flipped the sign to "Closed." My hands trembled slightly as I completed the familiar routine. Counting the till, banking the day's earnings, checking that everything was secure for the night. It went faster than usual since Mrs. Patterson had agreed to watch Beau for a few hours at my house.

Still, nothing felt familiar anymore. Nothing felt secure.

Papa had been gone for nearly twenty-four hours. I had no idea if he was safe, captured, or worse. Flynn Harper had promised to protect him, but promises from powerful men had proven worthless before. The weight of uncertainty pressed down on me like a physical thing, making each breath an effort.

I gathered my reticule and checked the back room one last time.

The bell above the door chimed as I prepared to leave through the front entrance. My heart leaped into my throat. I spun around, expecting to see Thurston's predatory smile or perhaps federal marshals come to arrest me for harboring a fugitive.

Instead, Flynn Harper stood silhouetted against the evening light, his tall frame filling the doorway. Dust clung to his clothes and his dark hair was mussed from riding, but his gaze was alert and focused entirely on me.

"Miss Beaumont." He removed his hat. "I hope I'm not intruding."

Relief crashed over me with such force that my knees nearly buckled. "Marshal Harper. No, not at all. I was just... Is there news? About Papa?"

"He's safe." The simple words carried such conviction that the terrible knot in my stomach finally loosened. "Hidden where no one will think to look for him. He's well-fed, protected, and in good spirits."

I pressed a hand to my mouth, fighting back the tears that threatened. For twenty-four hours, I'd imagined every possible disaster. Papa captured, tortured, killed. To hear that he was not only alive but safe felt like grace I didn't deserve.

"Thank you," I whispered, my voice thick with emotion. "Thank you for keeping your word."

Flynn stepped closer, his expression gentle. "I told you I'd protect your family. I meant it."

The sincerity in his voice, the way he looked at me like my gratitude actually mattered to him, sent pleasant tingles through me. Thurston had made promises too, sweet words designed to seduce and manipulate. But there was something different about Flynn Harper, something that called to the part of me that still believed in honor and integrity.

Before I could stop myself, I crossed the distance between us and threw my arms around his neck. The embrace was meant to be brief, a simple expression of gratitude, but the moment my face pressed against his shoulder, something shifted.

He smelled of leather and horses, of desert air, and

my pulse quickened. His arms came around me slowly, carefully, as if he wasn't sure he had the right to hold me. But when I didn't pull away, his embrace tightened. His solid strength, his warmth, chased away every fear I'd carried.

"Easy," he murmured against my hair, his voice rough. "Everything's going to be all right."

I should have stepped back then. Should have thanked him properly and sent him on his way before I did something foolish. Instead, I clung to him, drawing strength from his presence in a way that both comforted and terrified me.

When I finally pulled back, his hands lingered on my arms. My breath caught at the warmth in his gaze. Not the calculating assessment I'd seen in other men's eyes. Something that looked almost like wonder.

"I have some things to show you," he said quietly. "Evidence we've gathered. Information about who's really behind this conspiracy."

"Yes, of course." I stepped back, smoothing my skirts and trying to regain my composure. "Would you... that is, have you eaten? I was about to head home and prepare supper for Beau. You're welcome to join us, if you'd like."

The invitation tumbled out before I could think better of it. Having a man to dinner, especially a man who affected me the way Flynn did, was exactly the behavior that could destroy my carefully maintained reputation. But the thought of spending the evening alone with my worries was unbearable.

Flynn hesitated, glancing toward the street as if remembering his duties. "I don't want to impose."

"You wouldn't be. Beau would enjoy the company, and I... I'd be grateful for news about Papa. Whatever you can share."

Something shifted in his expression, and he nodded slowly. "If you're certain it's no trouble."

"None at all." I locked the mercantile's front door

and fell into step beside him as we walked toward Coronado Street. The evening air carried the scent of cooling earth and the distant aroma of wood smoke from supper fires. "Fair warning, though. Beau will likely talk your ear off about his wooden horses."

Flynn's smile transformed his entire face, softening the sharp angles and making him look younger, more approachable. "I think I can handle that."

We walked in comfortable silence for a few minutes, the wooden sidewalks creaking softly under our feet. I stole glances at him. He carried himself with a confident stride, his gaze constantly sweeping our surroundings. Even relaxed, he remained alert, ready to face whatever threats might emerge from the gathering dusk.

"Marshal Harper," I began, then caught myself. "May I ask you something?"

"Flynn," he corrected gently. "And yes."

"Flynn." His name felt strange on my tongue, too intimate, too personal. "Why are you helping us? I mean, truly helping, not just following orders or doing your duty. You could have arrested Papa yesterday and been done with it."

He was quiet for so long I thought he might not answer. When he finally spoke, his voice carried a note of something I couldn't quite identify.

"Because I know what it's like to have your family's name dragged through the mud by someone else's crimes." He paused, his jaw tightening. "And because seeing the way you love them, the way you'd sacrifice anything to protect them... It makes me want to be worthy of that loyalty."

The honesty in his words stole my breath. There was pain there, old wounds that ran deep. I wanted to know everything about what had shaped him into the man he was.

"Your family's name?" I asked softly.

"Galen Harper." The name came out flat, emotionless, but I caught the way tension rippled through his shoulders. "My father. He's the reason I became a marshal, and he's probably connected to whoever's framing yours."

I stopped walking, my hand instinctively reaching out to touch his arm. "Flynn, I'm so sorry."

"Don't be." He looked down at my hand on his sleeve, and his expression softened. "It taught me the difference between blood and family. Between the name you're born with and the one you earn."

We reached my front gate, the neat picket fence and carefully tended flowers a stark contrast to the darkness in his voice. I realized I was still touching his arm and reluctantly pulled my hand away.

"Well," I said, trying to lighten the mood. "I hope you're prepared for chaos. Beau's been building an entire civilization with his wooden animals."

The front door opened before we even climbed the porch steps, and Beau came running out with his favorite horse clutched in his small fist.

"Mama! You're home! I made Thunder jump over the sofa and he didn't break nothing!" He skidded to a stop when he noticed Flynn, his dark eyes going wide with curiosity. "Hello, Marshal!"

Flynn crouched down to Beau's eye level, his entire demeanor changing. Gone was the dangerous lawman; in his place was a man who clearly knew how to talk to children. "Your mama told me about your horses."

"Wanna see them? I have three now, and they all have names and everything!" Beau bounced on his toes with excitement.

"I'd like that very much," Flynn replied seriously. "After supper, maybe? Your mama was kind enough to invite me to stay."

Beau's face lit up like Christmas morning. "Really? We're having biscuits and gravy! Mama makes the best biscuits in the whole territory!"

"Is that so?" Flynn glanced up at me with the same

gentle smile. "Then I'm a lucky man indeed."

Heat rose in my cheeks at the way he looked at me, as if sharing a simple meal was somehow precious.

Mrs. Patterson laughed as she closed the door, stepping on the front porch. "That boy has more energy than a steam engine!"

"Thank you for watching him again."

"Any time, dear. He's a sweet child."

We wished Mrs. Patterson a good day before I turned my attention to my guest. "Come inside, both of you. Beau, wash your hands while I start supper."

The next hour passed in a blur of activity that felt both foreign and wonderful. Flynn insisted on helping, fetching water from the well and stoking the fire while I mixed biscuit dough and prepared the gravy. Beau chattered constantly, regaling Flynn with elaborate stories about his wooden animals' adventures.

"Thunder can jump higher than any real horse," Beau announced from his perch at the kitchen table. "And Lightning is the fastest. He's not mean, like some fast horses. Papa says mean horses are just scared. If you're kind to them, they get better."

"Your papa sounds like a wise man," Flynn replied, glancing at me over Beau's head. There was something in his expression. Understanding perhaps, or approval of the values Papa had instilled.

"He is! He teaches me to count and to be nice to people." Beau's voice carried confidence.

Flynn's expression grew thoughtful, and I wondered what he was thinking. His own father had clearly failed him in ways I could only imagine, yet here he was, patient and kind with a child he barely knew.

Having a man at our table, watching Flynn listen to Beau's stories with genuine interest and compliment my cooking with sincere appreciation, stirred longings I'd thought buried forever. This was what I'd dreamed of at sixteen. A home filled with warmth and laughter, a man who valued family above everything else.

Once we finished eating and Beau had shown Flynn his entire collection of wooden animals, I sent my son upstairs to prepare for bed. Flynn helped me clear the table and wash dishes, our movements creating an easy rhythm that felt natural despite the newness of it.

"You're good with him." I dried a plate, stealing a glance at Flynn's profile. "Children can usually tell when adults are just being polite."

"He's a good boy. You've raised him well." Flynn handed me another clean dish, his fingers brushing mine in the transfer. The brief contact sent warmth racing up my arm. "It can't be easy, doing it alone."

"I haven't been alone. Papa's been wonderful with him." I set the plate in the cupboard, then turned to face him fully. "Flynn, what you showed me today, about the evidence... How bad is this conspiracy? How much danger are we really in?"

His expression grew serious. I watched him weigh his words carefully. "Bad enough that your father needed to disappear completely. The people behind this... they have resources, connections, and no conscience about eliminating threats."

A chill ran down my spine. "Do you think they know Papa's been hiding at our house?"

"Probably. Which is why moving him was the right decision." Flynn dried his hands on the towel I offered, then leaned against the counter, studying my face. "Lavinia, I need you to understand something. This isn't going to end quickly or quietly. Before it's over, these people will likely try to use you and Beau as leverage."

Fear clawed at my throat. "What do you mean?"

"I mean they'll threaten what your father loves most to force his cooperation." His voice was gentle but unflinching. "Which is why I need you to trust me. Completely. If I tell you to do something, if I tell you to go somewhere or stay away from somewhere, I need your word that you'll listen."

The request stirred old fears, old wounds from another man who'd demanded my trust and used it to destroy me. But looking into his gaze, seeing the genuine concern there, I nodded.

"I trust you," I said quietly, surprised by how much I meant it.

Something shifted in his expression, and suddenly the kitchen felt smaller, more intimate. He was standing close enough that I could see the flecks of darker blue in his eyes, could smell the clean scent of his shaving soap.

"Lavinia." My name came out barely a whisper.

"Yes?"

"I need you to know... this isn't just about duty for me anymore." His voice was rough, uncertain in a way that made my heart race. "What I feel for you, for your family... it's making me think about things I never thought I'd want."

My breath caught. "What things?"

"A home. A family. Someone to come back to at the end of a long day." He reached up slowly, his fingers barely grazing my cheek. "Someone who makes me want to be better than I ever thought I could be."

The confession was everything I'd longed to hear and everything I feared. Because wanting led to trusting, and trusting led to being destroyed by men who used their power to take what they wanted.

But Flynn wasn't Thurston. Everything about him, from helping with dishes to his patience with Beau, revealed his understanding of what truly mattered.

"Flynn," I whispered, my voice shaky. "I'm falling for you, and it terrifies me."

"Why?" His thumb traced my cheekbone with infinite gentleness.

"Because the last time I trusted a man with power over me, he destroyed everything I thought I knew about love and left me to face the consequences alone." The words tumbled out in a rush, years of buried pain and fear finally given voice.

His jaw tightened, and something dangerous flickered in his gaze. "Thurston."

"Yes." I swallowed hard. "I told you the basic facts before, but I didn't tell you everything. I couldn't, not with Papa and Beau nearby."

He waited, his thumb tracing gentle circles on my hand. Patient. Listening.

"I was sixteen and foolish and completely in love with a man who saw me as nothing more than a conquest." The old shame threatened to choke me, but Flynn's gentle touch anchored me. "He took my virtue and my trust, then disappeared when I told him about the baby. Didn't even have the decency to face me. Just left town in the middle of the night."

"Sweet mercy." His voice came out rough. "Lavinia, I'm so sorry."

"Papa stood by me when everyone else turned away. He gave up everything—our home, our reputation, his business connections—to help me start over somewhere no one knew our story."

"And now someone's targeting him." Flynn's voice was deadly quiet. "Do you think it's connected? Your past and what's happening now?"

The question I'd been avoiding hit hard, like a cold wind through an open door. "I... I don't know. Maybe. The timing seems—"

Footsteps echoed on the stairs before I could finish, and Beau appeared in his nightshirt, clutching his wooden horse.

"Mama, I can't sleep. Thunder's worried about Papa too."

The moment shattered, but perhaps that was for the best. I was growing too attached to Flynn.

"Come here, sugar." I gathered Beau into my arms, breathing in the sweet scent of his hair. "Papa's safe and sound, remember? Marshal Harper made sure of it."

"Promise?" Beau's dark eyes looked between Flynn and me.

"I promise," Flynn said solemnly. "And I keep my promises."

The simple words carried such conviction that even I felt comforted. Beau nodded, apparently satisfied, and allowed me to carry him back upstairs for another attempt at sleep.

When I returned to the kitchen, Flynn was standing by the window, staring out at the darkened street. His posture was tense, alert. I realized he was watching for threats even in this quiet moment.

"You should go," I whispered, though everything in me wanted him to stay. "It's getting late, and people will talk if they see you leaving here."

He turned to face me. The hunger in his gaze made my knees weak. "I know. But leaving you here, unprotected..."

"I'm not unprotected. I have a gun, and I know how to use it." I moved closer, drawn by something stronger than common sense. "Besides, you said Papa was safe. Surely that means Beau and I are safe too."

"For now." His gaze dropped to my lips. "Lavinia, if something happened to you because of this case—"

"Nothing will happen." I reached up and touched his face, marveling at the roughness of his jaw under my fingertips. "You won't let it."

The simple declaration of faith seemed to undo him. His arms came around me, pulling me close. I could feel his rapid heartbeat beneath my palm.

"I should go." But he made no move to leave.

"Yes." I didn't step away either.

We stood there in my kitchen, holding each other while the lamp cast dancing shadows on the walls and the evening sounds of Holbrook drifted through the open windows. It was dangerous and foolish and everything I'd sworn to avoid.

It was also the most right I'd felt in ages.

Flynn's hand slid up to cup the back of my neck, his fingers tangling in my hair. "Lavinia."

The way he said my name, like a prayer and a plea, made something inside me break open. I rose on my toes, closing the distance between us. Our lips met in a kiss that was gentle and desperate all at once.

This was nothing like the fumbling kisses I'd shared with Thurston. This was something more honest, precious, filled with a promise I hardly dared believe.

When we finally broke apart, we were both breathing hard. Flynn tucked my head against his chest with tender care.

"I should definitely go now." His voice was rough.

"Yes." But my hands were still fisted in his shirt.

He pressed one more soft kiss to my lips, then stepped back with visible effort. "Lock the doors behind me. Keep that gun close. And if anything seems wrong, you send for me immediately."

"I will."

He collected his hat from the table, then paused at the back door. "Lavinia?"

"Yes?"

"What we just shared changes things. For both of us."

I nodded, not trusting my voice.

"I'll be back tomorrow. To check on you, to bring news if I can." His gaze held mine across the darkened kitchen. "And we're going to finish this conversation."

Then he disappeared into the night, leaving me with hope and fear tangled together. I locked the door and leaned against it, trembling.

What had I done?

I snuffed the lamp and climbed the stairs to check on Beau. I couldn't bring myself to regret it. For the first time in years, I'd felt like a woman, not just a mother and daughter. For the first time since Thurston had shattered my faith in love, I'd kissed a man and felt cherished. Not used. Not deceived.

Flynn Harper might be a man I could trust with my heart. The thought left me joyful. And terrified.

15 - The Connection

Flynn

THE TASTE OF Lavinia's lips lingered long after I left her front porch, sweet as desert honey and twice as haunting to a man's peace. I walked back toward the hotel through Holbrook's quiet streets. My boots echoed against the wooden sidewalks while my thoughts spun like a dust devil in a windstorm.

What in blazes had I been thinking?

The honest answer was I hadn't been thinking at all. One moment we had been talking about trust and second chances, and the next I'd been drowning in those brown eyes that held too many secrets and too much pain. When she looked at me like I might be different from the man who'd hurt her, something in me cracked wide open.

I walked away from the sweetest woman I'd ever known, heading back to a case that grew more tangled by the hour. How was I supposed to protect someone when feelings I shouldn't have were clouding my judgment?

Or maybe they were feelings I should have been harboring all along.

The thought stopped me mid-stride. I'd spent years

convinced that a man in my line of work had no business wanting a wife and family. Too dangerous. Too many ways to end up leaving someone behind the way Galen had abandoned us.

But holding Lavinia, feeling her trust despite everything she'd been through... it hadn't felt reckless. It felt right in a way I couldn't explain to Shane or anyone else demanding logical justification.

Lord, if this is Your doing, I'm going to need some clear direction here.

The prayer came easier than it would have a week ago. Maybe watching A.C.'s quiet faith in the face of disaster had worn down some of my resistance. Maybe Lavinia's determination to protect her son while trusting God with the impossible had shown me something I'd been too stubborn to see.

I didn't have all the answers. Wasn't even sure I was asking the right questions.

But if God had brought Lavinia Beaumont into my path for a reason beyond just solving a case, then I needed to figure out what that meant before I made promises I couldn't keep.

Shane was going to have plenty to say about this development.

The hotel lobby was empty except for the night clerk, who barely glanced up from his dime novel as I climbed the stairs to the second floor. My room felt stuffy after the cool evening air, so I slid open the window to let in the desert breeze.

I'd barely settled at the small table when footsteps in the hallway announced Shane's return. His knock was the same pattern we had used as children. Three quick raps, pause, two more. Some habits never changed.

"Door's open," I called.

Shane entered, dust still clinging to his clothes and the weary set of his shoulders showing another long day in the saddle. But his expression was sharper than I'd expected, alert in a way that meant he'd discovered something significant.

"Flynn." He closed the door behind him and moved to the chair, positioning himself where he could see both the window and the door. "We need to talk."

"That makes two of us." I gestured toward the papers spread across the table. "What did you find?"

Shane pulled several creased documents from his vest pocket. "B. Irving struck again. Yesterday morning. Moved another forty head through the railroad yards right here in Holbrook." He spread the papers on the table. "I've been tracking the shipping records. Found bills of sale signed by ranchers who swear they never sold a single head."

The weight of it hit me square in the chest. "When did this start?"

"Last week. Same time Thurston Blackwell arrived in Holbrook." Shane tapped one of the documents. "And look at this signature."

The handwriting was identical to A.C. Beaumont's supposed signature on the land fraud documents. Same flowing script. Same confident strokes. Same subtle flourishes. Pure forger's work.

And this time, A.C. had been hiding safely away.

"Son of a gun." I held it up to the lamplight. "It's the same hand."

"Gets better." Shane leaned back. "The cattle's been moving east on the Atlantic & Pacific. Not going to legitimate buyers. They're vanishing into holding pens and private railroad spurs that don't show on any official map. Over a thousand head in the past few months. Tens of thousands of dollars."

I thought about Thurston's expensive clothes, his cultured accent, the casual way he'd mentioned railroad investments. A man with those connections could move stolen goods across multiple territories without ever appearing on official records.

"They needed a fall guy," I said. "Someone respectable to take the blame if authorities got too close."

"A.C. Beaumont." Shane nodded. "Small-town merchant with an excellent reputation and no political connections. Perfect target."

Anger rose in my chest, hot and pressurized. Some ruthless criminals had tried to destroy an innocent man's life to protect their own profits. They'd put Lavinia and Beau in danger, threatened everything the Beaumont family had built.

And Beau... that little boy with wooden horses and a smile that could melt granite. He deserved better than a mother constantly looking over her shoulder, better than a grandfather forced into hiding.

That boy needed a father. A real one. Someone who'd teach him right from wrong, show him how to be strong without being cruel, demonstrate that a man's worth wasn't measured by his fists or his gun but by his character.

Someone like Shane had been for me.

The weight of that realization settled deep in my chest. Was God calling me to this? To be more than just the marshal who cleared A.C.'s name?

I'd spent my whole life proving I wasn't Galen Harper's legacy. Maybe it was time to build a different legacy entirely.

"There's more," Shane said. "I think I know how our father fits into this."

The words landed hard. "What do you mean?"

"Think about it, Flynn. Galen Harper was the most sophisticated cattle thief in the territory before Grady brought him down. He had forgers, inside connections, a network that stretched from Phoenix to Flagstaff. When he got arrested, all those resources didn't just disappear."

The logic was inescapable. "Someone took over his operation."

"Someone learned from it. Improved on it." Shane's expression was grim. "Galen always said rustling wasn't about stealing cattle. It was about making it look legal. Perfect paperwork, corrupted officials, shipping routes that bypassed normal oversight."

I thought about Kellerman's dying words about our family's connection to the evidence. What if he hadn't been talking about direct involvement? What if he meant our father's methods?

"Thurston Blackwell," I said.

"Has to be. A man with his background could have studied Galen's methods while our father was in prison. Maybe even contacted some of the same corrupt officials."

The pieces clicked together with terrible clarity. "Which means Lavinia and Beau are in more danger than we realized."

Something in my voice made Shane's eyes sharpen. "Flynn, what aren't you telling me?"

Heat crept up my neck. Shane could read me like tracks in fresh mud.

"I kissed her," I admitted.

The silence stretched between us. Shane didn't look surprised, just concerned.

"Lavinia Beaumont," he said finally. Not a question.

"Yes."

"The woman whose father's under federal investigation. Who lied about his whereabouts. Who is raising a five-year-old and guarding more secrets than the territorial legislature."

Put like that, it sounded worse than foolish. "I know how it looks."

"Do you?" Shane stood and moved to the window. "Because from where I'm standing, it looks like you're letting your heart overrule your head. And that's perilous for everyone involved."

"She's innocent in all this. She's just trying to protect her family."

"Maybe. Probably, even." Shane turned back to face me. "But Flynn, if this operation is as big as we think it is, if Thurston Blackwell really is connected to our father's old network, then anyone associated with the Beaumont name could be in danger. Including you, if they think you're compromised."

The truth of his words settled like lead in my stomach. "So what are you saying? That I should walk away from her?"

"I'm saying protect her. But don't jeopardize the investigation." Shane's voice softened slightly. "We need to be smart about this. Disciplined. Document everything. Gather enough evidence to bring down the entire operation, not just one man. Build a case that will hold up in court."

I nodded, though part of me chafed at the methodical approach. Every instinct screamed that Thurston was a direct threat to Lavinia and Beau, that waiting gave him more opportunities to hurt them.

"How long do you think we have?"

"Not long. If B. Irving moved cattle yesterday, they're feeling confident. That could benefit us if we move quickly."

I pulled out the papers from Kellerman's satchel, an idea taking shape. "We don't have enough direct evidence against Thurston. Not yet. But B. Irving? We've got cattle theft, forgery, blackmail, and interstate commerce violations."

Shane's eyes sharpened. "And we know who B. Irving really is."

"Galen." I stood, restless energy driving me forward. "An escaped convict using a known alias to commit federal crimes. We've got your eyewitness testimony connecting him to the forgery. The timing of the escape matches the start of this activity. The cattle theft evidence you've documented. Any honest judge would have to issue those warrants."

"Which judge?" Shane asked quietly.

The question hung between us, heavy with implication. Harrison Webb in Phoenix. A man with a reputation for being accessible to well-connected businessmen.

"We follow proper channels first," I said. "If Webb refuses to issue warrants for a known escaped convict, that tells us everything we need to know about how deep this corruption goes."

Shane studied me for a long moment, then nodded. "You're the Deputy U.S. Marshal. This is your jurisdiction. What's the procedure?"

I moved to the small desk, pulling out paper and pen. The familiar process steadied my racing thoughts. "I'll draft the warrant applications tonight. Document of all the evidence—cattle theft, forgery, blackmail, unlawful transport across state lines, escape from custody."

"And then?"

"We wire Webb in the morning with an urgent request. The telegram outlines the case. Full documentation follows by post." I began writing as I spoke, legal language coming easily. "The telegraph gives him enough information to issue provisional warrants until he receives the supporting documentation by mail."

Shane pulled his chair closer. "Spell out the link between Galen and B. Irving."

"Already planned on it."

The hours passed in focused silence. Shane reviewed each section as I completed it, suggesting improvements to the legal language and ensuring every claim was properly documented.

"What about the connection to Thurston?" Shane asked.

"Can't prove it yet. Not directly." I set down my pen. "But once we have Galen in custody, he might trade information about his associates for a reduced sentence."

"You think he'd turn on Thurston?"

"Galen is only loyal to himself." The bitterness in my voice surprised even me.

Shane's expression softened. "This isn't easy for you.

Filing warrants against Galen."

"Should be. He's a criminal who escaped from prison." I picked up the pen again. "Just another fugitive."

"He's also our father."

"He stopped being our father a long time ago. You've done more for me than he ever did. I'm a Deputy U.S. Marshal. He's an escaped convict. That's the only relationship that matters now."

Shane didn't argue, but I caught the concern in his expression. We both knew that confronting Galen Harper wouldn't be as simple as arresting any other criminal. Too much history. Too much pain. Too many years spent proving we weren't his legacy.

Dawn painted the eastern sky pale gold as I set down my pen. The warrant application lay before me. It was our best shot at turning the system against the men who'd twisted it.

"This is good work, Flynn." Shane's voice carried approval despite his obvious exhaustion. "You've documented everything properly. If Webb denies this, we'll know exactly where he stands."

After Shane left, I remained at the desk, studying the warrant application in the growing light. Somewhere across town, Lavinia was probably waking up, checking on Beau, going through the morning routines that gave structure to their precarious existence.

She was trusting me to keep them safe.

I bowed my head.

Lord, I'm not good at this. Never have been. But if You're listening, I need Your help with what's coming. Help me bring Galen to justice without becoming him in the process. Give me the wisdom to know when to fight and when to show mercy. Protect Lavinia and Beau from whatever Thurston's planning.

I thought about facing Galen again. The rage that would come, the temptation to settle old scores with a bullet instead of a badge. The darkness in me that wanted revenge more than righteousness.

And God, when I face him... keep me from becoming the monster he tried to make me.

The morning light strengthened. I didn't feel any sudden peace or divine assurance. No voice from heaven.

But the weight in my chest eased slightly. Like maybe I wasn't carrying this alone anymore.

Justice tempered with mercy. That's what A.C. had talked about. What Lavinia prayed for. What I'd spent my whole career ignoring in favor of swift, hard punishment.

Maybe it was time to learn a different way.

16 - A Tangled Webb

Flynn

THE TELEGRAPH OFFICE smelled of paper, ink, and the peculiar metallic scent that always clung to the machinery. Morning sunlight streamed through the front windows as Shane and I approached the counter, the warrant applications tucked in my vest pocket.

The operator, a thin man named Collins with wire-rimmed spectacles and ink-stained fingers, looked up from his work with the courtesy of someone who'd sent thousands of messages across the territory.

"Morning, Marshal Harper. What can I do for you, gentlemen?"

I pulled out the telegram and placed it on the counter. "Need this sent to Judge Harrison Webb in Phoenix. Urgent priority."

Collins adjusted his spectacles. "I can have it transmitted within the hour. I'll mark it urgent."

"How soon for a response?" I asked.

"Depends on his schedule, but I'd expect a reply by this afternoon at the latest." Collins began preparing the transmission. "I'll have any response delivered to your hotel immediately."

"Thank you, Mr. Collins." I handed him the payment for the transmission.

As we stepped out into the morning heat, Shane pulled his hat low against the glare. "How long do you think it'll take?"

"For a straightforward warrant request like this? With documented evidence of an escaped convict using a known alias?" I rubbed a hand over my chin. "Webb should review the applications, verify with Yuma prison if needed, and issue the warrants by end of business today. We've done the hard work. The rest is just procedure."

We spent the morning reviewing evidence and planning our next steps. I organized the documents we'd gathered, creating a comprehensive timeline that showed the clear connection between Galen's escape and B. Irving's criminal activities. Shane studied the evidence for his rustling case again, marking patterns in the cattle movements that suggested coordination across multiple jurisdictions.

The hours crawled. Every footstep in the hallway made me tense, waiting for Webb's reply. The afternoon sun climbed higher, casting sharp shadows across Holbrook's dusty streets.

"It's taking longer than I expected," I said finally, checking my pocket watch for the dozenth time. "Straightforward warrant approvals rarely require this much time."

"He might verify details with Yuma officials," Shane suggested, though his tone carried less conviction than before.

Unease curled around my spine.

The telegram finally arrived at three o'clock that afternoon. The hotel clerk brought it up personally, his expression suggesting he understood the message's importance even without knowing its contents.

I unfolded the yellow paper with steady hands. The message was almost dismissive in its brevity:

WARRANT APPLICATIONS REVIEWED
AND DENIED STOP
INSUFFICIENT EVIDENCE STOP
SUSPECT IDENTIFICATION
UNCONFIRMED STOP
WEBB

I stared at the words, reading them twice to make sure I hadn't misunderstood. Then I handed the telegram to Shane without speaking, too angry to trust my voice.

Shane read it slowly, his face growing increasingly hard. When he looked up, fury blazed in his eyes, an emotion I'd rarely seen in my calm older brother.

"Insufficient evidence?" His voice was deadly quiet. "Unconfirmed identification? We documented an escaped convict using his known criminal alias, provided witness descriptions, and showed a clear pattern of crimes." He looked back at the telegram, his jaw working. "Any honest judge would have issued those warrants without hesitation."

"He didn't even ask for additional documentation," I managed through clenched teeth. "Didn't request confirmation from Yuma prison officials. Didn't ask for more witness statements or evidence of the alias connection. He just denied them."

Shane crumpled the telegram in his fist. "Flynn." He moved to face me directly. "He denied arrest warrants for an escaped prisoner. Not because the evidence was insufficient. We both know it was more than adequate. He simply denied them."

The truth settled over me, cold as creek water in winter. "Webb knows exactly who B. Irving is. He knows Galen escaped from Yuma. And he's protecting him anyway."

"It's worse than that." Shane paced the length of the room, running a hand through his hair. "Think about what this means. A judge doesn't protect an escaped convict without reason. He must have history with Galen."

I sank into the chair, my mind racing through the implications. "You think Webb and Galen have been working together for years?"

"Has to be. The sophistication of this operation, the way it's survived Galen's imprisonment. It means protection at the highest level. None of that happens by accident." Shane turned to face me, his expression grim. "Our father built this network with judicial protection from the beginning. That's why he was so successful for so long. And now that he's escaped, Webb's still covering for him."

Rage climbed my throat, sharp and choking. Bad enough that criminals were destroying innocent lives for profit. But the legal system itself, the very institution I'd sworn to uphold, was actively protecting the man who'd terrorized our family.

"So, what do we do?" I asked. "If we can't use legal channels, if the judge is compromised, how do we stop them?"

Shane was quiet for a long moment, and I could see him weighing options, calculating risks. When he finally spoke, his voice carried the weight of a decision that would change everything.

"We need information. Get the facts straight about Webb's connection to Galen and who else might be involved."

"How do we get that without tipping our hand?"

"J.J. Westin." Shane's expression turned thoughtful. "He's working cases in Phoenix. And he's family."

I saw where he was heading. "You think J.J. can investigate Webb without arousing suspicion?"

"Better than we can. We've already put ourselves in Webb's sights after submitting those warrant applications. But J.J. has legitimate reasons to ask questions around the courthouse."

"We need to know who Webb's connected to, who's protecting him, how deep this corruption runs."

"What about Thurston Blackwell?" Shane asked.

The question stirred something sharp. In the chaos of Webb's denial, I'd almost forgotten about the immediate threat to Lavinia and Beau.

"Thurston's still operating freely," I said.

"Could have the same protection Webb's giving Galen. Which means we can't arrest him through normal channels either. We need to hold on to that evidence and deliver it to someone we can trust."

"Good thing I never mail the evidence until I have the warrant approval."

"Nice thinking."

"We need to know more about Webb." I moved to the small desk and began drafting my wire:

WARRANTS DENIED FOR GH STOP
NEED QUIET INQUIRY PHOENIX STOP
DISCRETION CRITICAL STOP
FLYNN

"I'll take this to Collins now," Shane said. "The sooner J.J. starts investigating, the better."

After Shane left, I moved to the window and looked out over Holbrook's quiet streets. Somewhere out there, Galen Harper ran free, shielded by the very system meant to bring him down. Thurston Blackwell prowled unchecked, bold enough to threaten Lavinia and Beau, knowing any warrant would rot on Webb's desk.

I thought about Kellerman's dying words on the Canyon Diablo bridge. "Bigger forces at play. Bigger than your badge." At the time, I'd thought he was just trying to rattle me. Now I understood he'd been trying to warn me.

We weren't just up against criminals. We were fighting the very institutions meant to stop them, corrupted by men who'd learned how to buy power and sell justice.

Shane returned a few minutes later, his expression thoughtful. "Collins will send it right away. J.J. should receive it within the hour."

"And if Thurston makes a move on Lavinia or Beau?"

"Then we protect them. But carefully, Flynn. Very carefully." Shane's voice carried warning. "We're about to walk a very dangerous line. Operating outside official channels, investigating a judge, protecting witnesses we can't officially recognize. If this goes wrong, we won't just lose our badges. We could end up in prison ourselves."

"Then we make sure it doesn't go wrong."

Shane studied my face for a long moment, then nodded slowly. "All right. Let's get back to work. We've got an outlaw gang to thwart and a corrupt judge to expose."

I turned back to the evidence spread across the table, my determination hardening into something cold and focused. Webb had denied our warrant applications, but he'd also shown his hand. Now we knew exactly what we were up against.

And knowing the enemy was the first step to defeating him.

The afternoon stretched ahead, full of planning and preparation. But for the first time since receiving Webb's denial, I felt something besides anger and frustration.

I felt ready.

The criminals thought they were untouchable behind their wall of corruption.

They were about to learn how far Harper justice could reach.

17 - The Devil's Hand

Lavinia

TWO DAYS HAD passed since Flynn's kiss, and the memory still sent warmth through me every time I allowed myself to think about it. But this morning, a gnawing anxiety tempered the warmth.

I dressed in the gray light of early morning, choosing a simple blue calico dress that was practical for store work. The house felt too quiet without Papa's familiar presence—no coffee already brewing, no rustling newspaper, no quiet humming. He'd been gone for days, hidden away somewhere safe while the marshal worked to clear his name.

At least, I hoped that's what was happening.

Yesterday, Flynn and Shane had moved through town with purposeful strides, their faces grim, their hands never far from their sidearms. But Flynn hadn't stopped by the store, nor had he sent word. My stomach twisted with worry.

Beau's cheerful voice drifted down from upstairs as he talked to his wooden horses, creating elaborate adventures that involved brave stallions and daring rescues. The innocent sound reminded me of what was at stake in this. Whatever my feelings for Flynn, Beau's safety had to come first.

"Morning, Mama!" Beau appeared in the kitchen doorway with his hair tousled from sleep and his favorite wooden horse clutched in one small fist. He climbed into his chair at the table, then looked around with curious brown eyes. "When is Papa coming home? I want to show him Thunder's new tricks."

The question still stung, even after two days of similar inquiries. I cracked eggs into a bowl, keeping my voice as normal as possible. "Papa's still away on his trip, sugar. I don't know exactly when he'll be back."

"But it's been forever!" Beau's small brow furrowed with concern.

"I know it feels like a long time. But he's somewhere safe, and Marshal Harper is helping make sure he can come home soon."

"Marshal Harper's nice," Beau said, his face brightening. "He played horses with me. Can he come back tomorrow?"

Heat crept into my cheeks despite my worry. "Eat your breakfast, sugar."

I served scrambled eggs and biscuits, but my own appetite had disappeared entirely. Flynn had promised Papa would be protected, and I was trying so hard to trust that promise. When he'd kissed me two nights ago, it hadn't felt like a man taking advantage. It had felt like someone offering something precious and real.

Trusting Flynn with Papa's safety was one thing. Trusting him with the truth about my past, about Beau's real father, was something else entirely. Could a federal marshal look past my fallen state to see the woman I'd tried so hard to become?

After breakfast, Beau and I walked to the mercantile through morning air that already promised another scorching day. My son chattered about his wooden animals, but I noticed how often he mentioned Papa in his stories. "Thunder misses Grandfather Horse," he said as we unlocked the store. "He wants to show him the new tricks he learned."

"Papa will love hearing about Thunder's tricks when he gets back," I assured him, though my heart ached with uncertainty about when that might be.

The familiar routine of opening the store helped settle my nerves. Mrs. Garrett stopped by for fabric, the postmaster's wife purchased flour and sugar, and old Mr. Cain bought his usual tobacco. Normal transactions with people who'd accepted us as part of the community.

The morning crawled past with agonizing slowness. Each time the bell above the door chimed, I looked up hoping to see Flynn's tall frame filling the doorway. But it was always just another customer, another ordinary transaction.

Around mid-afternoon, the bell chimed with a distinct, more ominous quality. I looked up from the inventory ledger. Thurston Blackwell entered the store.

His expensive suit was perfectly pressed despite the afternoon heat, and his dark hair showed not a strand out of place. But something had changed in his demeanor since our last encounter. The false charm was gone, replaced by cold calculation.

"Miss Beaumont." He closed the door behind him, then turned the lock with a soft click that made my blood run cold. "I hope you don't mind the privacy. We have important matters to discuss."

I glanced toward the back of the store where Beau played quietly behind the counter, then forced myself to meet Thurston's gaze with as much composure as I could manage. Without Papa here, without Flynn's protection, I was completely alone with my son and this dangerous man.

"The store is open for business, Mr. Blackwell. I don't conduct private meetings during working hours."

"Don't you?" He moved closer, his polished boots clicking against the wooden floor with measured steps. "I think you'll find our conversation worth the interruption."

Everything about his posture screamed danger. He positioned himself between me and the door, calculating assessment in his dark eyes. His subtle smile held no warmth whatsoever. This was the real Thurston Blackwell, the man who'd seduced and abandoned me.

"What do you want?" I kept my voice steady despite the terror crawling up my spine.

"Want?" He picked up a pair of gloves from the counter, examining them with apparent interest. "Such a direct question. I prefer to think of this as collecting what belongs to me."

Behind the counter, Beau's cheerful voice rose as he narrated his game. "Thunder's going to jump over the mountain and rescue the lost cows!"

Thurston's attention sharpened like a hawk spotting prey. "Charming boy. So full of life, so intelligent. He has such potential."

"Leave him out of this." I didn't bother softening my tone.

"Leave him out of what? I'm simply observing that the child shows remarkable qualities. Strength, intelligence, natural leadership. Traits that come from good breeding."

The way he said it, with that possessive emphasis on breeding, made my stomach turn. He wasn't just making conversation. He was staking a claim.

"Beau is my son," I said firmly. "He has everything he needs right here."

"Does he?" Thurston set down the gloves and moved closer, close enough that I could smell his expensive cologne. "A child being raised by an unwed mother and an aging shopkeeper who's now mysteriously absent? Lavinia, surely you can see that's no life for a boy with his heritage."

The casual reference to Papa's absence made my

heart skip. How much did Thurston know about our current troubles?

"Don't you dare question our family."

"Family?" Thurston's smile grew colder. "My dear, I'm not the one who created this unfortunate situation. I'm simply offering to rectify it."

"By doing what?"

"By giving the boy what every child deserves. A father. A proper name. Opportunities that extend beyond this primitive little town." He gestured dismissively toward the store's simple interior. "Education, refinement, a place in society that matches his natural abilities."

The casual arrogance in his voice made my hands clench into fists. Here was the same man who'd fled Georgia the moment I'd told him about the pregnancy, now claiming he wanted to provide for the child he'd abandoned before birth.

"You gave up any claim to him the day you disappeared. You have no authority over my son."

"Don't I?" Something dangerous flickered in his dark eyes. "Lavinia, I think you misunderstand the nature of a father's authority. Blood creates obligations that transcend circumstances."

The threat was subtle but unmistakable. In a territory where men's rights were paramount and unwed mothers had little legal protection, Thurston's biological connection to Beau could carry significant weight if he pressed the matter.

"Mama?" Beau's voice cut through the tension as he peeked around the counter. "Who's that man? Why does he sound angry?"

Terror shot through me as I saw Thurston's gaze focus on my son with renewed intensity. He studied Beau's features, cataloging the resemblances that confirmed his paternity. The dark hair, the firm jaw, the intelligent eyes.

"I'm not angry, son," Thurston said, his voice taking on a false warmth that made my skin crawl. "I'm just having an important conversation with your mother."

"I'm not your son," Beau replied with the simple honesty of childhood. "Papa's my papa."

"Is he?" Thurston crouched down to Beau's level, bringing his face closer to my child's. "And where is this papa today?"

"He's away on a trip. But he'll be back soon." Beau clutched his wooden horse protectively, sensing the undercurrents he couldn't understand.

"I'm sure he will be." Thurston's tone carried layers of meaning that chilled me to the bone. "But you know, sometimes men go away and don't come back. Sometimes, boys need new fathers to take care of them."

I moved quickly, stepping between Thurston and Beau with every protective instinct screaming. "Beau, sugar, go to the back room and play. Mama needs to finish talking to this gentleman."

"But Mama—"

"Now, please."

Something in my voice must have conveyed the urgency I felt, because Beau nodded and disappeared toward the storage area, his small footsteps fading into the back of the store. I waited until I was certain he was out of earshot before turning back to face Thurston.

"Get out of my store."

18 - Thunder's Flight

Lavinia

"YOUR STORE?" THURSTON straightened, towering over me with the physical intimidation of a man accustomed to getting his way. "How interesting that you should phrase it that way. Almost as if you have some legitimate claim to this establishment."

"I work here. I manage the day-to-day operations."

"Under your father's name. Using his reputation. Building on his foundation." Thurston moved to the window, looking out at Holbrook's busy main street. "It would be tragic if something were to undermine that foundation. If questions arose about A.C. Beaumont's character. His business practices. His fitness to have been raising a child."

The implications settled hard, like a stone in my chest. Thurston wasn't just threatening to take Beau. He meant to ruin Papa's name, to unravel everything we'd rebuilt.

"What do you want?" I whispered.

"I want what any father would want. A relationship with his son. The opportunity to guide his development, to ensure he reaches his full potential."

He turned to face me, and the chill in his eyes cut through the polish of his words.

"I want to take him somewhere he can receive a proper education, proper social training. Somewhere he can learn to be the man he was born to be."

"You want to take him away from everything he's ever known? From the only family he's ever had?"

"I want to give him opportunities you could never provide. Wealth, position, influence. A life that comes from having a father with resources."

The casual dismissal of everything Papa and I had given Beau made rage surge through me. "He has love. He has security. He has people who would die to protect him."

"He has poverty and limitations. A life of working in a small-town store, serving people who will never see him as more than a shopkeeper's..." He paused deliberately. "Well, let's be honest about what he is."

"And if I refuse?"

His smile was all teeth and no warmth.

"Then I suppose the good people of Holbrook might learn some interesting things about their respected merchant family. About the circumstances of the boy's birth. About certain irregularities in A.C. Beaumont's business dealings that federal authorities find so concerning."

The threat was plain as day. Comply with his demands or watch him tear down everything we'd built, one whispered rumor at a time, each revelation timed to do the most damage.

"You're behind Papa's troubles," I said as realization dawned with horrible clarity. "The federal charges, the wanted poster. You're the one framing him."

"Such a bright girl. I always admired your intelligence." His tone carried the same condescending approval I remembered from our courtship. "Yes, I've found A.C.'s identity quite useful for certain business ventures. Respectable men make excellent cover for less respectable activities."

"You're using his name to commit crimes."

"I'm using his name to conduct business. Whether that business meets federal approval is a matter of perspective." He moved closer again, backing me toward the counter. "But Lavinia, all of this unpleasantness could be avoided. Clear your father's name, restore your family's reputation, secure your son's future. All you have to do is cooperate."

"Cooperate how?"

"Allow me to take the boy for an extended visit. Let him see what life could offer beyond this dusty little town. Give him the chance to choose his own future once he understands his options."

The request sounded reasonable on the surface, but I knew Thurston well enough to recognize the trap. Once he had Beau away from Holbrook, away from me and Papa, there would be no guarantee he'd ever bring him back.

"No." The word came out stronger than I'd expected. "Absolutely not."

Thurston's expression grew colder, more dangerous. "That's disappointing, Lavinia. I had hoped we could resolve this amicably."

"There's nothing to resolve. Beau stays with his family."

"Does he?" Thurston pulled a folded document from his vest pocket, unfolding it slowly. "This is a letter to the territorial authorities. It details A.C. Beaumont's criminal activities, your own moral failings, and questions about your fitness to care for a minor child. One word from me, and you'll lose everything."

Terror clawed at my throat as I read the document. Thurston had been thorough. He'd laid out every detail of my shameful past to make me sound complicit.

"You wouldn't."

"I would. And I will unless you show some sense

about your son's future." He refolded the letter and returned it to his pocket. "I leave for Phoenix tomorrow morning. The boy comes with me, or this document heads for a judge by post tonight."

Either way, I lost everything. If I let him take Beau, I'd never see my son again. If I refused, he'd destroy our reputation and probably get Beau taken away anyway.

"I need time to think."

"Time is a luxury you don't have. The boy comes with me now, or the letter goes out within the hour."

Now. He wanted to take Beau now, while Papa was hiding somewhere and Flynn was across town, unaware of the crisis unfolding. I was alone, facing the same man who'd destroyed my life once before, and he was demanding the one thing I'd rather die than give him.

"Mama?" Beau's voice drifted from the back room. "Can I come out now? I want to show you what Thunder found!"

Thurston's smile became predatory. "Such a trusting child. So eager to please. He'll adapt quickly to new circumstances."

The casual reference to Beau's trusting nature as something to be exploited filled me with a fury that burned through my fear. This monster wanted to take my innocent son and twist him into another version of himself.

"Never," I breathed.

"Never is a strong word, Lavinia. Are you certain you want to stake your family's future on it?"

Before I could respond, Beau appeared in the curtained doorway, his wooden horse clutched in one small hand and his face bright with innocent joy.

"Mama, Thunder jumped over three whole boxes! And he found a treasure!"

Thurston moved with surprising speed, crossing the space between us before I could react. His hand settled on Beau's shoulder with false gentleness, but I saw the way his fingers tightened possessively.

"That's wonderful, son. Your horse sounds very brave."

Beau looked up at him with the wariness children showed toward strangers, but he didn't pull away. "He is brave. Papa says brave horses take care of their families."

"Papa's clever. But sometimes, brave horses need to go on new adventures. See new places. Learn things they could never learn staying in one place."

I saw what Thurston was doing, how he was subtly undermining Beau's sense of security while positioning himself as an exciting alternative.

"I like our place," Beau said. "Mama and Papa are here."

"Of course they are. But what if Papa can't come back? What if he goes away and never returns?"

The casual cruelty of planting such fears in a five-year-old's mind made my vision blur with rage. "Take your hands off my son."

"Your son?" Thurston's grip on Beau's shoulder tightened slightly. "I think you mean our son, Lavinia. And I think it's time he learned about his real father."

"Mama?" Beau's voice carried the first note of genuine fear I'd heard from him. "Papa's my papa."

"That's right, sugar. Papa's your papa, and he loves you very much."

"But blood tells a different story, doesn't it?" Thurston crouched down to Beau's level again, his voice taking on false warmth. "You see, son, sometimes children have more than one father. Sometimes they have the father who raises them, and the father who made them. I'm the father who made you."

Beau's brown eyes widened with confusion and the beginning of terror. He looked between Thurston and me, trying to understand things that had no place in a five-year-old's world.

"I don't understand," he whispered.

"You will in time. But right now, we need to go on a

little trip together. Just you and me, so we can get to know each other properly."

"No!" Beau jerked away from Thurston's grasp and ran to me, wrapping his small arms around my waist. "I don't wanna go anywhere! I want to stay with Mama!"

I held him close, feeling his small body trembling against mine. Over his head, I met Thurston's cold gaze with all the defiance I could summon.

"He's not going anywhere with you."

"Yes, he is." Thurston straightened, his pleasant facade finally falling away completely. "Because Lavinia, you're going to tell him to come with me. You're going to explain that it's for his own good, that he needs to trust his real father to know what's best for him."

"I'll do no such thing."

"Then I'll take him anyway." His hand moved to his vest, and I caught the glint of metal underneath the expensive fabric. A gun. He was armed and prepared to use force if necessary. "The boy comes with me. The only question is whether you make this easy or difficult."

Terror shot through me as I realized how trapped we were. Thurston was bigger, stronger, and armed. The store was locked, and no one would think to check on us until it was too late.

"Please," I whispered, hating the sound of my desperation. "Don't do this to him. He's just a child."

"He's my child. And I won't let him waste his potential in this godforsaken place any longer." Thurston moved closer. "Beau, come here. We're leaving now."

"No!" Beau's grip on me tightened. "I wanna stay with Mama!"

"What you want doesn't matter. You're too young to understand what's best for you. But in time, you'll thank me for this."

I looked around for some means of escape, some weapon, some way to protect my son from the monster. The front door was locked, but if I could reach it, unlock it, get help—

"Beau," I whispered, trying to keep my voice calm. "Remember what Papa taught you about Thunder? About how brave horses sometimes have to run very fast to stay safe?"

He nodded against my skirt, understanding flickering in his young eyes.

"I need you to be like Thunder now. Can you do that for Mama?"

"Enough games." Thurston's patience was clearly exhausted. "The boy comes with me now, or I take him by force. Your choice, Lavinia."

Before I could respond, Beau broke away from me and darted toward the back of the store as if he were playing one of his hiding games. Thurston lunged after him, but I threw myself into his path, clawing at his face and screaming at the top of my lungs.

"Help! Someone help us!"

Thurston backhanded me across the face with enough force to send me sprawling behind the counter. Stars exploded across my vision, and I tasted blood where my teeth had cut my lip. But the blow gave Beau precious seconds to disappear into the maze of storage areas and hiding spots he knew better than any adult.

"Beau, run!" I screamed. "Run to Marshal Harper!"

Thurston's face reddened and twisted as he pursued my son through the store, overturning displays and scattering merchandise in his haste. I could hear Beau's frightened sobs echoing from somewhere in the back, but I couldn't tell exactly where he was hiding.

I struggled to my feet, my cheek throbbing and my vision still swimming. The front door was just a few yards away. If I could reach it, unlock it, maybe someone would hear the commotion and come to help.

My legs felt unsteady as I started toward it, each step requiring concentration I barely had. Almost there. Just a few more feet.

But before I could reach the door, Thurston reappeared from the back room with Beau thrown over his shoulder like a sack of grain. My son was fighting desperately, hitting and kicking, but his five-year-old strength was no match for a grown man's determination.

"Mama! Help me! I don't wanna go!"

"Put him down!" I changed direction, lunging toward them, but Thurston pulled out his gun and aimed it directly at my chest.

"Stay back, or I'll make this much worse for everyone."

I froze, staring at the black barrel pointed at my heart. He would do it. I could see the resolve in his eyes, the same calculating nature that had allowed him to abandon me without a backward glance.

"That's better." He moved toward the back door, still carrying my screaming, struggling son. "Don't follow us, Lavinia. Don't make me do something we'll both regret."

"Please," I whispered, tears streaming down my face. "Please don't take him. I'll do anything. Give you anything. Just don't take my baby."

"You had your chance to cooperate. You chose defiance instead." He paused at the back door, looking over his shoulder. "Don't worry. I'll take good care of our son. After all, he's half mine."

Then they were gone, disappearing into the alley behind the store. I heard horse's hooves, fast and urgent, growing fainter as they carried my child away from everything he'd ever known.

I collapsed onto the floor behind the counter, my whole body shaking with sobs that seemed to tear something vital loose in my soul. Beau was gone. The light of my life, the reason I got up every morning—gone with a monster who saw him as property to be claimed.

But even as despair threatened to drown me, one thought burned bright in my mind. Flynn. I had to find Flynn. He'd promised to protect us. If anyone could bring

Beau back safely, it was the man who'd shown me what honor looked like.

I dragged myself to my feet and stumbled to the front door, unlocking it with hands that shook like leaves in a windstorm. The afternoon sunlight seemed impossibly bright after the horror of the last few minutes.

"Help," I called weakly, then louder. "Help! Someone help me!"

People turned at the sound of my voice. Mrs. Patterson ran across the street. The blacksmith's wife stopped sweeping her porch. They saw my bleeding lip, my torn dress, and the wild desperation in my eyes.

"My son," I gasped as they gathered around me. "A man took my son. I need Marshal Harper. Please, someone find Marshal Harper!"

The blacksmith's wife put a supportive arm around my shoulders while someone ran toward the hotel where Flynn was staying. Mrs. Patterson pressed a clean handkerchief to my cut lip, murmuring soothing words that barely penetrated the roar of panic in my ears.

All I could think about was Beau's terrified face as Thurston carried him away, the way he'd reached for me with small hands, the trust in his voice when he'd called me Mama for what might be the last time.

I had failed him. Failed to protect the most important person in my world from the monster who had created him. But Flynn would help. Flynn had to help. Because if he couldn't bring Beau back safely, I didn't know how I'd survive the guilt and loss.

In the distance, I could hear running footsteps and urgent voices as word spread through town. Soon Flynn would know what had happened. Then I would see if his promises meant anything when the stakes were this high.

My baby was out there somewhere with a man who saw him as a possession rather than a person. And I was powerless to save him alone.

But maybe if I could find the courage to trust completely, I wouldn't have to face this nightmare by myself.

19 - The Long Night

Flynn

I WAS STUDYING the evidence on the hotel room table when the sound of a commotion drifted through the open window. Raised voices, running footsteps that made my instincts prick like a hound catching a scent.

"You hear that?" Shane looked up from the document he'd been examining, his face creased with concern.

"Sounds like trouble." I moved to the window, scanning the street below. People were gathering near the mercantile, their voices urgent and worried. Mrs. Patterson pointed toward the store while the blacksmith's wife gestured frantically.

Then I caught sight of a familiar blue dress, and my blood turned cold.

Lavinia stood in the middle of the crowd, her hair disheveled and something dark staining her lip. Even from this distance, I could see she was shaking, her arms wrapped around herself as if trying to hold the pieces together.

"Sweet merciful heaven." I grabbed my gun belt and hat, already moving toward the door. "Shane, something's happened to Lavinia."

"Flynn, wait—"

But I was already taking the stairs two at a time, my heart hammering against my ribs. Every instinct I possessed screamed that the woman I'd kissed was in danger, and nothing else mattered except getting to her side.

I pushed through the hotel's front doors and ran down the street, my boots pounding against the wooden sidewalk. The crowd parted as they saw me coming, and I caught fragments of worried conversation.

"—took the boy—"

"—man with a gun—"

I reached Lavinia just as her knees buckled. My arms went around her automatically, pulling her against my chest as her whole body shook with sobs.

"Lavinia." I kept my voice low despite the fury coursing through my veins. "What happened? Are you hurt?"

She looked up at me with eyes that held more pain than anyone should have to bear. Blood had dried on her lower lip, and I could see the beginnings of a bruise on her left cheek. Someone had hit her. Someone had put their hands on my Lavinia and hurt her.

When I found out who it was, they were going to answer for it.

"He took him," she whispered, her voice broken. "Flynn, he took Beau."

The words landed hard, sending fire through my veins. "Who took him?"

"Thurston Blackwell. He came to the store, and he..." Her voice dissolved into sobs again, and my blood boiled with nearly murderous intent.

The name hit me like a fist to the gut. Thurston Blackwell. The man who'd courted Lavinia when she was barely more than a child. The man who'd gotten her pregnant and abandoned her to face the shame alone.

Beau's father.

The connection snapped into place with sickening

clarity. This wasn't just a kidnapping. This was a man who'd tried to erase the consequences of his sin years ago, and now he'd come back to claim what he'd once wanted destroyed. The evil of it stole my breath.

My hands trembled with the urge to mount up and ride. To hunt him down like the predator he was and deliver swift justice that made evil men regret drawing breath. But even as that familiar fury burned through my veins, something else rose to meet it. Something cleaner, harder, more focused.

Standing here with Lavinia shaking in my arms, I understood. Real justice wasn't just about punishment. It was about standing between evil and the people it tried to destroy.

Thurston Blackwell had abandoned his responsibilities, threatened Lavinia's family, and now stolen an innocent child. That made him a terror in need of facing justice.

And I would be the one to deliver it.

"Mrs. Patterson," I called to the older woman hovering nearby. "Would you help me get Miss Beaumont inside the store?"

"Of course, Marshal. Poor dear's been through something terrible."

Together we guided Lavinia toward the mercantile. The front door stood wide open, and I could see signs of a struggle inside. Overturned displays, scattered merchandise, a child's wooden horse lying abandoned on the floor.

I bent and picked up the toy, the smooth wood still warm as if small hands had just been clutching it. The simple carved mane, the careful paintwork. Beau had loved it. My fingers closed around it, and fresh rage surged through my veins. Some monster had terrorized a five-year-old boy badly enough that he'd dropped his treasure.

"Flynn?" Shane's voice came from behind me as he caught up. "What's the situation?"

"Kidnapping. Thurston Blackwell took Lavinia's

son." I kept my voice low, but Shane would hear the barely controlled fury underneath. "I'm going after him."

"Hold on." Shane's hand settled on my shoulder. "Think this through. Where would you go? Which direction? How long ago did this happen?"

The questions hit me hard, forcing my mind to engage despite the emotional storm raging within me. Shane was right. Charging off without a plan would only waste precious time.

Mrs. Patterson settled Lavinia on a stool behind the counter and began dabbing at the cut on her lip with a damp cloth. "There now, dear. Just a small cut."

"How long ago did this happen?" I asked.

"Maybe twenty minutes, Marshal," Mrs. Patterson replied.

Twenty minutes. Thurston had a significant head start, but not insurmountable if we moved wisely and quickly. I turned to Shane, forcing myself to think like a lawman instead of a man whose heart was breaking for the woman sobbing on the other side of the counter.

"We need to track which way he went. Check for witnesses, fresh horse signs, anything that points us in the right direction."

"Agreed. I'll check the alley behind the store, see if I can pick up a trail." Shane was already moving. "You stay with her, get the details. Find out if she knows where he might be headed."

I nodded and crouched beside Lavinia, taking her hands in mine. Her skin was cold as a winter morning, and I could feel the fine tremors that revealed shock setting in.

"Lavinia, look at me." I kept my voice firm but quiet. "I need you to tell me exactly what happened. Every detail you can remember."

She met my eyes, and I saw her fighting to pull herself together. My brave, sweet Lavinia.

"He came to the store about an hour ago. Locked the door behind him, said we needed privacy." Her voice was steadier now, though tears still tracked down her cheeks. "He said he wanted to take Beau. Said my son deserved better than what we could give him."

"Did he say where he was taking him?"

"Phoenix. He mentioned leaving for Phoenix tomorrow morning, but..." She hesitated, shame flickering across her features. "Flynn, back then in Georgia, he tried to make me get rid of the baby. When I refused, he threatened to destroy Papa's reputation if I ever told anyone the truth." Her voice broke. "He abandoned us. And now he comes back claiming to be Beau's father?"

Fire crawled up my spine, and I forced my shoulders to stay relaxed instead of tensing for a fight that would never come because the man who'd hurt her wasn't here to face me.

He'd tried to make her kill their baby. Then threatened to destroy her father when she refused.

My jaw tightened until my teeth ached. Being a sire didn't make a man a father any more than a badge made a man just. Fatherhood was earned through sacrifice, staying when others fled, putting a child's needs above your own comfort. A.C. Beaumont had been more father to Beau than Thurston would ever be.

Scripture rose unbidden in my mind. Our oath. *When justice is executed, it is a joy to the righteous but a terror to evildoers.* I'd always heard it as a call to hunt down the guilty and make them pay. But now I understood something deeper. Protecting the fatherless. Defending the vulnerable. Refusing to let wickedness win. That was justice too.

I couldn't undo what Thurston had done years ago. But I could stand in the gap now. Could bring Beau home safely. Could prove that some men kept their promises even when it cost them everything.

I pulled her into my arms, feeling her sob against my chest. Mrs. Patterson discreetly moved to the front of the store, giving us space.

"Listen to me," I whispered. "None of this was your

fault. You were sixteen years old, and he knew exactly what he was doing. He manipulated you, threatened you, and now he's terrorizing you again. But it stops today."

She looked up at me, hope and fear warring in her expression.

"I'm going to get Beau back," I continued. "And when I do, Thurston Blackwell is going to face justice for everything he's done. The kidnapping. All of it."

"I want to come with you." She pulled back, desperation replacing the momentary hope. "Flynn, I can't just sit here while my son is out there with that monster. I have to do something."

"No." The word came out harsher than I intended, and I softened my tone. "Lavinia, I understand. But you need to trust me on this."

"Trust you?" Her voice rose. "How can I trust anyone when—"

"Because I'm not him." I cupped her face gently, careful of the bruise. "I'm not Thurston. I don't make promises I won't keep. And I promise you, I will bring Beau home safely."

The bell above the door chimed as Shane returned. "Found fresh tracks heading west. Two horses, one carrying double. Trail's clear for now."

I looked between Shane and Lavinia, torn between the desperate need to pursue and the knowledge that she needed me here right now.

"Flynn, we need backup." Shane's voice was quiet but firm. "I'll wire J.J. and Grady. We should wait for them."

Wait. The word felt like a betrayal of the terrified child somewhere out there. But Shane was right. Charging off into the dark without a plan wouldn't help Beau.

I turned back to Lavinia. "I need you to stay here. Stay safe. Because rushing in without the lay of the land and backup could get Beau hurt in the crossfire."

"But—"

"If you're out there in danger, I'll be distracted trying

to protect you instead of focused on getting him back." I lifted her chin so she had to meet my eyes. "I need to know you're safe so I can focus on bringing him home. Can you understand that?"

The internal struggle played out across her features. Finally, she took a shaky breath.

"You really believe staying here is the right thing to do?"

"I do. And I believe you're brave enough to do the hardest thing of all. Wait and trust." I squeezed her shoulders gently. "After everything Thurston put you through, I know how hard it is to trust any man's promises. But I'm asking you to trust me now."

Something shifted in her expression, and I saw acceptance replacing the wild desperation.

"All right," she whispered. "I'll stay. But Flynn, promise me you'll send word if you can. I need to know he's all right."

"I promise. Mrs. Patterson," I turned to the older woman. "Would you mind staying with Miss Beaumont?"

"Of course, Marshal. I'll take good care of her." Mrs. Patterson wrapped a supportive arm around Lavinia's shoulders. "We'll keep the coffee hot and say our prayers."

I squeezed Lavinia's hands one more time, then pressed the small wooden horse into her palm, folding her fingers around it. "Hold on to this for him. When I bring Beau home, he's going to want his horse back."

Her breath caught as she looked down at the toy, and fresh tears spilled over. But she nodded, clutching it against her chest.

"Thank you," I whispered. "You're doing the right thing. The brave thing."

"Just bring him home."

"I will."

I headed outside to meet Shane.

"Telegrams sent. J.J. and Grady will be on the first train tomorrow morning." He studied my face. "What's the plan?"

Every instinct I possessed screamed to mount up and ride. To chase down Thurston's trail while it was still fresh, to push hard through the night if necessary. The old Flynn Harper would have done exactly that.

But as I looked back through the mercantile window at Lavinia, something shifted inside me. She'd made her choice to trust me despite everything her past had taught her about trusting men.

And that trust demanded more than reckless action. It demanded wisdom.

"We wait until morning," I heard myself say.

Shane's eyebrows rose slightly. "You sure about that?"

"No." The admission came easier than I expected. "Every part of me wants to ride out right now. But Thurston's got at least an hour head start, and we don't know if he's actually headed to Phoenix or if that was misdirection. Charging off blind in the dark won't help Beau."

I turned to face Shane directly. "Most of the businesses are already closed for the night. Come first light, we canvas the town. Talk to the railroad clerk, the livery owner, anyone who might've seen Thurston preparing to leave or heard which direction he took. We nail down his actual route." I glanced toward the setting sun, already touching the horizon. "By the time J.J. and Grady arrive tomorrow afternoon, we'll know exactly where we're headed and have a solid plan."

Shane studied me for a long moment, then gripped my shoulder. "Smart. We'll start at first light."

I nodded, the weight of the decision settling over me. Somewhere out there, Beau was scared and confused. But rushing into the darkness without knowing where I was going wouldn't bring him home safely.

"Get some rest," I said. "Tomorrow's going to be a long day."

Shane headed toward his room, then paused. "Flynn?

This was the right call. I'm proud of you."

My chest tightened, and I stood taller. I watched the man who'd been more father to me than the devil Galen as he disappeared from view.

After he left, I stood alone on the hotel's front porch, staring out at the darkened street. The waiting felt like swallowing hot coals. Every minute that passed was another minute Beau spent in Thurston's custody.

But rushing in blind wouldn't save him. It would only put him in more danger.

I'd spent years operating on instinct and fury, letting my rage at injustice drive me forward. It had made me effective, but it had also made me reckless. Tonight I'd chosen strategy over impulse. Planning over immediate action.

It was the hardest decision I'd ever made.

I glanced toward the mercantile, dark now. Lavinia was at home, probably unable to sleep, trusting that I would bring her son home safely.

"I will," I whispered to the darkness. "I promise you I will."

I leaned against the porch railing, staring up at the stars scattered across the desert sky. The night was quiet except for the distant yips of coyotes and the soft sounds of Holbrook settling in for sleep.

"God," I whispered, "I need You to help me understand this."

With Beau's life hanging in the balance, I had nowhere else to turn.

"My sisters say You care about the fatherless. That You put people where they're meant to be." My hands gripped the railing hard. "If that's true, then I'm asking You to help me bring Beau home. Not because I'm worthy of the asking, but because he's innocent and scared. Protect him."

The still night offered no immediate answer, but something shifted in my chest. A steadiness I hadn't felt before. Maybe it was faith. Maybe it was just the result of making a hard choice and seeing it through.

I thought about Lavinia's trust. About A.C. Beaumont's years of proving that family was built through choice and sacrifice, not blood alone. About Beau, who'd called me Mr. Flynn with such innocent confidence that I'd protect him.

Tomorrow I'd ride out with a plan, with backup, with everything a smart lawman needed to face a dangerous situation.

Tonight I'd wait. I'd trust that the delay wasn't weakness but wisdom.

"Make me a man who deserves their trust," I finished quietly. "One who brings that boy home safe and proves that evil doesn't get the final word."

Peace settled over my shoulders like a well-worn coat. I'd made my choice. Now I had to live with it and pray it was the right one.

20 - First Light

Flynn

THE MORNING SUN climbed steadily higher as Shane and I made our way down Holbrook's main street, the heat already building despite the early hour. One day had passed since Thurston Blackwell kidnapped Beau, and every minute felt like an eternity. But charging in blind wouldn't bring the boy home safely. We needed to find out what we were up against first.

"Railroad office?" Shane suggested, gesturing toward the depot at the end of the street.

"Good place to start." I kept my voice steady despite the urgency thrumming through my veins. "If Thurston bought tickets, the clerk will remember."

The depot smelled of coal smoke and machine oil, and the rhythmic clack of the telegraph key echoed through the space. The railroad clerk, a nervous man with ink-stained fingers, looked up from his ledger when we approached.

"Morning, Marshal. Detective. Something I can help you with?"

Shane leaned against the counter, his badge catching

the light from the window. "We're looking for information about a well-dressed gentleman who might have purchased tickets recently. Probably had a young boy with him."

The clerk's eyes widened with recognition. "Oh yes, I remember him. Hard to forget a transaction like that."

"Tell us everything you remember," I said.

"Well-dressed gentleman, yes, sir. Bought two tickets to Phoenix on the morning train. Had a young boy with him, maybe five or six years old." The clerk adjusted his spectacles, his expression troubled. "The child seemed upset."

"How upset?" Shane asked.

"Crying and nervous. The man kept telling him they were going on an adventure, but the child didn't seem convinced." The clerk shook his head slowly. "Truth is, something felt wrong about the whole thing. The boy kept looking back toward town as if he was hoping someone would come after him."

My hands clenched into fists at my sides. Beau, frightened and confused, was taken from everything he knew. The image made my stomach roil and my muscles coil.

"Did they board the train?" Shane's voice remained steady.

"No, sir, that's the peculiar thing. Bought the tickets, but then the gentleman said they'd changed their minds. Wanted to travel by horseback instead. Asked about the best routes to Flagstaff."

Shane and I exchanged glances. That was a deliberate misdirection.

"Did he ask about any specific routes?" I pressed.

The clerk frowned, thinking. "He seemed interested in the main road at first, but then asked if there were any less-traveled paths. Said something about preferring privacy."

"Thank you for your help." Shane straightened from the counter. "If you remember anything else, we're staying at the hotel."

The morning air hit hard, like stepping into a forge. I pulled my hat lower against the glare.

"Classic misdirection," Shane observed. "He's smarter than I had hoped."

"Let's try the livery," I suggested. "If he didn't take the train, he needed horses."

The livery stable sat at the edge of town, a weathered structure that smelled of hay and leather. The owner, a man named Carson, was shoeing a bay mare when we arrived. He straightened when he saw our badges, wiping his hands on his leather apron.

"Marshals. You here about that Blackwell fellow?"

"You know him?" I asked.

"Know of him. He arranged everything three days ago." Carson gestured toward the stalls. "Wanted two of my best trail horses, and supplies for hard riding. Paid cash in advance and specified he'd need mounts that could handle rough country."

Three days ago. Before the kidnapping. This wasn't a crime of opportunity. Thurston had planned every detail.

"What kind of supplies?" Shane asked.

"Grain for the horses, jerky, hardtack, enough water for two days of desert travel. But here's what struck me as odd." Carson moved closer, lowering his voice. "He also asked about the old mining trails north of town. Specifically wanted to know about routes that avoided the main roads."

"Mining trails?" I frowned.

"Abandoned silver prospecting routes from the eighties. Most folks don't even know they exist anymore, but they'll take you through country where you won't see another soul for days." Carson's weathered face creased with concern. "Marshal, if he's got a child with him on those trails, that's dangerous territory. No water sources, rough going, and easy to get lost if you don't know the way."

"Did he seem familiar with the area?" Shane asked.

"He had maps. Good ones too. Not the kind you pick up at a general store. These were detailed survey maps showing elevation, water sources, the whole works." Carson shook his head. "That man came prepared."

After thanking Carson, Shane and I continued our canvassing. The barber remembered Thurston asking questions about local ranches two days earlier. Mrs. Patterson recalled him carrying rope and other supplies that seemed odd for a businessman. Each piece of information painted a picture of meticulous planning and deliberate deception.

By late morning, the heat had grown oppressive. Sweat trickled down my back beneath my shirt. Shane and I sought the shade of an awning outside the barbershop, where old Pete Morrison sat whittling a piece of pine.

"Marshal Harper," he called when he spotted us. "Heard you boys are looking into that business with the Blackwell fellow."

"That's right, Pete." I moved closer, grateful for any information. "You see or hear anything that might help?"

Morrison glanced around nervously, then motioned us closer. His voice dropped to just above a whisper. "Maybe. Been hearing stories about that old Broken Arrow Ranch. Place has been empty for three years, but lately..."

"Lately what?" Shane pressed.

"Riders coming and going at night. Lights in the windows when there shouldn't be anybody there." He paused, clearly uncomfortable. "And there's talk that the ranch is connected to some unsavory characters. Including..." He hesitated, his eyes flicking to my face.

"Including who?" My voice came out harder than I intended.

"Including Galen Harper."

My father. Of course he would be involved. The corruption, the carefully planned crimes, the outlaw gang operating under our noses. It all bore his mark.

Shane's hand settled on my shoulder, a steadying weight. "You certain about this, Pete?"

"Can't swear to it in court, but it's what people are saying. And Marshal," he looked at me directly, "if it's true, you might be riding into more than just a kidnapping."

After Pete left, Shane and I stood in silence for a moment. The street bustled with normal activity around us. Wagons rolled past, creating plumes of dust spiraling into the air. Shopkeepers swept their storefronts. Children played in the shade of the general store. Normal life continued while somewhere out there, a frightened boy waited for rescue.

"Flynn," Shane began.

"Don't," I cut him off. "Whatever you're about to say about him, I don't want to hear it."

"I was going to say that we need to be smart about this. If Galen's involved, this is bigger and more dangerous than we thought."

I nodded, swallowing the anger that always came with thoughts of my father. "I know."

"We wait for J.J. and Grady. We plan carefully. We do this right." Shane's tone left no room for argument.

"Agreed." The word tasted like ash in my mouth, but he was right. Beau's safety depended on us being careful, not reckless.

We started back toward the hotel, our boots clomping against the boardwalk. As we passed the mercantile, the movement in the window caught my attention. Lavinia stood behind the counter, her silhouette visible through the glass. Even from this distance, I could see the tension in her shoulders, the way she kept glancing toward the door.

She looked up as we passed. Our eyes met through the window, and something in her gaze reached straight through me. Then she was moving, swift and sure, like a woman chasing hope before it vanished.

The bell chimed as she burst through the doorway, her blond hair slightly disheveled, her brown eyes wild with fear and frustration.

"Marshal Harper," she called, her voice carrying an edge I'd never heard before. "I need to speak with you. Now."

Shane stepped back slightly, giving us space while remaining close enough to observe. I approached Lavinia, noting the way her hands trembled slightly at her sides.

"Miss Beaumont," I began, but she cut me off.

"It's been a day." Her voice shook with barely controlled emotion. "A whole day, and my son is still out there. What are you doing to find him?"

The accusation in her words stung, even though I understood its source. "We're running down some leads. Making sure we know what we're walking into before we—"

"Really?" She took a step closer, her eyes blazing. "A dangerous man has kidnapped my five-year-old son, and you're standing around town talking to people?"

"Lavinia." I kept my voice low, calm. "I understand your fear—"

"Do you?" She wrapped her arms around herself, a gesture of protection against pain I couldn't shield her from. "Do you understand what it's like not to know where your child is? To imagine all the terrible things that might be happening to him? To lie awake at night wondering if he's crying for you?"

"No," I admitted quietly. "I don't. But I do know that charging in without a plan will get Beau killed."

She flinched as if I'd struck her. "Don't say that."

"It's the truth." I glanced at Shane, who nodded slightly. I moved closer to Lavinia, close enough to speak without the entire street hearing. "Thurston planned this carefully. He had maps, supplies, and alternate routes. He knew exactly what he was doing. If we rush in blind, we play right into his hands."

"So you're just going to wait? While my son—" Her voice broke, and she pressed a hand to her mouth.

"We're not waiting," Shane interjected gently. "We've

been working all morning gathering information about Thurston's movements, his destination, his resources. We need to know what we're facing."

"Shane sent wires yesterday to two of the best lawmen in the territory," I added. "They're arriving this afternoon. With four of us, we'll have the manpower to mount a proper rescue."

Lavinia's eyes searched mine. "Four lawmen against one man. That's enough to bring him home safely."

My jaw tightened. She deserved the truth. "Thurston isn't working alone. At the ranch where we believe he's taken Beau, there are multiple men—an outlaw gang. This is bigger than one kidnapping."

"How much bigger?" Her voice had dropped to barely above a whisper.

"We don't know yet. That's why we need to be smart about this." I wanted to touch her, to offer some physical comfort, but we stood on a public street with dozens of eyes watching. "Lavinia, I swore I'd bring Beau home safely. I meant it. But I can't do that if I'm dead or captured because I rushed in without preparing properly."

She closed her eyes, and I watched her visibly struggle for control. When she opened them again, tears glistened on her lashes, but her voice was steadier. "How long?"

"My brothers-in-law arrive this afternoon. We'll plan our approach, then ride out at dusk. We'll reach the ranch around dawn, which gives us daylight to observe and time to find the best way to get Beau out safely."

"Dawn," she repeated. "That's tomorrow morning."

"Yes."

"He'll have been gone for two days by then."

The accusation hung between us, and I had no defense against it except the truth. "I know. And every hour that passes makes this harder. But a failed rescue attempt doesn't help anyone."

She stared at me for a long moment, and I saw the internal battle playing out across her face. The mother who wanted to demand immediate action warred with the woman who understood the necessity of patience. Finally, she nodded, a small, jerky movement.

"Promise me," she said. "Promise me you'll bring him home."

"I promise I'll do everything in my power to bring him home safely." I couldn't promise success, and I wouldn't insult her intelligence by pretending I could guarantee an outcome in a situation this dangerous. "And Lavinia, you need to trust that I care about Beau almost as much as you do. That I won't take unnecessary risks with his life."

Something in her expression softened slightly. "I do trust you. That's what makes this waiting so hard. If I didn't trust you, I could at least be angry instead of terrified."

Before I could respond, a train whistle echoed across town, the sound carrying clearly in the afternoon heat. I pulled out my pocket watch and checked the time.

"That'd be our backup now," Shane observed, straightening from his position against the mercantile wall.

Lavinia looked toward the depot, then back at me. "Go. Do what you need to do to bring my son home." She paused, then added quietly, "And Marshal? Come back safely yourself. Beau's going to need you when this is over."

The words stole the air from my lungs. She wanted me. In her future. In her son's future. The impact reverberated through my chest. I wanted the same thing.

I held her gaze, seeing the fear and something deeper in those brown eyes. Something that made my heart hammer against my ribs in a way that had nothing to do with the coming confrontation.

"I'll come back," I said, my voice rougher than I intended. "I promise."

She turned and walked back into the mercantile, her spine straight despite the weight she carried. The bell chimed softly as the door closed behind her.

"That woman's stronger than railroad iron," Shane murmured as we started toward the depot.

"She is," I agreed. "And she's terrified."

"So are you."

I shot him a sharp look, but he met my gaze steadily. "Nothing wrong with being afraid when the stakes are this high. Just means you care about the right things."

The afternoon train from Phoenix wheezed to a stop at the depot in a cloud of steam and dust, its whistle echoing off the adobe buildings. Shane and I stood waiting on the platform, watching as the livestock car doors slid open with a metallic screech.

Two familiar figures led their horses down the ramp. J.J. Westin moved with the easy confidence of a man who'd spent most of his life in the saddle, his weathered face breaking into a grin when he spotted us. Behind him came Grady Thatcher, stockier but no less capable, his bay gelding stepping carefully onto the platform.

"Flynn Harper, you ugly cuss," Grady called out, dropping his horse's reins to pull me into a back-slapping embrace. "Justine wants to know when you're coming down for a proper visit. The kids are growing like spring weeds, and Lee's been asking when Uncle Flynn's going to teach him to track."

Despite the circumstances, some of the tension left my shoulders. There was something about family that reminded a man he wasn't facing the world alone.

"Tell Justine I'll make it down as soon as this business is settled." I meant it. "How are Amy and Lee?"

"Amy's reading everything she can get her hands on, and Lee's determined to be a lawman like his uncle." Grady's expression sobered. "When we got Shane's wire about a kidnapped child, there wasn't any question about coming."

Shane stepped forward to clasp J.J.'s hand. "How's married life treating you, brother?"

J.J.'s grin widened. "Well, let's just say Hayley keeps me on my toes. Woman's got more fire than a branding iron and twice the determination. But I wouldn't have her any other way." He tied his horse to the post, his expression turning serious. "Now, what's this about Galen Harper and a missing boy?"

"Let's head to the hotel," Shane suggested, glancing around at the curious faces studying us. "This isn't a conversation for public ears."

We walked down the dusty street, four men united by bonds of family and shared purpose. Whatever we faced at the Broken Arrow Ranch, whatever dangers lay ahead, we'd face them together.

This wasn't just about justice anymore. It was about family. The family Lavinia and Beau had become to me, and the family of brothers who'd answered the call when I needed them most.

21 - The Hunt Begins

Flynn

THE HOTEL'S SMALL lobby was empty except for the desk clerk, who nodded respectfully and disappeared into the back room when four lawmen walked in. Shane led us to a corner table near the window where we could speak freely while keeping an eye on the street.

"All right," J.J. said once we'd settled in our chairs. "Shane's wire was short on details. What exactly are we dealing with?"

I filled them in on everything. Thurston's kidnapping of Beau, his relationship to Lavinia, the evidence pointing toward the Broken Arrow Ranch, and the troubling connection to our father's criminal network.

Both men's expressions grew increasingly somber as the story unfolded. Grady'd brought down Galen Harper's rustling ring years ago and had seen firsthand the scope of his criminality.

"So you think the old man's gang is still running?" Grady asked when I finished.

"Has to be," Shane replied. "An organization that sophisticated doesn't just disappear when the leader gets arrested. Somebody took it over, probably expanded it."

"And now they've got a five-year-old boy." J.J.'s voice was quiet. "That changes everything."

I appreciated that neither man questioned our commitment to the rescue. Family was family, whether by blood or by choice, and the Harpers had learned long ago that you protected your own.

J.J. glanced toward the lobby entrance, then leaned forward and lowered his voice. "Before we discuss the tactical details, there's something you need to know. Something that changes what we're facing here."

I straightened in my chair. Shane's hand stilled on the table.

"Hayley and I uncovered hard evidence about Judge Harrison Webb," J.J. continued, his words careful and deliberate. "He colluded with Galen Harper to facilitate the prison escape."

The air seemed to leave the room. I stared at J.J., my mind racing through the implications. Webb's name had been hovering over this investigation like a vulture since those warrant denials, but having it confirmed felt like a kick in my gut.

"You're certain?" Shane's voice remained even, but I saw the muscle working in his jaw.

"Absolutely certain. Well, it was really Hayley. Former Pinkerton and all." J.J.'s expression held equal parts pride and concern. "She interviewed three prison guards who were too terrified to report what happened. Webb threatened their families with false crimes if they didn't facilitate Galen's escape. Manufactured charges, planted evidence, the whole apparatus of federal power turned against innocent people to force cooperation."

Grady muttered something under his breath, his weathered face hardening. "Good grief. A federal judge."

"She's still sorting through what happened with the guards' families," J.J. added. "Documenting everything, building a case that can't be dismissed. But Flynn, Shane, this means you've been operating under the nose of a judge who's actively protecting the criminals you're pursuing."

The full implications crashed over me. Every denied warrant, every legal obstacle we'd faced, every moment of wondering why the system seemed to work against justice instead of for it. All of it traced back to Webb's corruption.

"If Webb finds out we're going after Galen and Thurston," I said slowly, "he could have us all arrested. Federal prison for interfering with his protected criminals."

"Not just you two," Grady pointed out. "All four of us. We're about to ride into a rescue mission against men hiding behind a crooked judge's robes. If Webb wants to, he can make this look like rogue lawmen exceeding their authority."

The weight of that reality settled over the table. We weren't just risking our lives on this mission. We were risking our freedom, our careers, everything we'd worked to build as lawmen.

J.J. met my eyes, then Shane's. "I won't lie to you. This is dangerous in ways that have nothing to do with bullets and outlaws. But that boy needs us. And sometimes doing the right thing means risking everything."

Shane pulled a toothpick from his case and clamped it between his teeth, his eyes distant as he processed the implications. "Agreed. We didn't become lawmen to hide behind corrupt judges. We took these badges to protect the innocent, even when the system itself is broken."

I thought about Beau, probably scared and confused somewhere in the darkness ahead. About Lavinia's trust that we'd bring her son home safely. About A.C. Beaumont, framed by this same outlaw gang that had federal protection. About all the other victims across the territory who'd suffered because evil men corrupted the very institutions meant to stop them.

"Then we do this by the book where we can," I said. "We document everything, we follow proper procedure, and we make sure that when this is over, even Webb can't twist it into something criminal."

"And we watch each other's backs," Grady added. "All four of us. If Webb tries to come after us, he'll have to explain why four decorated lawmen with spotless records all suddenly went rogue at the same time."

J.J. allowed himself a tight smile. "Strength in numbers. I like it." His expression sobered again. "But we need to understand what we're walking into. We're alone out here, gentlemen. No legal backup, no guarantee the courts will support us, no safety net."

"We've never needed a safety net before," Shane said quietly. "And we're not alone. We've got each other, and we've got the truth on our side."

"An we've got God with us," J.J. added.

I looked around the table at these men who'd answered the call without hesitation. J.J., who'd married into our family and proved himself worthy of Hayley's fierce loyalty. Grady, who'd married our sister Justine despite our outlaw father's involvement in the death of his parents. Shane, my brother, unwavering even when the world seemed to crumble around us.

Whatever we faced at the Broken Arrow Ranch, whatever consequences came from defying a corrupt federal judge, we'd face it together.

"When justice is executed," I said, "it is a joy to the righteous but a terror to evildoers."

"Amen." Shane squeezed my shoulder.

"All right," I said, pulling myself back to the immediate mission. "Let's talk tactics."

Shane spread a detailed map across the table, marking locations as we discussed our approach. "Here's what we know. Destination is almost certainly the Broken Arrow Ranch."

I pointed to the marked location. "Abandoned property with connections to criminal activity. And possibly our father."

Grady leaned forward to study the terrain. "Distance from here?"

"Forty-three miles southwest," Shane calculated. "Through rough country with limited water sources."

"Time to reach it?"

"We could be there by dawn," Shane estimated. "That gives us daylight to observe and plan our approach."

J.J. pointed to several locations on the map. "These ridgelines here and here would give us good observation points. We could study the ranch layout, count men, and identify defensive positions."

"What about weapons and ammunition?" Grady asked.

I inventoried my equipment aloud. "Colt Peacemaker with thirty-six rounds of .45 Long Colt. Winchester rifle with twenty rounds. Boot knife."

"Winchester rifle with forty rounds," Shane reported. "Single Colt, twenty-four rounds total."

J.J. nodded approvingly. "Winchester M94 lever-action, forty rounds of .30-30. Twin Remington six-shooters, forty-eight rounds between them. Winchester M97 pump-action shotgun with twelve shells of buckshot. And the fastest horse this side of the grave."

Grady's arsenal was equally impressive. "Winchester rifle with thirty rounds. Single Colt, twenty-four rounds total. Plus a few items Justine doesn't know I carry." He patted a small leather pouch on his belt.

"Explosives?" Shane asked with raised eyebrows.

"Small charges. Sometimes you need to make a door where there isn't one."

"If we're dealing with Galen Harper's old network," J.J. said, "we need to assume they're well-armed and experienced."

"Agreed," I replied. "He never worked with anyone who wasn't competent with weapons and tactics. If his people are involved, they'll be skilled marksmen."

"How many men might we face?" Grady asked.

Shane contemplated the question. "Probably eight to ten, knowing Galen, if this is their hideout."

"Weapons?"

"Assume rifles and handguns, possibly military surplus," I said. "Superior firepower was always one of his principles."

J.J. traced potential approach routes on the map. "We'll need to account for sentries, especially if they're expecting pursuit."

"They might not be," Shane pointed out. "Thurston thinks he's dealing with a frightened woman and an old man. He might not expect anyone to stand against him."

"Don't count on it," I warned. "If this really is connected to Galen's gang, they'll have contingency plans for everything."

We discussed signals, backup plans, and what to do if things went wrong. Each man contributed expertise gained from years of dangerous work in hostile territory.

"Priority one is the boy's safety," J.J. emphasized. "Everything else is secondary."

"Understood," we all agreed.

"Priority two is taking prisoners for interrogation," Shane added. "We need to know the full scope of this gang."

"And priority three," I said, "is making sure they don't threaten anyone else's family."

We spent the next hour preparing our equipment. We checked weapons, cleaned and oiled mechanisms, and counted ammunition twice. Each man verified his gear was secure and accessible. Horses were inspected, shoes checked, and saddles adjusted for the long ride ahead.

Grady crouched beside me as I sketched a rough perimeter on the map with the butt of my knife. "We'll split into two teams. J.J. and I will take the southern ridge—best vantage point for the rail siding and main house. You and Shane circle west, approaching from the blind side. If they've got sentries, that's where they'll be weakest."

"Agreed," Grady said, nodding. "We'll signal with the mirror if we spot movement. One flash for patrol, two for armed response."

"Three if they spot us," I added. "If that happens, we fall back to the juniper grove and regroup."

J.J. leaned in, his brow furrowed. "What's our breach plan?"

"Two options," I said. "If Beau's in the house, we go quiet. Take out the sentries, extract the boy, and disappear before they know what hit them. If he's in the rail cars, we'll need a distraction. Grady's charges or a fire near the stables."

Grady grinned. "I can make noise."

"Just don't make a crater," Shane muttered.

We ran through contingencies, fallback routes, and rendezvous points. I kept the pace brisk and focused. Every man here had been in shootouts before.

When the planning was done, we stood in a loose circle beneath the stars. The wind stirred the sagebrush, carrying the scent of dust and pine. I cleared my throat.

"Before we move," I said, "I think we ought to pray."

J.J. nodded. "I was hoping you'd say that."

We bowed our heads. No flowery words, no theatrics. Just quiet conviction.

"Lord," I said, voice low, "we're riding into danger. Not for glory. Not for vengeance. But for a child. For justice. For the kind of world You told us to build. Watch over us. Guide our hands. And if it's our time, let us fall with honor."

"Amen," the others echoed.

We broke the circle and turned to our gear. I checked my Colt, spun the cylinder, and felt the weight settle into my palm like an old friend. The Winchester got a fresh oiling. I ran my fingers along the stock, remembering the first time I'd fired it training with Shane in the hills behind our childhood home.

Grady packed his charges with care, wrapping each in oilskin and tucking them into his saddlebag. J.J. adjusted the sling on his shotgun, his face grim but steady.

I paused, staring at the horizon. Somewhere out there, Beau was waiting. Lavinia's son. My son, if God allowed it. I'd never asked for fatherhood, never imagined it. But the moment I saw that boy's eyes—so much like hers—I knew I'd fight to my last breath to protect him.

And Lavinia… she'd trusted me with everything. Her heart. Her child. Her hope. I wouldn't let her down.

I cinched my saddle tight and mounted up. The others followed suit, four shadows against the fading light.

By the time we were ready to ride, the sun was touching the western horizon and painting the desert sky in shades of orange and purple. Four horses stood saddled and ready, their riders armed and prepared.

"You sure about leaving the woman behind?" Grady asked as we prepared to mount up.

"She agreed it was necessary," I replied, though the words felt like gravel in my throat. "Besides, this kind of operation requires complete focus. Can't have anyone acting on emotion instead of training."

"Even if that someone is the boy's mother?"

"Especially then." I swung into the saddle, the leather creaking beneath me. "Grady, you have children. You know how fierce a parent's love can be. But you also know that love can make people take risks they shouldn't."

He nodded slowly. "Justine would want to come too, if it were Lee or Amy. And I'd have to tell her the same thing you told Miss Beaumont."

"Exactly."

Shane moved his horse closer to mine. "You ready for this, Flynn? If we're right about the Galen Harper connection, if he's somehow involved..."

"Then it's time to finish what we started," I said simply. "Time to prove that justice can triumph over everything he represents."

J.J. and Grady exchanged glances, understanding the deeper currents running beneath this mission. They'd seen what our father's abandonment and abuse had done to the Harper children, had helped us build something better from the wreckage he'd left behind.

"Well then," J.J. said, settling his hat more firmly on his head. "Let's go get that boy and put an end to this once and for all."

We rode out of Holbrook as twilight settled over the high desert, four lawmen united by bonds of family and shared purpose. Behind us, the town settled into its evening routines, unaware that its safety might depend on what we accomplished in the hours ahead.

The desert wind whispered across the sage as we rode southwest toward the Broken Arrow Ranch, carrying the scent of cooling earth. The horses settled into a ground-eating lope, their hooves kicking up small clouds of dust.

"How's the hand?" Shane asked, riding alongside me.

I flexed my fingers, feeling the pull of healing skin. "Good enough."

"Good enough to shoot straight?"

"Always."

The conversation fell away as we focused on the ride. Miles passed beneath our horses' hooves. The landscape changed gradually, flat desert giving way to rolling hills, then steeper terrain dotted with juniper and pinyon pine. Stars emerged overhead, a vast canopy of light that seemed close enough to touch.

We stopped twice to rest the horses and verify our route. Each time, Shane consulted his compass and the detailed maps we'd acquired. Each time, we moved closer to whatever waited at the Broken Arrow Ranch.

Around midnight, we spotted lights in the distance. Not the warm glow of a ranch house, but the harsh illumination of work lamps. Multiple lights, suggesting significant activity.

"That's not an abandoned ranch," Grady observed.

"No," I agreed. "It's not."

We approached cautiously, leaving our horses tethered in a grove of juniper a half-mile out. Moving on foot, we worked our way to a ridgeline that overlooked the ranch complex.

What we saw made my blood run cold.

The Broken Arrow Ranch sprawled across a small valley, but it was the railroad siding that drew my attention. A private spur line, complete with a small locomotive and six freight cars. Men moved around the train, loading crates under the harsh glare of work lamps.

"Good Lord," Shane breathed beside me.

J.J. pulled out a pair of field glasses, studying the scene. "I count at least eight men. All armed. Military bearing on most of them."

"Professional crew," Grady confirmed.

I took the field glasses from J.J., scanning the workers below. Most were strangers, but then a figure emerged from one of the freight cars, and my heart stopped.

Tall, lean build. Confident stride. The way he moved, the particular arrogance in his shoulders.

Galen Harper.

My father stood fifty yards away, shouting orders to rough men loading stolen goods onto railcars.

"Flynn?" Shane's hand settled on my shoulder.

"That's him," I growled.

J.J. and Grady moved closer, all of us watching. Stolen cattle. Forged documents. Land fraud. A.C.'s stolen identity. And now Galen's man had taken Beau.

He was behind it all.

We stayed low and silent. The men below hauled crates and drove cattle under the devil's sharp gaze. My father—the man who'd escaped Yuma and crawled back into our lives like a venomous snake—ran this gang of outlaws.

The wind shifted, carrying the scent of cattle and

smoke. Down there, somewhere in those buildings, a five-year-old boy waited in terror. And between us and Beau stood the man whose blood ran in my veins.

My chest tightened. I was about to face the devil himself.

My hand moved to my revolver.

The reckoning had come.

22 - Desperate Measures

Lavinia

THE SILENCE IN the mercantile pressed heavy around me, thick with Beau's absence. I stood behind the counter where he'd played with his wooden horses, my hands gripping the smooth oak until my knuckles ached. The evening shadows stretched long fingers across the floor, marking each minute he drifted farther from safety.

More than a day. Beau had been gone for more than a day, and the wait was wearing me down, splinter by splinter.

My eyes burned, but no tears came. I'd cried them all out hours ago after Flynn and his posse left. Now only this hollow ache remained, pressing tight against my lungs with every breath. I closed my eyes and let my forehead rest against my white-knuckled grip on the counter's edge.

"God." The word came out broken, barely a whisper. "I don't have the right words. I never do."

The admission felt like a confession I'd never meant to speak aloud. Good Christian women knew how to pray properly, knew the right phrases and reverent tones. But all I had were these desperate fragments, this raw panic clawing at my throat.

"You know where he is right now. You see him when I can't." My voice cracked. "Please... please keep him safe until I can reach him. I know I don't deserve to ask. I know what I've done, the mistakes I've made. But he's innocent. He's just a little boy who needs his mama."

The store remained silent around me. No voice from heaven, no sudden peace flooding my soul. Just the creak of settling wood and the distant sound of horses passing on Main Street. I'd prayed for forgiveness a thousand times over the years, begged God to wipe away my shame. And somewhere deep down, I believed He had. Papa's gentle words echoed in my memory: *God's grace covers even our worst mistakes, darling.*

I knew it was true. Had clung to that truth through every sleepless night, every whispered rumor, every fearful glance over my shoulder. But knowing and feeling were different things entirely, and right now, crushed under the weight of terror for my son, grace felt as distant as the stars.

"I can't just wait here." The words came out fierce, determined. "Sitting idle while he's in danger."

God had given me legs to ride and arms to fight. He'd given me a mother's fierce love and the strength to protect what was mine. Trusting His providence didn't mean doing nothing while evil men carried my boy into the desert. It meant believing He would guide my path even as I rode into the darkness.

I released my death grip on the counter and smoothed my skirts with trembling fingers. Standing here accomplished nothing while my boy was in danger. I needed to do something, needed to help somehow. Even if all I could do was to follow and pray.

Last night I had paced the length of my home, jumping at every sound, praying Flynn would return with my boy before dawn. When morning came without word, I had forced myself through the motions of opening the store, serving customers with a smile I'd stitched into place. Then the confrontation with Flynn—his promises, his determination, the fierce protectiveness in his eyes.

I'd believed him. Trusted that he would bring Beau home.

But now Flynn had ridden out hours ago with his brothers, following whatever trail they'd discovered. Hours of promises to stay safe, stay put, let him handle the rescue. Hours of trying to be the reasonable woman who trusted the capable lawman.

I couldn't do it anymore.

The bell chimed as I pushed through the front door, my eyes scanning Main Street in the fading light. The street stretched quietly in both directions, normal evening business continuing as if the ground hadn't shifted beneath me a few days ago.

But where could I even begin? Flynn had mentioned tracking, following trails, but I didn't know which direction they'd headed. The thought of riding blindly into the desert while precious time slipped away made my stomach clench.

The barbershop. Pete Morrison and Obadiah Cain spent their evenings there when the weather was fair, watching the street, hearing everything that happened in town. If anyone had seen which way Flynn went, it would be them.

I hurried down the wooden sidewalk, my heeled boots clicking sharply against the boards. The evening air carried the scent of cooking fires and the sound of families settling in for supper. Normal life continued while everything I knew was coming apart.

The two old men sat in their usual chairs outside the barbershop, but their relaxed postures straightened when they saw me approaching. Pete Morrison's weathered face creased with concern, and Obadiah Cain removed the tobacco plug from his mouth.

"Miss Lavinia?" Pete stood, his hand automatically

moving to steady me as I swayed slightly. "What's wrong, honey? You look like you ain't slept."

"I haven't." The words came out cracked and desperate. "Did you see which way Marshal Harper and his men went when they left town?"

The effect on both men was immediate. Pete's jaw tightened until the muscles jumped beneath his weathered skin, and Cain's eyes blazed with fury that had probably served him well during his Army days.

"They rode out maybe three hours back," Pete said without hesitation, his gray eyes never leaving my face. "Southwest toward the old Flagstaff trail. Had rifles and looked like they meant business." He stepped closer, studying my face with gentle understanding. "This about young Beau?"

"Someone took him." I struggled to keep my voice steady. "Yesterday afternoon. A man named Thurston Blackwell. He claims to have rights to Beau."

"Rights?" Cain spat tobacco juice into the dust with violent precision. "What kind of rights would a stranger have to our boy?"

Our boy. The simple phrase pierced my heart. Somehow without my realizing it, Beau had become part of this community. These gruff old men thought of him as belonging here, belonging to all of them.

"I need to follow them. I can't just sit here while he's in danger. I know Marshal Harper told me to wait, but I can't. I just can't. Not another night of not knowing, not being there if he needs me."

Pete and Cain exchanged a knowing look, decades of friendship passing between them. When Pete turned back to me, his expression was resolute.

"You ain't going alone," he said firmly. "Obadiah and me know those trails better than most. We'll ride with you."

"I can't ask you to—"

"You ain't asking," Cain interrupted, already moving

toward the barbershop door. "We're offering. That sweet boy of yours has brought more joy to this town than you probably realize. Ain't nobody taking him from his mama on our watch."

"But Marshal Harper expects me to stay here. He'll be furious when he discovers—"

"Marshal Harper will understand when he sees we kept you safe," Pete said with quiet confidence. "Man like that, he knows what it means to love someone enough to risk everything for them."

The certainty in his voice brought unexpected comfort, but worry crept in like a shadow. What would they think if they knew the whole truth? If they discovered what kind of rights Thurston claimed?

"There's something you should know." I whispered the words, my throat tight and painful. "Thurston Blackwell isn't just a criminal. He's Beau's natural father."

The silence that followed hung heavy in the air. I kept my eyes fixed on my hands, unable to bear seeing disappointment or judgment replace the kindness in their weathered faces.

When Pete finally spoke, his voice was rough with emotion, but not the kind I'd expected.

"That snake." The words came out harsh. "He took advantage of you, didn't he? When you were young and trusting."

I nodded, still not looking up. "I was sixteen. He promised to marry me, said he loved me. When I told him about the baby, he disappeared. Never saw him again until he showed up in our store."

"Son of a—" Cain caught himself, glancing at me apologetically. "Beggin' your pardon, Miss Lavinia. But that kind of man ain't fit to call himself anybody's father."

"But legally, he might have rights. Claims to Beau. What if—"

"What if nothing," Pete interrupted firmly. "Blood don't make a man a father any more than laying an egg makes a hen a rooster. That boy's got a papa. Your father's been raising him with love and care. And he's got Marshal Harper looking out for him now."

I finally raised my eyes, expecting to see pity or condemnation. Instead, I discovered fierce protectiveness and paternal pride.

"You think we didn't suspect?" Cain's voice turned gentle now, almost tender. "Honey, you came to town with a baby and no husband. Your father told folks he was adopting the boy, giving him the family name. We ain't blind. Just decent folks who mind our own business."

"We could see what kind of woman you are," Pete added. "How you work hard, take care of your family, treat everybody fair and honest. Whatever happened in your past, it don't change who you are now."

Their words struck like a horse's kick, jarring loose something I'd kept cinched tight in my chest for years. I'd spent so long trying to earn acceptance through perfect behavior, through never making another mistake, through working myself to exhaustion to prove I was worthy of a second chance.

But grace didn't work that way.

The truth settled over me like the hush of a fire-lit room. These men weren't accepting me because I'd been good enough, worked hard enough, or hidden my shame well enough. They accepted me simply because that's what decent people did. Just like God's grace wasn't something I could earn through endless striving. It was something freely given, waiting for me to stop trying so hard and just accept it.

Tears I'd been holding back for hours finally spilled over. "You don't think less of me?"

"Think less of you?" Cain stood and spat emphatically. "Girl, we think more of you. Takes real strength to build a good life after someone betrays your trust. Takes courage to raise a boy right on your own." He paused, his weathered face softening. "The good Lord forgave you long ago, honey. Maybe it's time you forgave yourself."

The words pierced straight through every defense I'd built. God's grace included forgiveness and the strength to move forward, to trust again, to believe I could make better choices. I'd been so afraid of repeating my mistakes that I'd stopped trusting my judgment entirely. But faith wasn't the absence of wisdom; it was wisdom guided by grace.

"And that boy of yours, he's a credit to your raising," Pete said, his voice thick with emotion. "Polite, smart, and kind to everybody. That's not an accident. That's good mothering and good grandfathering."

"Marshal Harper's more of a daddy to that boy than any scoundrel who ran off," Cain declared, and something in my chest loosened at his words.

He was right. I'd seen the difference so clearly these past days. Thurston's cold possession versus Flynn's warm protection. Thurston saw Beau as property, something to own and control. But Flynn saw him as a person to cherish and guide. Thurston's fatherhood was selfish, demanding rights without accepting responsibility. Flynn's was selfless, offering protection and demanding nothing in return.

Just like the difference between earthly fathers who failed us and the heavenly Father who never did. God didn't abandon His children when they became inconvenient or disappointing. He pursued them, protected them, fought for them. The same way Flynn was fighting for Beau right now, risking everything to bring him home safe.

That was what real fatherhood looked like. Not the man who'd sweet-talked me into ruin and disappeared, but the man who'd ridden into danger for a boy who wasn't even his own.

"Now come on," Pete said, offering me his arm. "Obie, get your old Colt and whatever ammunition you got. I'll fetch the horses." He turned back to me. "Miss Lavinia, you got any riding clothes? This won't be a Sunday social."

As I hurried toward home, my mind raced with everything that needed doing. Change clothes, arm myself, close the store, leave word for Flynn somehow. The familiar tasks helped steady my nerves, giving me something concrete to focus on instead of the sick twist low in my belly.

The house felt hollow and strange without Beau's presence. I changed quickly into a split riding skirt, sturdy boots, and a cotton blouse that wouldn't restrict my movement. Papa's old service revolver hung in its holster on a peg in his bedroom closet. Its weight was familiar. Papa had taught me to shoot.

As I lifted the gun belt from its peg, my hands trembled. Was I doing the right thing? Flynn had told me to stay, to trust him. Was following him a lack of faith in his abilities? Or worse, was it a lack of faith in God's protection?

I thought of my desperate prayer in the store, the plain truth of admitting I didn't have fancy words or proper phrases. That prayer had been real in a way my careful, proper prayers never were. And somewhere in that honesty, I'd recognized a truth I'd been avoiding.

Faith wasn't sitting idle and calling it trust. It was taking action and trusting God to guide the path. Abraham had to get up and walk when God called him. Moses had to raise his staff over the Red Sea. David had to pick up the stones before he could face Goliath.

God gave me a mother's love and the strength to fight for my child. Using those gifts was my faith in action.

I buckled the gun belt around my waist, adjusting it for my smaller frame. The weight felt right, solid and reassuring. In the mirror, I caught sight of myself—a desperate mother preparing for battle. The woman staring back at me bore little resemblance to the respectable shopkeeper who'd served customers that morning.

Good. Respectability wouldn't save Beau. But a mother's fierce love, guided by faith and supported by good men, might be enough.

I hurried to the kitchen table and found paper and pencil, and I wrote a note to Flynn.

I left the note propped against the sugar bowl where he'd be sure to see it, then gathered what supplies I could carry, such as water, dried meat, and ammunition for Papa's revolver.

True to their word, Pete and Cain waited outside with three horses. Pete's mount was a sturdy bay that could travel all day without complaint. Cain rode a gray mare with intelligent eyes and the lean build of a distance runner. The third horse, a chestnut gelding with a gentle face, stood saddled and ready.

"Borrowed him from the livery," Pete explained, noting my questioning look. "Carson said to bring that boy home safe."

I mounted with hands that had steadied somewhat, grateful for the hours Papa had spent teaching me to ride during our first years in Arizona. The saddle leather creaked as I settled in, and the horse shifted beneath me, sensing the urgency that surrounded us.

"You sure about this, Miss Lavinia?" Cain asked quietly. "Once we leave town, we're committed to whatever comes. Could be dangerous country ahead."

"I'm sure." The words came out stronger than I felt. "He's out there with an evil man. I won't abandon him to face that alone."

"Then we'd better get moving," Pete said, checking his rifle one more time. "Every minute we waste is another minute they get ahead of us."

We rode out of Holbrook as the last light faded from the western sky, three unlikely companions united by love for a little boy and determination to bring him home. Behind us, the town settled into its evening routines, unaware that a desperate mother and two old soldiers were riding toward whatever confrontation waited on the trail ahead.

The desert stretched before us in the gathering darkness, vast and unforgiving. Somewhere out there, Flynn was trailing Thurston's path, believing I was safe at home. Somewhere out there, Beau was waiting—frightened, confused, too young to understand, but hoping someone was coming.

He wouldn't wait in vain. I was riding out, and I wouldn't ride alone. God had given me faithful companions and the courage to face whatever waited on the trail.

His grace was enough. Not because I'd earned it, but because He gave it freely.

And that grace carried the strength to fight for the ones I loved.

23 - Convergence

Flynn

THE ABANDONED FLAGSTAFF & Northern rail siding stretched across a natural clearing, surrounded by corrals and loading chutes that hadn't seen use in years. But today, the facility bustled with activity. A locomotive sat coupled to six freight cars, steam wisping from its stack while men swarmed around the loading dock.

Cattle filled the holding pens. Hundreds of head bearing a mix of brands I didn't recognize. Men with running irons worked methodically to alter the marks. The acrid smell of burning hide drifted on the morning breeze, mixing with wood smoke and locomotive coal.

"Sweet mercy," J.J. breathed beside me. "This isn't just cattle rustling."

I studied the layout, counting men and noting weapon positions. At least twenty workers now, most carrying holstered sidearms. Four guards with rifles were positioned around the perimeter. A group clustered near the locomotive, distinguished by their finery and the deference the workers showed them.

"Range to target?" Grady asked, pulling out his Winchester and checking the action.

"Four hundred yards to the locomotive." Too far for accurate pistol work, but manageable for rifle fire. Shane made his own calculations, noting wind direction and elevation. "But we've got the boy down there. We can't risk a long-range engagement."

My systematic scan of the valley froze. My blood ran cold.

Tall, lean, silver-haired. Moving with the grace of a hunting cat. Twin Colts with ivory grips riding his hips. The man who'd shaped my childhood with brutality and abandonment. Who'd taught me that strength meant taking what you wanted and destroying what you couldn't control.

Galen Harper. My father. Free and running this band of outlaws as if he'd been born to it.

"Flynn?" J.J.'s voice came from beside me. "What is it?"

"It's him," I whispered. "Galen Harper. My father."

A movement near the locomotive caught my eye. Two men stepped down from the lead passenger car.

Thurston Blackwell still dressed in that fancy suit despite the heat and dust. Beside him, a small figure. My throat tightened.

Beau. Alive. Unharmed, from what I could tell. But scared. His little hands wrapped tight around the train car's iron railing, knuckles pale against the dark metal.

"There," I said, pointing them out to Shane. "Passenger car near the front."

Shane adjusted his glasses, then nodded grimly. "I see them. Boy looks frightened but unhurt."

I studied the situation with forced calm, pushing down the fury that demanded immediate action. The train sat on the main line, ready to depart. Steam pressure was up, which meant they could move within minutes. Once that locomotive got up to speed, we'd never catch them on horseback.

"Four-way approach," I decided after studying the terrain. "Grady, you take the eastern bluffs with that Winchester. J.J., circle around to the north with your M94. Shane, you take the western ravine. I'll work my way down through the rocks on this side."

"Crossfire pattern," J.J. agreed, understanding the strategy immediately. "We can cover all the escape routes and provide mutual support."

"Signal when everyone's in position," Shane added. "Nobody moves until we're all ready."

I watched them disappear into the rocks, then began my approach down the eastern slope. The terrain was treacherous. Loose shale that could start a slide, scattered boulders providing cover but also concealing potential threats. I moved carefully, testing each foothold before committing my full weight.

Halfway down the slope, I paused behind a large boulder to reassess the situation. The guards had shifted positions slightly, responding to some order I couldn't hear. One man now stood near the locomotive itself, close enough to Beau's position to be a direct threat.

I continued my descent, using the rocky cover to mask my movement. Fifty yards from the rail siding, I spotted an ideal position behind a fallen log, offering a clear sight line to the locomotive. From here, I could cover the distance to Beau in seconds once the shooting started.

The morning sun slanted, casting shadows across the railyard. Movement on the northern bluffs caught my eye. J.J.'s signal. Three quick flashes from a mirror fragment. He was in position and ready. A moment later, Grady signaled acknowledgment from the eastern rocks, followed by Shane from the western ravine.

I checked my weapons one last time. The Colt's weight settled familiar in my palm, cylinder loaded with six rounds. My Winchester leaned against the boulder beside me, ready if I needed the range. Everything was in place. Everything except the certainty that I could do what needed doing without becoming the devil.

My brother Ike's voice echoed across the years, *Maybe we should pray.* He'd been fourteen years old, dying of starvation, clutching his own wooden horse—so much like Beau—and still believing God might listen. If Ike could have that kind of faith when we had nothing, maybe I could find enough faith now to make the right choice instead of the easy one.

"God," I whispered, the words rough in my throat. "I need help here."

The prayer didn't come easy. Never had. But standing fifty yards from my father with a five-year-old boy's life in the balance, I had nowhere else to turn.

"My sisters say You care about the righteous when they execute justice. That it brings You joy." My grip tightened on the Colt. "But I don't feel righteous. I feel like I'm about to walk into Galen's world, and I'm scared I won't walk back out the same man."

The wind whispered through the rocks, carrying the smell of cattle and wood smoke.

"Help me choose right when it counts," I finished. "Help me be different than him. Please."

The prayer settled something in my chest. Not peace exactly, but purpose. I was going into that railyard not as Galen Harper's son, but as a man who'd chosen a different path. A lawman. A protector. Someone who stood between evil and the innocent.

I rose from cover and prepared to face the man who'd taught me everything I'd spent my life trying to forget.

My first shot took the nearest guard in the shoulder, spinning him around and sending his rifle clattering across the rocky ground. The sharp crack of my Colt echoed off the canyon walls, followed immediately by the boom of Grady's Winchester from the eastern bluffs. His bullet punched through the locomotive's water tank, sending a geyser of steam and scalding water across the railyard.

"Federal marshals!" I shouted, moving fast toward the train while chaos erupted around me. "Drop your weapons!"

Muzzle flashes bloomed from behind cattle cars and loading equipment as Galen's men returned fire. J.J.'s Winchester M94 cracked repeatedly from the northern position, efficient and deadly accurate. Shane's shotgun boomed from the west, the sound echoing off the canyon walls like thunder.

I reached the cover of the first freight car just as a rifle bullet carved splinters from the wooden planking beside my head. Through the gunfire and noise, Beau's crying sliced straight into my gut. This fight wasn't just about justice anymore. It was about him.

Hoofbeats. Distant but closing fast.

Not from the railyard, but from behind me. Riders approached fast from the direction Shane and I had come. My blood turned cold. We were caught between two forces, and if these were more of Galen's men...

The riders burst into view just as I prepared to wheel around and face this new threat. But instead of outlaws, three familiar figures appeared. Lavinia riding a chestnut gelding, flanked by Pete Morrison and Obadiah Cain.

They were riding straight into Galen's trap.

My father stepped from the shadows, Colts bright as bone in the morning light. He looked like judgment come to call. But he wasn't alone. Two of his men stepped up beside him, rifles trained on the approaching riders. They'd been waiting, watching, ready to spring their snare.

"Hold your fire, boys!" Galen's voice carried the same sinister authority that had once terrorized a frightened boy. Now it just made me angry. "Let's see what the desert wind blows in."

Lavinia's horse shied as armed men emerged from cover, surrounding the three riders quickly. Pete and Obadiah reached for their weapons, but a dozen rifle barrels swung toward them with deadly intent.

"I wouldn't," Galen warned. "Dead heroes don't rescue anybody."

The gunfire in the railyard stuttered to a halt as both sides realized the stakes had changed. J.J.'s Winchester fell silent from the bluffs. Grady's rifle stopped its methodical thunder, and Shane's shotgun went quiet.

Galen smiled, and I recognized those cold eyes that had haunted my childhood nightmares. He'd aged since I'd last seen him, silver threading through hair that had once been as dark as mine. Prison had hollowed his cheeks and added lines around his eyes, but he still carried himself like a man who expected the world to bend to his will.

"Flynn Harper!" he called out. "My prodigal son, come home at last. Step out where I can see you, boy. We need to have a conversation."

I stayed behind the freight car, mind racing through tactical options. From my position, I could see Beau huddled near the locomotive, tears streaming down his face. Thirty yards in the opposite direction, Lavinia sat frozen in her saddle while armed men surrounded her.

Two targets. Two people I loved more than my life.

And only one of me.

"Come now, don't be shy," Galen continued, his tone mockingly paternal. "After all these years, surely you want to greet your old man?"

Slowly, I stepped out from behind the freight car, keeping my Colt ready but not pointed at him. Galen's smile widened as he took in my appearance. The badge on my vest, the marshal's star that represented everything he despised.

"Look at that," he said, genuine amusement in his voice. "My boy, wearing a badge. After everything I taught you about the weakness of the law. Power comes from taking what you want."

"You didn't teach me anything worth learning," I replied. "Except maybe how not to be a man."

His laughter was as sharp as breaking glass. "Is that

so? Well then, let's see what you've become." He gestured toward Lavinia with one of his revolvers. "Beautiful woman. And the boy crying by the locomotive? Sweet child. Reminds me of you at that age. All tears and weakness."

The cruelty in his voice made my trigger finger itch, but I forced myself to remain still.

"Here's the situation, son," Galen continued. "You're going to make a choice. That's what separates men from boys. The ability to make hard decisions when everything you care about hangs in the balance."

He nodded toward his men, and a dozen rifle hammers snicked back in unison. "My boys have clear shots on both targets. You can save one, but not both. Choose quickly. My patience has limits."

The world seemed to slow around me. Save Lavinia, the woman I loved, or save Beau, an innocent child who depended on me for protection.

"Tick tock, Flynn," Galen said. "Clock's running. What's it going to be?"

My gaze flicked to Lavinia. I read the terror in her brown eyes mixed with something else. Understanding. Acceptance. Her chin lifted slightly, that stubborn strength I loved unmistakable even now. Her lips pressed together, holding back words she wouldn't speak. Then she nodded, just once. A release. Permission. Forgiveness for what I had to do. The gesture engraved itself into my memory like a brand, searing away everything except the knowledge that this woman trusted me to save her son even as I failed to protect her.

Something twisted in my chest. Beau was about Ike's age when Shane had given him that wooden horse. The one birthday gift that said he mattered. I'd watched my little brother clutch that carved toy like it was the only proof he deserved to exist. Now, Beau needed someone to show him the same thing. That he was worth protecting. Worth sacrificing for. Worth choosing.

"Children are expendable, boy," Galen said. "Always

have been. I threw away six of them without a second thought. But a woman can give you more children. She can warm your bed, cook your meals, and serve your needs. Choose wisely."

The words revealed the depth of his depravity. This was the man who'd shaped my earliest years, who'd tried to teach me that strength meant crushing the weak.

A memory slammed into me. Lying in that loft, too weak to stand, my body so skeletal I could count my own ribs. Galen hadn't just abandoned us. He'd burned our food stores in retribution for sneaking our sisters to safety. He'd left Shane, Ike, and me to starve, knowing we'd probably die, and he hadn't cared. We'd come within days of death before Grady and his partner found us.

"You think you're different from me?" he continued. "Prove it. Save the one you can't replace. Stop pretending to be some noble hero and make the practical choice."

But Lavinia's eyes held absolute faith that I'd choose right. Even if it meant her death for Beau's life. She wasn't just willing to die for her son. She was asking *me* to make that choice. She believed in me more than I believed in myself.

And in that moment, I understood what Galen had never grasped. Real strength was about protecting those who couldn't protect themselves, even when it cost you everything.

"You're wrong," I hissed. "Children aren't expendable. They never were."

I turned toward Beau, raising my Colt toward the men guarding him. "All of you! Take care of Lavinia!"

Galen's roar of rage split the air. "You weak-minded fool! You're choosing sentiment over sense!"

The gunfire erupted again, but this time I moved with purpose. Grady's Winchester boomed from the eastern bluffs, and Pete Morrison's old Army Colt barked behind me as the elderly rancher proved he still remembered how to fight. Obadiah Cain's rebel yell echoed off the canyon walls. J.J.'s Winchester M94 cracked repeatedly, while Shane's shotgun thundered from the western ravine.

I sprinted toward the locomotive, weaving between freight cars while bullets whined around me. A guard stepped out to block my path, and I put two rounds in his chest without breaking stride. My boots pounded against the wooden ties as I closed the distance to where Beau cowered beside the great iron wheels.

"Flynn!" The boy's cry of relief nearly unmanned me as I scooped him up with my left arm, keeping my gun ready with my right. He clung to me with desperate strength, his small body shaking.

"I've got you," I breathed against his hair. "You're safe now."

A shadow fell across us as Thurston Blackwell emerged from behind the locomotive, his expensive suit now dusty and torn. His cultured face twisted with rage as he raised an ornate pistol toward my head.

"You should have minded your own business, Marshal," he snarled. "The boy is mine by right of blood."

"Blood doesn't make a father," I replied, shifting Beau behind me while keeping my Colt trained on Thurston's chest. "Love does."

"Touching sentiment." Thurston's finger tightened on his trigger. "But blood trumps sentiment in courts of law."

The shot that ended his threat came not from my gun, but from J.J.'s on the northern bluffs. Thurston's head snapped back as the bullet took him high in the chest, spinning him around before he collapsed beside the locomotive's drive wheels. His eyes stared at the darkness coming for his soul.

Relief flooded through me. Beau would never again cower under this man's cruelty. Lavinia would never again fear his threats or manipulation.

"Beau!" Lavinia's voice cut through the chaos as she broke free from the confusion. She ran toward us with her skirts flying, tears streaming down her face. The old-timers had done their job. She was alive and unharmed.

I set Beau down just as she reached us, and he launched himself into her arms with a sob of pure relief. She gathered him close, pressing kisses to his hair.

"Thank you," she whispered, looking up at me. "Thank you for choosing him."

Around the railyard, the fight was over. Galen's men lay scattered. Some were dead, wounded, or fled into the desert. Shane and J.J. were already moving among the survivors, securing weapons and binding prisoners. Grady descended from the eastern bluffs while Pete and Obadiah corralled the horses.

But Galen himself stood untouched near the locomotive, his revolvers still holstered. Shane approached him cautiously, shotgun ready, while I kept my Colt trained on his chest.

Grady moved in from the side, his face granite-hard as he reached for Galen's guns. Those twin Colts with their distinctive ivory grips slid free from their holsters, and for just a moment, Grady's jaw tightened. He'd seen these weapons before. Recognized them. His fingers closed around the grips with a restrained fury that spoke volumes.

Then he stepped back, the Colts secure in his belt, and Shane secured Galen's hands with iron manacles.

"Galen Harper," Shane said in his official voice, "you're under arrest for cattle rustling, conspiracy, and too many federal crimes to count."

My father's laugh echoed across the railyard. But instead of defeated rage, his eyes gleamed with malicious amusement.

"Arrest me?" He threw his head back and laughed harder. "You think this changes anything? You think arresting me matters?"

He leaned forward, his eyes glittering with triumph. "I've got Judge Harrison Webb in my pocket, boy. Had him for fifteen years. You arrest me, and I'll be out before the ink dries on the warrant."

My gut tightened. Fifteen years. Webb had been protecting Galen since before he'd been captured the first time.

"Shut up, you fool!" One of the bound prisoners, a man in a suit too fine for railyard work, had gone pale. "Keep your mouth shut!"

But Galen ignored him, too arrogant to recognize danger. "Webb's been covering for me since the beginning. How do you think I built my outfit so big with no one stopping me? How do you think I got those prison guards to look the other way?"

He grinned at me. "Even with you wearing that marshal badge, boy, you couldn't touch me. None of you could."

My vision narrowed until it included only Galen's face. Here was the man who'd beaten Shane for protecting us. Who'd used Justine as bait in his schemes. Who'd abandoned all of us to pursue his ambitions. Who'd corrupted everything he touched, including the institutions meant to stop men like him.

And he was laughing.

My finger tightened on the trigger. One squeeze. One bullet. Swift justice, the way Galen himself had taught me.

I could end it right here. No one would question a marshal defending himself against an escaped convict. Clean. Final. Just.

When justice is executed, it is a joy to the righteous but a terror to evildoers.

But which was I in this moment? Righteous or evildoer? The line blurred when I looked down the barrel of my Colt at my father's sneering face.

"God, help me," I breathed. The prayer came out ragged, desperate. "Help me choose right."

My hand shook. Sweat ran down my face despite the morning chill. Every fiber of my being screamed to pull the trigger. To watch Galen Harper's blood soak into the Arizona dirt where he'd spilled so much innocent blood himself.

"Flynn." Shane's voice cut through the red haze. Not loud, but carrying absolute authority. "Don't. Be better than him."

I didn't look away from Galen, but Shane's words landed like a fist to my jaw, rattling awake my conscience.

"You pull that trigger, you become what he is," Shane continued, moving closer. "Doesn't matter what badge you wear. Doesn't matter how justified it feels. You kill him in cold blood, and you cross a line you can't uncross."

"He deserves it," I hissed.

"Maybe he does." Shane stepped into my peripheral vision, his presence steady as granite. "But killing him doesn't serve justice. It serves rage. And rage has been Galen's master his whole miserable life. Don't let it be yours."

Shane. He'd created the bandanna system to keep us safe when we were too young to protect ourselves. He'd given up pieces of his soul to buy Ike one day of joy. He'd starved and taken beatings meant for us. Shane knew what it cost to choose justice when everything screamed for revenge. He'd been making those choices since he was thirteen years old.

The Colt trembled in my grip. My finger rested on the trigger, a hairsbreadth from ending everything. One bullet. One choice. One moment that would define who I was for the rest of my life.

Movement caught my eye. Beau, clinging to Lavinia, watching. Those innocent eyes would remember what happened here. Remember what I chose.

And suddenly Lavinia's voice echoed in my memory, clear as if she said it aloud. *You're not like him. You're nothing like him.*

The internal war raged through me. Vengeance screamed for blood. But justice whispered a harder truth—if I killed Galen now, a new outlaw would rise to take his place. Webb would walk free. The corruption would continue. More families would suffer.

But if I kept him alive, Galen could testify. Could expose Webb's fifteen-year conspiracy. Could bring down the entire gang that had terrorized the territory.

Shane had made this choice years ago. He'd found Galen's evidence room—enough proof to stop our father—and instead of using it for revenge, he'd held onto it. Waited. Built a case that sent Galen to prison. I'd been too young to understand it then, but Shane had taught me that real justice was worth more than personal satisfaction.

Slowly, fighting every impulse that screamed for violence, I eased my finger off the trigger. The Colt remained pointed at Galen's chest, but my hand had stopped shaking.

"You're right," I spat. "They called me Swift Justice. But you know what I learned, Galen?"

I holstered my weapon with deliberate care. "Swift justice isn't always real justice. Sometimes the harder path, the one that costs you everything you want, is the one that actually serves something bigger than revenge."

Galen's confident smirk faltered. "What are you doing?"

"I'm keeping you alive. And you're going to testify against Judge Harrison Webb." I stepped closer. "You're going to expose every corrupt official you ever worked with, every crime you committed under his protection. And then you're going to spend the rest of your miserable life in prison, knowing that your own testimony destroyed everything you built."

"You can't make me testify."

"I don't have to make you." I gestured toward Shane, J.J., and Grady. "You're going to volunteer. Because the alternative is every single crime you admitted to just now, including your relationship with Webb, gets testified to in court by four lawmen who heard every word."

I leaned close enough that only he could hear. "You

taught me to be ruthless, Galen. You just never thought I'd use those lessons against you in the name of actual justice."

Shane moved to my side, his hand gripping my shoulder. No words, but his approval came through solid and sure.

"Time to go, Galen."

As they led my father away, still sputtering threats that rang increasingly hollow, I turned to where Beau stood with Lavinia. The boy's eyes were wide, processing everything he'd witnessed.

I kneeled down to his level. "You alright, partner?"

Beau nodded slowly, then threw his arms around my neck. "You came," he whispered. "I knew you would come."

The words pierced straight through me. I had prayed for the same as a boy, waiting for a rescue that came too late. Shane had tried. He'd done his best.

But I was here now. For Beau.

I held the boy close, feeling the rapid beat of his heart against my chest, the dampness of tears soaking into my collar.

When I looked up, Lavinia's face was wet with tears, but her smile held everything I'd been afraid to hope for.

"Thank you," she whispered.

I stood, and she stepped into my arms, Beau still clinging to my side. The weight of them both against me felt right in a way nothing else ever had. Not the badge. Not the reputation. Just this—protecting the people I loved.

Around us, my brothers secured the prisoners. Horses stamped and snorted. Somewhere in the distance, a coyote called to the darkening sky. The scent of dust and sage hung heavy in the cooling air.

But all of it faded compared to Lavinia's hand pressed against my chest, right over my heart.

"It's over," she breathed.

I tightened my hold on her and Beau, looking past them to where Shane stood coordinating the cleanup. My brother caught my eye and nodded once.

"The worst of it, yeah," I said. "But there's still work ahead."

Lavinia pulled back just enough to meet my eyes. "Then we'll face it together."

Together. The word settled into my chest like a promise I intended to keep.

24 - The Reckoning

Flynn

THE SPRAWLING WOODEN structure of the Aztec Land and Cattle Company's headquarters came into view as the sun touched the horizon. Lanterns already burned in the windows, and I could see riders moving between the corrals and outbuildings. Our procession of lawmen with bound prisoners created a spectacle cowboys would recount for years to come.

Shane, J.J., and Grady rode behind me, each man bearing the exhaustion of a hard fight well won. Pete Morrison and Obadiah Cain brought up the rear, looking like two old roosters who'd just run off a pack of coyotes. The remnants of Galen Harper's outlaw gang rode between us, secured with iron manacles and rope.

Beau sat secure in my arms, his small hands still gripping my shirt as if he never intended to let go. The boy had finally stopped crying about an hour back, exhausting himself into a fitful doze against my chest. Every so often, he'd jerk awake with a small gasp, then relax when he realized he was safe.

Lavinia rode beside us on the borrowed chestnut. She

kept her eyes on Beau, tracking every slight movement he made against my chest. For the first time since I'd met her, the tension had left her shoulders.

As we rode into the ranch yard, movement on the porch caught my attention. Burton Mossman stood on the front porch of the main house, his reddish hair catching the last rays of sunlight. His alert eyes tracked our approach with keen interest. Beside him stood A.C. Beaumont. Finally Lavinia's father could walk freely.

"Flynn, Shane." Mossman's greeting carried genuine warmth as they dismounted. "Looks like you boys had success."

"More than we expected," Shane replied, his voice carrying the bone-deep weariness we all felt. "We'll need help to arrange transport for federal prisoners."

Mossman nodded, already moving into action. "I'll wire the U.S. Marshal's office in Phoenix. They'll want to send an escort for this many prisoners, especially with Galen Harper among them." He paused, studying the handcuffed men. "That's quite a haul."

"We kicked over one rock and found a whole mess of scorpions," J.J. said, stretching his back with an audible pop.

"And a few vipers," Grady added grimly.

I dismounted carefully, keeping Beau secure against my chest. Shane stepped forward to help Lavinia down from the chestnut while the boy woke fully, tightening his grip on my shirt. Once she had solid footing, I transferred Beau into her waiting arms. He wrapped himself around his mother's neck and held on tight.

A.C. hurried down the porch steps toward them, his careful composure crumbling at the sight of his grandson safe and whole.

"Beau." He reached out to touch the boy's hair with trembling fingers. "Thank the good Lord."

"Papa!" Beau's delighted cry brought smiles to several hardened lawmen. "We're home! Flynn saved me from the bad men!"

While Mossman's ranch hands helped secure the prisoners in a fortified storage building, the rest of us gathered near the water trough to clean up and catch our breath. The Beaumont family stood together on the porch. A.C. held his grandson while Lavinia leaned against her father's shoulder, all three of them finally able to breathe without fear.

I was cleaning dust from my rifle when Mossman emerged from the ranch house with a telegram in his hand.

"Flynn, Shane," he called, gesturing toward a spot away from the main group. "J.J., Grady, you should hear this too."

The four of us exchanged glances and followed him to a quiet corner of the porch where we could speak privately.

"Got a wire from your sister about two hours ago," he said without preamble. "U.S. Marshal Davis arrested Federal Judge Harrison Webb in Phoenix this morning."

My hand tightened on the porch rail. Webb arrested. After all these years of operating above the law.

"On federal charges." Mossman's tone rang with vindication. "Corruption, obstruction of justice, conspiracy to aid escaped convicts, and about a dozen other counts. The U.S. Attorney General's office has been building a case against him for months."

Shane's hand found my shoulder. "What changed?"

Mossman looked at me directly. "Your sister's investigation into the prison guard intimidation gave them what they needed. Hayley figured you'd want to know right away."

Something loosened in my chest. We'd made the right call.

"Webb's facing serious federal time," Mossman continued. "The corruption charges alone could put him away for twenty years."

"Well, butter my biscuit," J.J. said. "Hayley pegged

Webb as crooked from the get-go. Woman's got a nose for corruption like a hound's got a nose for bacon."

"Every case Webb dismissed, every warrant he denied—all of it can be revisited now," Shane said.

I nodded slowly. "Including Galen's escape."

"According to Hayley, Webb's already trying to make a deal," Mossman said. "Offering testimony against his criminal associates. Including Galen Harper."

The irony wasn't lost on me. I'd kept Galen alive hoping his testimony could expose the corruption. Now Webb was doing the same, each man betraying the other to save himself.

"Webb's arrest changes everything," Shane muttered. He pulled a toothpick from his case and clamped it between his teeth.

Real justice had been served. Not the quick vengeance I'd once craved, but something that would protect future victims and expose the full scope of the corruption that had poisoned the territory.

Across the yard, Lavinia stood with her father and son on the porch. A.C. had Beau on his hip now, and the three of them were talking quietly, the first private moment they'd had as a family in far too long. Watching them, I felt the last knot of tension in my chest finally release.

Galen Harper captured. Judge Webb arrested. Thurston Blackwell collected by the Grim Reaper for his final judgment.

The chains of vengeance shattered, freeing me for a future I could finally claim.

25 - Safe Harbor

Lavinia

TEARS BLURRED MY vision as I watched Papa hold Beau close, his weathered face folding with emotion he could no longer contain. He'd been in hiding, unable to hold his grandson, unsure if any of us were still breathing. Now, with all of us whole and within reach, the restraint finally broke.

Papa looked up from Beau, his eyes locking onto mine across the dusty yard.

"Lavinia-girl," he breathed, extending one arm to draw me in. "When I heard what happened, when I thought I might lose you both…"

I stepped into the familiar shelter of Papa's arms, the place that had steadied me through every storm since Georgia. Beau wriggled between us, chattering about trains and gunfights and how brave Flynn had been, his mind already reshaping fear into legend.

"Everyone's safe," I whispered against Papa's shoulder, breathing in the scent of his shaving soap and the faint trace of pipe tobacco that always clung to him.

"Mr. Beaumont." Flynn's voice pulled my attention as

he approached, hat in hand, respect etched into every line of his posture. "I believe we have some things to discuss."

Papa straightened, keeping one arm around my shoulders and the other wrapped protectively around Beau. Despite everything Flynn had done, despite the heroism we'd witnessed firsthand, Papa's old wariness flickered. For weeks, Flynn's presence had meant danger. Pursuit. Fear.

"Marshal," Papa said carefully. "I understand I owe you a considerable debt."

"No debt," Flynn replied, his voice firm, and something in it made my heart stutter. "Justice has been served."

"A.C.," he continued, "you're a free man. The charges are being dropped. You can go home."

Papa's shoulders dropped, the tension he'd carried finally releasing. The lines around his eyes softened. For the first time since I'd seen his face on a wanted poster, we both breathed easier.

"Exonerated."

Beau tugged at Papa's shirt, his brow furrowed. "Papa, what's ex-on-er-ated mean? Is it a bad word?"

Papa crouched to meet his grandson's eyes, and I watched the change come over him. He looked like himself again. The steady, kind grandfather Beau had always known.

"It means," Papa said gently, "we can go home. No more hiding. No more being scared. We get to live like a family again."

Beau's face lit up. "And Flynn can come too, right? He's part of our family now, isn't he?"

My breath caught as Flynn's features softened. This man had risked everything to bring my son home. Had stepped into the role Beau needed without hesitation. The way he looked at my child with fierce affection and quiet protectiveness sent my heart racing with possibilities I hadn't dared to imagine.

"That depends," Flynn said, his gaze drifting from Beau to me, "on whether your mama thinks there's room in your family for a lawman with a questionable past and an uncertain future."

The unasked question hung in the desert air, heavy with everything we'd endured. Everything we'd learned about trust, about love, and about courage. Papa's gaze rested on me, expectant. And I sensed the other men nearby, pretending not to listen.

"Flynn Harper," I said, my voice steady despite my racing pulse. "You put Beau first. Even over me."

Hope flickered in his eyes, growing brighter as he searched my face. I saw the restraint in him, the way he fought not to reach for me, holding himself still out of respect—for my father, for the moment.

"That's when I knew."

"Are you saying what I think you're saying?" he asked, voice low.

"I'm saying I've been waiting my whole life for a man who'd protect my son the way you did." I reached up and touched his face, no longer caring who saw. "You've been part of our family since the moment you chose us."

Flynn's hand covered mine, warm and solid. His eyes held mine, and I saw everything I wanted reflected there.

"What about me?" Beau's voice piped up from somewhere near our knees.

I looked down to find him tugging at Flynn's pant leg, his small face earnest and determined.

Flynn crouched to meet him, his expression turning serious in a way children recognize and trust. "Beau, I'd be honored if you'd let me be your papa. Not instead of your grandpapa but as someone else who loves you and wants to take care of you. Would that be all right?"

Beau looked at Flynn, then at me, then at Papa, as if weighing the entire world in his small hands. Finally, he nodded.

"Okay. But… can I still call Grandpapa 'Papa' like

always?"

"Of course you can," Flynn whispered.

"Then yes," Beau declared emphatically. "You can be Papa Flynn."

Papa cleared his throat. When I turned to him, tears shimmered in his eyes. "Marshal Harper—Flynn—I don't know how to thank you. Not just for bringing my grandson home, but for seeing the best in us when you had every reason not to."

Flynn rose and extended his hand. "A wise man once told me justice isn't just about punishment. Sometimes it's about making sure love wins out over everything that tries to destroy it."

They shook hands, my father's quiet strength meeting Flynn's hard-won integrity, and something shifted inside me. The fear I'd carried for years, the belief that our past made us unworthy of happiness, crumbled under the weight of grace.

This was redemption. Not perfection. Not the absence of struggle. But mercy and love amid it.

"Well," Burton Mossman said, "I imagine you folks are eager to get back to Holbrook."

"Holbrook," Papa repeated. "I can walk down Main Street again."

Flynn retrieved something from my saddlebag before joining us again. He opened his hand to reveal Beau's wooden horse. The one he'd dropped during the kidnapping. The one Flynn saw me holding on the ride here.

"I believe this belongs to someone," Flynn said.

"Thunder!" Beau cried, clutching the carved figure to his chest. "I thought I lost him forever!"

"Sometimes," Flynn said, his eyes meeting mine over Beau's head, "the things we think we've lost forever find their way back to us."

I settled into my saddle with Beau secure in front of me. Flynn caught my eye.

"Ready?" he asked.

"Ready," I said.

Together, we rode toward home. Toward our future as a family.

Epilogue

Flynn

THE MORNING SUN slanted through the windows of the sheriff's office, casting light beams across the neat desk where I'd just finished reviewing the night reports. Three minor disturbances, one dispute over grazing rights that I'd mediated with coffee and common sense, and a drunk cowboy who'd spent the night in my jail sleeping off his overindulgence. About as exciting as wearing a badge got in Holbrook these days, and that suited me just fine.

I leaned back in my chair, the leather creaking softly, and looked out the window toward Main Street. The town bustled with its usual morning activity, but now I saw it through fresh eyes. Not as a federal marshal passing through, but as a man whose roots ran deep into this dusty desert soil.

Sheriff Flynn Harper. Still sounded strange sometimes, but it felt right in ways I'd never expected. The badge on my vest carried the same weight of responsibility as my old marshal's star, but it came with what my federal position never had. I'd be home for dinner every night. I could watch my son grow up day by day instead of missing months at a time chasing criminals across the territory.

Six months had passed since that evening when I'd proposed to Lavinia in front of the entire town. Six months since the community had officially welcomed me as their permanent sheriff and embraced the Beaumont family as the pillars of society they'd always deserved to be. I'd witnessed a remarkable transformation in my life and in Lavinia's.

She'd blossomed into the strong, confident leader I'd always known she could be. She'd thrown herself into community life with the same determination she'd once reserved for protecting her family. Now she organized church socials, led the ladies' auxiliary in their efforts to improve the school, and had somehow convinced the town council to approve funds for a new library. The women of Holbrook looked to her for guidance, and the men respected her judgment. She'd become a natural leader who inspired others through her courage and compassion.

Even A.C. had emerged from his ordeal stronger than before. The false accusations proved his character to everyone. His reputation for honesty and fairness had only grown, and his mercantile had become the unofficial community center where folks gathered to discuss everything from politics to the weather.

The bell above the door chimed, and I looked up to see Shane walking in with his easy stride. My older brother looked trail-worn but content, his territorial ranger badge catching the morning light as he settled into the chair across from my desk.

"Morning, Sheriff," he said with a grin that made him look years younger. "Heard tell you've got this town so well-tamed that folks are complaining about the lack of excitement."

"Can't say I'm sorry about that. New badge?"

"Arizona Ranger. Mossman recruited me."

I stood and walked over to the stove. Then I poured

coffee from the pot on the stove and handed him a cup. "How long you staying this time?"

"Few days, maybe a week. Got some rustling reports down near Tucson that need investigating, but I figured I'd stop by and see how married life's treating my little brother."

I thought about that question as I sipped my coffee. How was married life treating me? Like nothing I'd ever imagined, that was certain. Lavinia had transformed from the guarded woman protecting her family's secrets into a partner who challenged me, supported me, and loved me with a devotion that still took my breath away.

Beau had taken to calling me Papa without the "Flynn" attached. I'd fully earned his trust. Every morning he burst into our room asking if today was the day he could wear my badge, and every night he fell asleep recounting his adventures with the solemnity of a seasoned lawman.

And last night, my precious wife had told me our little family was expanding.

I'd stood there in our bedroom, Lavinia's hand pressed against her still-flat stomach, and felt something crack open inside my chest. Another child. A baby who would know from the first breath that they were wanted. Loved. Protected. Everything I'd spent years believing I didn't deserve.

"Better than I deserve," I said finally.

"That so?" Shane's eyes twinkled with amusement. "And how's fatherhood suiting you?"

Before I could answer, the sound of running footsteps on the wooden sidewalk reached us through the open door. A moment later, Beau burst into the office, his dark hair tousled and his brown eyes bright with excitement.

"Papa!" he called, launching himself toward my desk with enthusiasm. "Mama sent me to tell you dinner will be ready in one hour, and you better not be late because she's making your favorite pot roast."

I caught him in a hug, marveling as I always did at how completely this child had accepted me into his life. Not as a replacement for the grandfather who'd raised him, but as a father who'd chosen to love him.

"Well, we can't keep your mama waiting," I said seriously. "She might decide to give my pot roast to Uncle Shane instead."

"Uncle Shane!" Beau noticed my brother for the first time and ran to give him an equally enthusiastic greeting. "Are you staying for dinner? Mama always makes extra when family comes to visit."

"I'd be honored," Shane replied, ruffling the boy's hair. "Been looking forward to your mama's cooking since I left Prescott."

"Can you tell me more stories about when Papa was little?" Beau asked hopefully. "The ones about him getting into trouble?"

"Beau," I warned, but Shane was already grinning.

"Oh, I've got plenty of those stories," he said. "Like the time your papa caught a rattlesnake with his bare hands because he thought he could train it to do tricks."

"I was eight years old," I protested.

"Old enough to know better," Shane countered. "And there was the time he tried to ride a wild mustang he'd been tracking, just to prove it could be done."

Beau's eyes widened with delighted horror. "Really? What happened?"

"Let's just say your papa learned some horses aren't meant to be ridden," Shane said solemnly. "But he was too stubborn to give up, so he kept trying until that horse finally decided he wasn't worth the effort."

I listened to their easy banter as peace settled in my chest. This was what family was supposed to feel like. Laughter and stories and the comfortable certainty that these people would stand by me no matter what. Not the fear and violence that had defined my childhood.

"Beau," I said, "why don't you run back to Mama and tell her Uncle Shane will join us for dinner? And see if Grandpa needs help with anything at the store."

"Yes, Papa!" Beau gave us both quick hugs and dashed out of the office with the same energy he'd brought in.

Shane watched him go, then turned back to me with an expression I couldn't quite read. "Good boy. You've done well with him."

"He was already a good boy when I met him. I just try not to mess him up too badly."

"That's all any father can do." Shane's voice carried a note of wistfulness. "He's lucky to have you."

"I'm the lucky one." I studied my brother's face, noting the lines that hadn't been there a year ago, and the restless energy that never seemed to leave him. "Shane, when are you going to stop wandering long enough to find what I found? When are you going to let yourself have a family of your own?"

Shane was quiet for a long moment, staring into his cup as if it held answers to questions he wasn't ready to ask. When he looked up, his expression was thoughtful but resolute.

"Flynn, I spent fifteen years holding our family together after Galen Harper walked out on us. Fifteen years as a father to you, Ike, and the girls, making sure everyone was safe and fed and had what they needed." He paused, choosing his words carefully. "I'm proud of that time, don't get me wrong. But now you're all grown up, building your own families, making your own lives. Maybe it's time I figured out who Shane Harper is when he's not responsible for everyone else."

I understood that better than he probably realized. The weight of responsibility could define you until you forgot there might be other ways to live. But I also saw loneliness in his eyes that he might not recognize himself. A loneliness that no amount of duty could fill.

"Just don't wander so far that you forget to come home," I said.

"Home." Shane tested the word like he wasn't sure it applied to him. "Speaking of which, how's A.C. adjusting to having his reputation back?"

"Better than expected. Turns out, being falsely accused of federal crimes made him something of a celebrity around here. Folks respect a man who can survive that kind of ordeal with his integrity intact." I grinned, remembering the stream of customers who'd made special trips to the mercantile just to shake A.C.'s hand. "Business has never been better."

"And the real criminals?"

"Galen Harper's back in Yuma Territorial Prison, this time with extra security and no chance of another escape. We completely dismantled his gang. Webb has been moved to a federal prison back east. The other gang members are dead or serving long sentences." I felt the satisfaction that came with seeing justice properly served.

"Good." Shane's hands fisted slightly at the mention of our father, but the anger was old now, worn smooth by time and distance. "Think he'll stay put this time?"

"Prison officials assured me that Galen Harper will never see the outside world again. And even if he did somehow escape, he knows I'll be waiting for him."

But I barely thought about our father anymore. His power to hurt me, to define who I was or what I could become, died the day I had saved Beau. I was free of Galen Harper's shadow in ways I'd never thought possible.

"What about you?" I asked. "This new assignment is in southern Arizona. Anything I should know about?"

Shane's expression grew more serious. "Cattle rustling. Professional. Reminds me of what we dealt with last year, before we captured Galen. Could be isolated, could be larger."

"Need any help?"

"From a married sheriff with a family to think

about?" Shane shook his head with a smile. "Thanks, but no. I'll be required to disappear for weeks at a time with no one worrying about me coming home."

I wanted to insist that I could still handle dangerous assignments, but we both knew he was right. My priorities had changed the day I'd pinned on this sheriff's badge. My first duty was to Holbrook, to Lavinia and Beau, to the family I'd chosen to build instead of the criminals I'd spent years chasing.

"Just promise me you'll be careful," I said. "And that you'll write more than twice a year. Lavinia worries about you, and when she worries, she makes me worry."

"I'll try to do better on the letter-writing front," Shane promised. "And I'll be careful. Got too much to live for these days to take unnecessary risks."

"Such as?"

"Such as watching my little brother raise his family. Such as spoiling my nephew rotten every time I come to visit. Such as making sure this Harper generation finally gets the happy endings we never thought we'd see."

The church bell chimed the hour, reminding me that Lavinia's pot roast dinner was probably about ready. I stood and reached for my hat, then paused as I caught sight of my reflection in the window glass. The man in the glass bore little resemblance to the angry, driven deputy marshal who'd ridden into Holbrook a year ago.

This man had peace in his eyes instead of fury. Purpose instead of restless energy. The badge on his vest represented protection and service to his community rather than a personal crusade against injustice. He was a husband, a father, and a pillar of the community he'd chosen to call home.

He was who I'd always wanted to be, even when I'd been too lost to know it.

"Come on," I said to Shane, settling my hat on my head. "Let's go home for dinner. And Shane?"

"Yeah?"

"Thanks. For everything you did to get us all here. For being the father we needed when we didn't have one. For teaching me that being a Harper could mean something good."

Shane's smile was brighter than the Arizona sun streaming through the office windows. "Just returning the favor, little brother. You taught me something too."

"What's that?"

"That sometimes the best way to honor the family that raised you is to build something better for the family that comes after."

We walked out of the sheriff's office together, two Harper brothers who'd survived the worst childhood and emerged as men worthy of the badges we'd earned. Behind us, Holbrook went about its peaceful business, secure knowing that its sheriff would keep them safe.

And ahead of us waited the family I'd never dared dream I could have. A wife who loved me despite knowing all my flaws, a son who called me Papa with complete trust, and a father-in-law who'd welcomed me as if I'd always belonged.

When justice was executed, it truly was a joy to the righteous. But I learned that sometimes the greatest justice was simply the chance to love and be loved in return, to build something good from the broken pieces of the past, and to know that tomorrow would bring new opportunities to protect what was important.

As we headed toward home and family and the pot roast that was surely getting cold while we talked, I sent up a silent prayer of thanksgiving for the grace that had brought me to this place, this moment, this life I'd never believed I deserved.

My maverick marshal days were over, and with them, the last shadow of Galen Harper erased from my life. I'd found my purpose as a godly father, loving husband, and protector of the innocent.

Author's Note

NOT EVERYTHING IN *The Maverick Marshal* is historically accurate, and I'll own at least one deliberate liberty.

The bridge where Flynn refuses to let go is real. Known today as the Hell's Canyon Railroad Bridge near Drake, Arizona, it spans a 300-foot drop that is every bit as terrifying as it sounds. I called it Canyon Diablo in these pages to bridge it to the world readers entered in *The Rustler Hunter* (pun fully intended.) Except that bridge wasn't completed until 1901, two years after Flynn's opening scene. When my friend K.W. put that image in my head, I couldn't let it go. Some stories are worth bending the calendar for.

Holbrook needed no embellishment. By 1899, the town had fully recovered from the devastating 1888 fire that leveled most of its buildings and grown into the county seat of the newly formed Navajo County. Its handsome new courthouse was built in 1898, just one year before Flynn and Shane visited its records office. For several years, the basement of that courthouse served as the county jail. I like to think Flynn noticed.

Burton Mossman was every bit the formidable presence he appears in these pages. He was still managing the vast Aztec Land and Cattle Company, the famous Hashknife brand spanning over a million acres, when Flynn rode onto the land in 1899. Around 1900, the company liquidated its assets. Mossman relocated to Douglas in southern Arizona and opened a cattle slaughterhouse. Like many men of that era, Mossman rarely followed a straight path, pivoting from cattle to butcher to law enforcement without missing a step.

Then in 1901, Governor Nathan Oakes Murphy came calling with a new assignment to organize and lead the newly formed Arizona Rangers. Mossman served as the Rangers' first captain, and though his time in that role lasted less than two years, the structure he built shaped the organization for years to come.

The invitation waiting for Shane at the end of this story? That part is history. Read his story in *The Traitor's Badge*.

R.J. Sloane

About the Author

R.J. SLOANE CAPTURES the raw spirit of the American frontier in action-packed westerns that don't shy away from the harsh realities of territorial justice. Drawing inspiration from modern classics like *Longmire*, *Yellowstone*, and *Murdoch Mysteries*, R.J.'s stories blend historical authenticity with the timeless struggle between law and lawlessness.

A passionate student of Southwest history, R.J. spends countless hours researching the legendary lawmen of the region—from the Arizona Rangers to the territorial marshals who tamed pivotal frontier towns like Phoenix, Tombstone, Prescott, and beyond. Growing up watching John Wayne, James Garner, and Clint Eastwood westerns with dad on lazy Sunday afternoons instilled a deep appreciation for authentic frontier storytelling. This combination of classic western influence and dedicated historical research brings depth and authenticity to every story.

The Harper Justice series follows a family of territorial lawmen as they navigate the dangerous transition from frontier chaos to civilized order, where doing what's right often means defying what's legal.

Website: https://www.rjsloanewesterns.com
Facebook: rjsloane.westerns
X (twitter): @RJSloaneWest

Books by This Author

The Harper name once struck fear in honest folk across the Arizona Territory. Now it strikes terror in outlaws. The six children of notorious criminal Galen Harper have turned their family legacy inside out, becoming the very lawmen their father spent his life outrunning. As Pinkerton agents, federal marshals, and territorial rangers, they're hunting down men just like the one who raised them. In the untamed frontier of 1898–1904, justice has a new name: Harper.

Blood Justice (Prequel) – Grady Thatcher

The Rustler Hunter (Book 1) - Hayley Harper

The Maverick Marshal (Book 2) - Flynn Harper

The Traitor's Badge (Book 3) – Shane Harper

Desert Life Media

There Is Life in The Desert

Entertainment-first Christian fiction set in the Southwest, featuring redemption, family, and faith

Publishing clean, wholesome, and uplifting fiction since 2010

If you enjoyed R.J. Sloane's The Rustler Hunter, check out more Western Adventures on our website:

desertlifemedia.com

The Traitor's Badge

In a land ruled by grit and gunfire, even the badge can lie.

Arizona Ranger Shane Harper built his reputation on quiet competence and unshakable resolve. In 1904, that reputation is tested when a raid goes wrong and he's forced to seek shelter at the Duncan ranch where he meets a woman who challenges everything he thought he knew about strength.

Tessa Duncan has been fighting to keep her ranch and raise her two children alone since her husband's death. She's got a sharp wit, a sharper tongue, and no patience for men who think she needs rescuing. When the stoic Ranger shows up wounded on her doorstep, she's tempted to turn him away. Instead, she finds herself drawn to the man who treats her children with unexpected gentleness and respects her independence.

But someone wants Tessa gone. The pressure on her ranch escalates from petty harassment to outright violence. As Shane investigates the sophisticated rustling operation threatening her livelihood, he uncovers a trail of deception that leads disturbingly close to home.

Information leaks where it shouldn't. Traps get turned against them. And the deeper Shane digs, the more he begins to question the loyalties of those he once trusted with his life.

In a territory where justice is hard-won and betrayal cuts deep, Shane must decide who to believe and how far he's willing to go to protect the innocent when brotherhood itself is on the line.

Buy Now:
https://books.rjsloanewesterns.com/the-traitors-badge

www.ingramcontent.com/pod-product-compliance
Lightning Source LLC
LaVergne TN
LVHW010644110826
845149LV00014B/2951

* 9 7 8 1 9 6 0 2 1 7 7 4 5 *